Cold November Rain
The Doc Series #2

BY
Lisa Beth Darling

Moon Mistress Publishing USA

Moon Mistress Publishing
New London, CT 06320

Copyright 2015—Lisa Beth Darling-Gorman
ISBN: 978-0692401750
ISBN: 069240175X
Cover Art Designed by Lisa Beth Darling
Edited by: Donna Ruggeri and Cathy Chester
Text set in Calibiri 11

Carmelita-Copyright 1976-
Words & Music by Warren Zevon

In Memory of
Ebony Clarke

Dedicated to:

G.H. & H.L.

And, as always,
To The Big Guy

Chapter One

Summer was long gone, the leaves on the trees turned from their lush supple green to brilliant reds and oranges before drifting to the ground signaling the coming of winter. On this chilly November night, the fallen leaves crackled and crunched beneath Doctor Mason's feet as he wound his way to the neighborhood bar. This would be the seventh time he'd made this trip since summer. The seventh time he would be hoping to run into her, to see her sitting at that far corner booth, alone, martini in hand.   Every night she haunted his dreams, her breath hot against his neck as she whispered 'Doc' in that sultry way of hers.   Even in his waking hours, just thinking of the way those three little letters rolled off her tongue was enough to make him hard.   There was no denying his Mystery Woman somehow wormed her way into his head and if he didn't see her tonight Rick thought he'd go crazy...or worse yet, he would simply combust leaving nothing behind but dry ash.

As he did every time he took this walk, when he got to the El Royale Hotel, he looked up to the windows of the room on the fourth floor to see if her light was on. More often than not, it was dark up there but a few times, he'd passed by to see the light on and to catch glimpses of people moving around up there. He'd stand across the street looking up wondering who she was with and what she was doing for him. Wondered why he'd had the bad luck to miss her again.

Tonight the window was dark. Rick felt the uneasy tinge of loneliness settle over him as he continued his short journey.

The bar was busy tonight, it was filled with cold lonely people looking for a little warm company or just a few laughs.

"Hey, Doc!" Tony the bartender called out to him.

At first, Rick didn't hear him over the din but soon enough he raised a hand in the bartender's direction as he limped toward an empty stool. His hungry blue eyes were scanning the crowd looking for any sign of her. It seemed Fate was with him tonight, just as he settled upon the stool, he saw her sitting there in the far corner booth. If he didn't know her face so well, he might have missed her, between August and November she dyed her hair from that stunning strawberry red to a deep rich auburn. She was smiling and dipping her fingers into the last drops of her martini so she could get the olives and tease the man sitting across from her.

Rick felt his heart drop; she was here but she'd already picked out her prey for the night.

Feeling his jaw clench as he tried to decide if he should stay or go, Tony put a glass of scotch on the bar for him. There wasn't any sense in letting good booze go to waste. Turning his back to his Mystery Woman, Rick retrieve the drink only to discover the large mirror behind the bar gave him a better angle on her companion for the evening; male, maybe thirty, good looking. Lucky guy didn't know what he was in for tonight. The Mystery Woman raised her empty glass to catch Tony's attention and, like a good bartender, Tony went right over to her with a fresh Martini. Downing the double-shot, Rick gazed in the mirror to stare at her reflection, she was staring at his back from the corner of her pale green eyes as she chatted with the man across from her.

Rick looked away wondering if it was just coincidence or if she'd noticed him sitting there so he gave it a few moments while he lingered over his drink before glancing into the mirror again. This time she wasn't taking a sneak peek at him from the corner of her eye she was looking directly at him, past him, at his reflection. When she saw him staring back at her, she smiled for him. Shy. Precocious. Full of promise.

Was she wishing he'd come over there? Maybe. Only one way to find out.

Rick eased himself off the barstool and made his way over to where the couple was engaged in light conversation. "Excuse me," he said to the man in the booth, "You're in my seat."

"Pardon?" The man asked as he looked from him to her. "Were you waiting for this guy?"

"Actually," she said softly, "I was." She was surprised and delighted by the Doc's forthrightness. "Hi, Do-c."

There it was, 'Do-c', just the way she said in it his dreams, with that extra little coy kick she gave the 'c'. It made him want to melt. "Hi." Rick said to her. "Three's a crowd." He said to the man. "Go on beat it."

"What the hell?" The man complained. He'd been doing so well with her, he was sure he was going to get laid tonight from the way she was undressing him with those haunting eyes. "I hate games."

"So do I." She said to him and gently put her hand over his wrist. "I'm sorry if you got the wrong idea, here; let me pay for the drinks."

"You got it, sister." He got up and Rick stepped back to let him pass. "She's all yours." He took a seat at the bar and ordered another drink.

"How are you tonight, Doc?" She asked as Rick took a seat across from her. "Long time no see."

Richard Mason didn't like games either, "You want to keep going with this? Another drink. A little chitchat? Or should we just go up to your room now?"

"No need to be crude, Do-c." She admonished quietly. "The least you can do is sit with me for a moment or two while I have another drink. After all, I did let you chase my date away."

Rick leaned across the table. Damn, she looked fine tonight, sitting there with her deep auburn hair pulled back in a braid, her lips glistening with pink gloss and the way that deep green sweater dress clung to those curves made his lower regions tingle. He found her more intoxicating than moonshine. Rick had his share of Working Girls and she wasn't one of them, not by a long shot. She might sleep around but she wasn't a slut, in fact, she had a certain quiet elegance about her. "Date? Is that what you call it? I bet you don't even know his name."

Tony's shadow fell over the table and she sat back to allow the bartender to put the drink in front of her. "Here," she said to him as she handed over a fifty. "Please put the gentleman's....no, the gentlemen's...drinks on my tab."

"You want to pay for him for the whole night?" Tony hitched a thumb to the rejected would-be lover.

"Just that last one, please. You keep the change."

"You got it. You want another one, Doc?"

"Yes, he does." She answered for Him. When Tony walked she leaned over the table. "I see your patience isn't your strongest suit, Doc."

"Gonna tell me your name tonight?" He said impatiently.

The woman sighed deeply. "What is it with you, Doc? My name, his name, your name...what difference does it make?" She drank the martini that had been sitting in front of her while Tony came back with Rick's scotch.

8

Grateful for the fresh round, he picked it up and drank down half of it. "Call me crazy but I just like to know who I'm getting in bed with."

"So do I, however, it didn't seem to bother you too much last time." She returned with silky ease.

How could she possibly know who she was getting into bed with if she didn't know so much as their names? The woman truly had a major screw loose somewhere in that very pretty head of hers. Under the table he felt her bare foot slide over his ankle and slowly make its way up to his inner thigh. She sat there drinking her drink and looking at him oh so innocently as she licked the drops of alcohol from her lips moistening an already inviting tongue. Ok, fine, who cared what her name was? Still, "How 'bout a hint?"

Across the table that shy smile turned into a full grin and she shook her head. "Poor, Doc." She cooed. "I already told you, didn't I? A rose by any other name would smell as sweet."

"Romeo and Juliet," Rick mused quietly, "Shakespeare fan?"

"Does that surprise you?"

"Then, that's what I'll keep calling you...Rose." Across from him she smiled a shy grin. "By the way, Rosie, everything you do surprises the hell out of me." He took a long drink letting the warm amber liquor slide down his dry throat while her eyes sparkled at him.

"Is that good or bad?"

Rick shook his head, "I'm not sure yet."

One delicate hand around her glass and the other gliding over the back of his hand, she leaned across the table, "Don't try to figure me out, Doc, just go with it, I promise I won't hurt you. Who knows? You might even have a little fun along the way."

Oh, yes, she was oodles of fun in a very small package. There had to be a catch. Things this good weren't free and he feared that at the end of whatever this was there would be a high price to pay for the feel of her milky flesh against his. "You're not going to tell me anything, are you?"

"Nothing you don't need to know," she said softly and withdrew her hand from his. "What do you say? After you, Doc?"

Watching her slide across the booth to stand up, he plucked the heavy cashmere shawl from the coat rack at the end of the booth. It was soft, fuzzy, and deep green like her sweater dress. He draped the cloak around her shoulders taking in the shortness of the dress clinging to her legs several inches above the knee, the black stockings and matching green stiletto heels. He held back the smile thinking of the last time he'd asked her about those shoes and how she'd 'gotten them for a song'.

Wrapped in warmth, she looked up at him. "Thank you," she said in a whisper that was almost sad.

"I am a gentleman or, well, I try sometimes anyway." He held out his free arm to her, she looked up at him for a moment trying to judge if he was serious or not. In the end, she looped her arm through his and he escorted her from the bar while the man he'd booted out of her bed tonight scowled at them in the mirror from behind a rather large glass of Jack Daniels. "Gee, Rosie, I don't think I made a friend." He commented.

Beside him the woman laughed. "Neither do I, Doc." Unseen by them, tonight's jilted would-be lover wasn't the only one watching them in the mirror and seething.

The hotel room was just as he remembered it and just as he'd seen it a hundred dreams between now and the last time he saw her. The door opened to the bedroom, off of which, to the right, was the bathroom, straight ahead was the living area and those windows he was so accustomed to looking at from the street.

Although he didn't know it, there were many nights she'd sat in the chair by the window in the darkened living area and watched him stroll down the street on his way to the bar or on his way to wherever home was for him. Often he stopped under the streetlight and looked up to her window while she wondered if he would have the courage to come to up to her room on his own. He never did, he just stopped, gazed and then went on his way. As he walked by her windows on those nights, she couldn't help wondering if he was looking for her. Had he gone down to the bar in search of her and, if so, what would happen if she should wander in a few minutes after him? Being the type of woman who, in large part, liked leaving things to Chance and to Fate, she never followed him. If she should run into him again then that would fine. Perhaps they would take it from there but she wouldn't actively chase him or any man. Besides, while she came here to this hotel room more often than she should, she didn't go to the bar until the loneliness became unbearable and the ache in her wept for comfort.

"Why don't you make yourself comfortable?" She invited as she laid the shawl in the chair and put her purse on top of it. "I have to use the Ladies Room." She disappeared into the bathroom.

All of that booze in her had to find its way out sometime and he took the opportunity to pop two Oxies into his mouth. His hip was acting up again, a little memento from Operation Desert Storm. Now that the weather was turning cold and damp, it ached like a bad tooth.

Rick learned to live with the injury and tonight he intended to do many things that would cause his hip a great deal of discomfort but bring so much pleasure to the rest of him. Make yourself comfortable she said and so he did, Rick tossed his jacket to the nearest chair, kicked off his sneakers before quietly sliding open the nightstand drawer to see the same assortment of toys and a new box of condoms. Behind him the bathroom door opened to reveal tonight's theme was black.

11

Black push-up bra embroidered with lacy flowers, matching panties under a black garter belt holding up black silk stockings, the old-fashioned kind with the seam running up the back racing from her tiny ankles to those lovely thighs. Mason's lips dried even as his mouth watered and his heart began to throb.

"Been looking for me, Doc? Waiting for me?"

Rick pulled the t-shirt over his head and then patted the empty space of bed next to him. "Not anymore."

The Doc was very striking especially for an older man. She'd never had much interest in older men until he caught her eye, those she usually left with from the bar were her age—which was 38—or younger. He had a flat stomach and tight chest whereas most men of his age had rather large spare tires, back hair, and man-boobs. Those things were altogether unappealing as far as she was concerned. Not the Doc. Even with that bum leg of his, he was in fine shape. She liked his gray/silver hair as it went very well with those striking blue eyes.

Sitting there on the bed watching her wind her way over to him, Rick fully appreciated the way her hips rocked from side to side and the way her lips glistened after her tongue lapped along them. Slowly reaching behind her back, Rose unhooked the bra and let it fall to the floor. The nipples on those pert little breasts were still pink and they were very hard as her hand ran along their curves making his cock hard.

She appreciated the tent he was pitching in those faded blue jeans. Her eyes sparkled and she bit down ever so coyly upon her bottom lip as she reached out for it. "Been thinking about me?"

Long graceful fingertips ran over her body from her breasts, down the curve of her waist, past her hips, "Incessantly." Rick admitted without feeling as though he should hold back. He reached up to touch her and run his hands along her flesh so smooth and alabaster that it seemed to glow in the full moon of late autumn. "You're in my head." Morning, noon, and night she was in his head and now she was finally back in his bed. He wasn't going to let any of the night slip by him. She leaned into him and he took one pert pink nipple into his mouth as he breathed deeply of her scent. Rick was slightly disappointed not to have the sweet scent of honeysuckle greet him. The one he remembered it so well in his dreams and swore he caught whiffs of during the day. Disappointment turned to arousal as the heady aroma of cinnamon settled into his brain. With his lips and tongue sucking at her nipples, his head buried against her chest he heard her heartbeat pick up the pace.

Like the last time, she pushed him down on the bed and straddled him. She stared down at him with hungry sparkling eyes. "I've been waiting for you too, Doc." She whispered. That was true; she had been waiting for him. She'd been elated when she saw him walk into the bar tonight. She tried hard not to show it but she immediately began coming up with ways to politely ditch the much younger man she'd been considering for her evening company. When Doc came over to the table and dismissed the other man as though he were nothing more than an annoying fly, she was very turned on. Yes, she liked a man who knew when to be a man and take charge of the situation. Doc seemed like that type of a guy to her.

Rick's warm hands planted themselves on each of her hips and then slowly made their way up the curve of her supple back to the braid at the back of her head. Untying the ribbon keeping her hair in place, he ran his fingers through her dark fiery tresses until they was loose, wild and hanging free wisping about her face and breasts. It was much longer than he remembered it being this past summer, then it had only cascaded to her shoulder blades. Cupping her pretty face in his hands, he brought her down and in for a long kiss taking in the taste of her and the scent of cinnamon hanging heavy in the air.

Cinnamon.

The scent of Fall. Of crisp leaves, hot cider and warm apple pie. Of nights by the fire, glasses of wine and sweet kisses such as this.

Straddled over him, her hips slowly ground down on him making the crotch of faded jeans steamy. Lips and chests pressed together, skin to unfettered skin; she reached down between her own legs to undo the restrictive clothing he was still wearing. Before she could free him, Rick rolled her over onto her back and pinned her hands behind her head with one hand. She let out a deep sighing moan and her back arched off the bed.

He knew she liked it rough, question was- how rough? Getting a firm grip on her wrists, he picked them up as he reached into the drawer by the bed to produce the handcuffs. She didn't complain in the slightest when he harnessed her to the bed. Now his hands were free and she was secure.

From below him, in a heavy whisper she asked, "What are you doin', Doc?"

"Nothing you don't want me to, Rosie." Rick whispered back. With devilish delight, he put the key between her breasts so that she could see it but she couldn't get to it. Looking back at her it was clear to see that she was so hot right now she was almost glowing. Those limpid eyes sparkled with anticipation. Yes, this was the way she wanted it. However, chances were she didn't want it too rough. Like last time, just rough enough to let her know who was in control tonight. He was going to take as much delight as he possibly could in finding out just where she drew that line.

Over and over, in his dreams one thing haunted him more than anything else, even more than those pale eyes and sweet sighs. He didn't get to indulge in it the last time they were here. Now that he had her in such a submissive position, and she was enjoying the hell out of it, he was going to indulge himself in that act from the tip of his nose, to his lips, his chin and by the end of it, hopefully he'd be soaked to chest with it. Slowly, he made his way down her naked body from neck to shoulder to nipple and further still. Hands and mouth roaming wherever he pleased, lingering as long as he wanted all while he listened to her sigh and took in the enthralling scent of her. Turns out Medical School is good for more than medical situations. An intimate knowledge of female anatomy did wonders outside of the hospital. In fact, he couldn't remember a class he enjoyed more and was hard-pressed to think of one that he'd put into practical use more often. Seemed she liked it too. There were so many subtle places to touch and taste a woman's body. So many places other men passed by without a single thought, but they didn't understand about nerve endings, pressure points, and endorphins. Hell, let's face it; most guys didn't know the difference between a moan of pleasure and a groan of pain.

Most guys were idiots.

He wasn't most guys.

She definitely wasn't in any pain.

The closer he came to that smooth place between her legs, the more the musky scent of her overpowered what cinnamon she wore, mixed with it, made it stronger as musk mingle with spice. Black satin panties slid over the silk black thigh-highs and past her shoes to the floor. He thought about taking off the stockings then thought better of it, she could leave those and the shoes on if she wanted. Making his way back up those lovely legs, Rick was almost drooling before he got to where he really wanted to be, he just kept breathing in deeper and deeper trying to pull more and more of her into him. That scent seemed to fill so many barren places.

Hot breath brushed against her lower lips making the waiting space between tingle and ache to be touched. How many men had cum and gone between now and the last time she saw her

Doc? Was it eight? Maybe ten? She'd even found herself scoping out older men as of late in hopes of replacing him but she didn't have any luck with that. No, none of them were like him. None of them would do.

Her restrained hands pulled against the cuffs on her wrists wanting to reach down and touch him, run her fingers through that silver hair and over his shoulders. The frustration of knowing she couldn't only made her want him more as the caress of the palm of his hand roamed over her inner thigh. Her eyes closed as she let out heated moan.

That soft mound of smooth flesh rose up to bring him more of that wanton scent that made his mouth water. She wanted him to taste of her and that was good because now it was time to find out how many steps there were to that line. Perched between her legs, the tip of his tongue twitching in his mouth, he looked up at her with just his eyes. "Beg me, Rosie." She stared back at him with those hungry eyes, the ones that drove him wild, the ones that pleaded for him to do whatever he wanted.

"Please, Doc?"

By her unquestioning willingness to comply, Mason thought the trip to the edge of that line could be very long and extremely pleasurable, "Again."

"Oh, please, Do-c? Taste me."

What a sweet invitation. It would be rude to say no now wouldn't it? Hearing her wasn't enough, he wanted to see her face too. He didn't close his eyes as the tip of that waiting tongue flicked out to get its first taste of her. Above him, secured to the bed, she let out a quick moan as her eyes closed and that back arched even closer to him. She was just as tangy and sweet as that musky scent told him she would be. He wanted more. Much more. To that end, he slid his index finger into that hot moist place and she quivered. A few slow thrusts in and out and, mercilessly he stopped. He waited for her eyes to open again; when they did, they were hazy and puzzled. "More?"

He was going to tease her endlessly! "Bad Doc," she chided and watched him give her a sly grin as her inner thighs tingled from the softness of the whiskers on his face.

"Horrible," he agreed from between her legs. "More?"

"Yes," she sighed, "Please?"

"Please? Please what, Rosie?"

Involuntarily her hands strained at the cuffs again as she tried to reach for him. Taunting her between her rising and falling breasts lay the key that would free her from this prison. "Please more...please, Doc, don't stop."

"That's better." He looked past her face to her hands straining against the cold metal cuffs as she tried to reach for him. Rick had to hold back the smile lest she think him...evil. He'd let her go soon enough but not before her arms fell asleep and were useless to her for a while. "Sometimes, Rosie, you have to ask for what you want." He'd tell her to demand it but, while Rosie loved and to tease and to flirt, she didn't like to be the dominant one and even if he told her to do it, she might shy away. Shying away was the last thing he wanted her to do tonight, he'd waited too many months for that.

"I've missed you, Doc."

That surprised him such words were unexpected. Maybe it was just part of the mind game she was playing out in this room night after night. Rick didn't doubt that on nights such as these there was much more than animal sex involved, at least in her head. Something drove to her this and he would very much like to know what it was. The words led him to think that, perhaps in her mind or maybe even her heart, it was a whispered plea to a lover that never returned. He wished he knew her real name but the one he was using was pleasant enough. "Missed you too, Rosie." Rick whispered with his mouth poised over that wet waiting place. His hot breath met the tender sensitive flesh there and made goose bumps arise on the thighs on either side of him.

Soft, wet tongue and gentle commanding finger found their home. She thought she'd lose her mind. Nobody did it like the Doc. All of the men who'd cum and gone over the last sixteen months...nobody did it like the Doc. He seemed to know and somehow even to understand what these nights were all about for her. He used that knowledge to both their advantage. The other men were cumbersome, they were ungraceful, awkward and lacked in self-confidence. That was the best of them. Others were...selfish. They were...brutish. Some were even...cruel. They took advantage of what she offered so freely and greedily robbed her of it.

Not The Doc. He was confident, maybe even a little arrogant and cocky but he wasn't a boor or a brute. He didn't seem to have a cruel bone or bad intention in his slim body. Adventurous ones, yes, but cruel and demeaning, no.

For almost two years she'd watched him before her chance finally came that fateful night when he walked into the bar last August. She just couldn't let that chance slip away. No, not after all the times she'd sat quietly in the shadows listening to him as he fought for one patient or another hearing the passion and zeal rising in his voice watching it take hold of his handsome face. He took chances. He took risks. In the end, he was almost always right. He was a very strange creature indeed, in that, in spite of all of the chances he took, The Doc was a man who could admit when he was wrong. Perhaps he didn't like to do so...who did? But he *could* do it, she'd even go so far as to say that he knew *when* to do it.

To her it seemed that The Doc knew when to do just about everything.

Very strange indeed. Then again, perhaps doctors weren't all bad and they did have their advantages in the bedroom.

Lost in her thoughts and the pleasure between her legs, she didn't notice when she began to cum and so she didn't hold back.

It was just the coolest thing in the world when a hot dream became an even hotter reality. Before Rick knew it, he was drenched in her hot wet juices from nose to chest just as he wanted when he started this.

Thank you, Professor Collins and your Female Anatomy Class. They were the best four credits in the whole world.

That's what Rick thought as he made his way up her, tongue leaving a long slick trail from the space between her breasts to the key between them. Her arms were good and tired now, yep, they surely were. His eyes glanced over at the items in the drawer but dismissed them. Maybe later he'd like to use that dildo but not just now. Rosie's misty eyes followed him as he plucked the key from its resting place, letting his hand linger there a long moment to feel the rapid beat of her heart before he unlocked the cuffs. "Come with me." He grabbed a condom out of the box.

Anxious to see what he had in mind, Rosie did as he asked, and followed him away from the bed. She found that her arms were heavy almost as though someone replaced the bone with lead.

Rick looked around the room. The wall with the dresser had space but it adjoined the room next door, he didn't want to disturb the neighbors. The wall where the chair sat—the chair looked interesting too but he'd get to that later along with the dildo—there was room there and there was another wall between them and then nothing but the street beyond. "Over here." He took her hand and led her over to the empty space. She was short but not too short and those heels would definitely help, they were turning him on just looking at the way they led from the floor, up those black stockings to her bare ass. Against the wall, if he bent deeply at the knee, which would be to his advantage in the end though it would be murder on his leg later. It was a small price to pay for reaching such heights of pleasure. "Face the wall, Rosie." The eyes that had looked at him with curious desire now did so with trepidation. He took another step toward the line. "Do it."

Heart skipping a beat, she turned to the wall, put her hands against it and waited. The next thing she knew, his hand was between her shoulder blades pushing her further into the cold wallpapered sheet rock. She tried to push him away but her arm wouldn't move, when she tried to force it her shoulder cried out in protest. Behind her The Doc pressed his naked body against her and gave his next command.

"Spread 'em." Rick whispered in her ear. "Wide."

"Doc?"

Rick grabbed a handful of silky auburn hair with his free hand and gave it a firm yank. "Do it." Rosie hesitated but she didn't say 'no' and she didn't say 'stop'. "Now, Rosie, nice and wide." When his lips met the nape of her neck those lovely legs parted to shoulders width. When he bit down they spread a little further still and her firm ass arched out toward him.

He knew there was still a ways to go before he found that line.

Rosie was ready and Rick was beyond ready as he tore open the wrapper to do the right thing before sliding into her.

Her face pressed to the wall as she moaned out his name; "Doc."

He wanted to see that beautiful face and he used that handful of hair to turn her head as he began to surge in and out of that hot tight hole. The one he'd been dreaming about.

The one she'd been waiting for him to fill again.

Maybe a Viagra would have been a good idea. Next time.

Next time?

Yeah, oh yeah, definitely...next time.   He didn't come here tonight only to walk out with lighter balls. He wanted a name, a phone number, an email address at least.

The way she was turned to him exposed her neck, so vulnerable and tasty as it started to shine with a sheen of sweat. Burying his whiskered face in the space he breathed in the scent of Cinnamon and sex, he marveled at the way she changed her scent with the seasons. Did she do that on purpose? She must. Rosie smelled light and breezy in summer and heady in fall, it was all just another way to attract the right prey. Like him.

Lucky fucking him.

Lost in his own thoughts and desire, his eyes rolled back in his head behind closed lids, Rick was completely oblivious when the nibbling turned into gnawing and then a strong bite. It wasn't until the salty tang of blood met his tongue that he pulled back but not at first, no not right away. He let it linger on his tongue and dribble down the back of his throat before realizing he had to be hurting her. If he kept going, just a little more pressure from his teeth would break the skin and he might well come away with a chunk of flesh in his mouth. Glancing down at the corner of his eye, he saw one of those too tired to raise arms trying to reach back and push him away.   Another thing he didn't realize was that his thrusts were matching the pressure of his jaw. The slender fingers on that helpless hand flexed and stretched and flexed and stretched. Below his chest, her breath came shallow and controlled.   The legs below her, the ones that ended in those come-fuck-me pumps threatened to give out. It seemed without knowing it, Rick found that line.

Still she didn't say 'no', she didn't say 'stop'. No, what Rosie did say, what she managed to croak through a tight throat was;

"Do-c?"

Pain wasn't the object of The Game, not for him and as much as she might put up with it, not for her either. Maybe it was true and most guys really didn't know the difference but Rick lived with enough pain to know it when he heard it and had a feeling that Rosie did too. Nights like this were for walking along the razor's edge not for crossing over it. Although it took a bit of doing and an amount of self-control that he was very unaccustomed to exercising Rick pulled back and eased off. He forced his jaw open to release the tender flesh caught there, he let his tongue lap along the wounded place taking up the last of her blood even though he knew he shouldn't. It was so tender and sweet, when his tongue rang along it and his lips kissed it, she seemed to melt against the wall. The hand that was flexing and trying to bat him lay still as it tried to hold its owner on her stilettoed feet. She didn't mind the strength of his thrusts...not too much judging from the way she once again arching that fine ass toward him...it was his teeth on her neck. He'd use that lightly from here on out. The hand in her hair gave another firm yank. Her eyes fluttered open and she let out a moan that would make the angels cry. He was back to the right side of the razor's edge. "I know you've been waiting for me, Rosie. You dream about me." He didn't know if he was right when he uttered the words but her response gave him all he needed for confirmation of its truth. Another truth was that he couldn't hold out much longer. Bending deeply at the knee Rick gave a long slow upward thrust. "Come on, Rosie, I've been dreaming about you too."

Was that true? Did The Doc dream about her? What did it matter if it was a lie? The whole thing was a lie, why not enjoy it while it lasted and before the illusion shattered? Where was the harm in that?

At the moment, it was nowhere that she could see.

"Do it, Do-c. Go on. Take it the way you want it. Fuck me."

At the last two words hit him like a slap in the face and it was Rick's turn to flinch. He didn't know why he should find them so ugly right here and right now. After all, what else were they doing if not fucking? Yet the word was repulsive and part of him wished she hadn't cheapened this moment. Then again, maybe that was what she needed to get through it all. "Fuck you good." He whispered in her ear. Her back to his chest, he felt her cringe and quiver as the word came from his lips. She didn't like it either but she needed it.

Pressed against the hotel room wall, the woman Rick knew as Rosie, surrendered to him and the rest of the night.

By the time dawn threatened to arrive, the box of Trojans was empty, every hole in her had been filled, and all of the toys had been used. Exhausted and feeling as though all of his bones had somehow been replaced with helium, Rick rose from the bed. "Where are you goin', Doc?"

"I don't like to wake up alone." That was where she left him the last time; alone. If that was going to happen after a night like this then he'd rather do it in his own bed.

She shouldn't. No she shouldn't. Absolutely. Positively. Should not. She never did this. She swore to herself when this started that she never would do this!

"Stay, Doc." Rosie pleaded from the bed as she reached out for him. "You won't wake up alone."

He took off the t-shirt and climbed back into the bed to take her up in his arms.

In the morning, when he woke, she was still there. Sleeping peacefully on his shoulder and smiling slightly as she dreamed. Looking toward the window he saw that it was raining. It was Sunday. He had nowhere to go and nothing to do. No one was expecting him. If he wanted to, if she wanted him to, then he could spend the day here in this bed with her. At the thought of it he found he had a good deal of morning wood. How could that be after last night? Yet it was. There she was, soft and warm and waiting. Quietly he reached for the box only to remember it was empty.

What did it matter now? He took in her blood last night and if she had anything that was treatable but not curable, he was already at risk. He was clean, he knew that because he got tested twice yearly. Working Girls and all, AIDS was a real draw back. Rosie wasn't sick, the worst that could happen...maybe...was that she'd get pregnant. Gazing down at her, watching her sleep, he thought that wasn't such a bad idea. He could fall for her and he didn't even know her name.

Danger, Will Robinson! Danger! Danger!

Outside the rain fell gently against the window casting a soft gray glow over the room. Rick rolled the sleeping woman onto her back and straddled her just as her eyes opened. "Mornin', Rosie."

"Mornin', Doc." She cooed. She'd been so sure he'd sneak off in the middle of the night. He was still here and he was sliding into her again..and.... he hands reached out and caught his hips before he could slide all the way inside. "Doc?" There was no condom between them. Finally, they were flesh to flesh. Men often complained that condoms made sex feel weird or that they couldn't feel anything, but what they didn't realize was that the same was true for the female involved.

Holding himself on one elbow, he used the other hand to pull away. He laced his fingers through hers and pinned her arm by

24

her head on the bed. "It's ok, Rosie, don't be afraid. It's ok, I really am a doctor."

I know...that was what she wanted to say. *I know, you're Doctor Richard Mason and you're one-third owner The Mountainside Wellness & Research Center where you're the Head of Exploratory Medicine.* Of course, she said no such thing.

The incredible sex they'd engaged in last night and that of a few months ago didn't come close to what they did next on that rainy Sunday.

She could fall for him. She mustn't but she could. For now, she could feel and she could dream.

Rick and his lovely lady Rosie passed the day making love in the hotel room.

II

Richard Mason didn't leave the El Royale Hotel until nearly 6pm on Sunday evening and when he did the man behind the desk gave him a strange smile that irked him. "What?"

"Nuttin'," the young man mused, "just, ah, I seen a lot of guys come and go from there," he pointed upward to the room on the fourth floor with a skinny finger. "You're the only one I've ever seen twice. She must like you."

Rosie liked him all right just not enough to tell him her name. Not what she did. Where she lived. Where was from or where she thought she was going. She was still a complete mystery even though he knew her most intimately. He had no plans to see her again nor a way to get in touch with her other than to look for the light when he passed by on the street.

Chapter Two

Monday morning came and Rick dragged himself out of his lonely bed where he'd collapsed right around 9pm the night before. After a hot shower in which he very much regretted washing away the scent of her, and three Oxies to relieve the pain in his overly strained oh so pleasantly over used bum hip, he slept deeply the whole night through.

His underlings were waiting for him in his office, waiting for the day to start, Mason was late again. Most of them wondered if the man even owned an alarm clock let alone knew how to use one. As they sat there making chit-chat about what they'd done over the weekend an odd sound began to drift down the hall from outside the office.

"Is someone whistling?" Goodspeed asked as they sat around the differential table.

The whistling stopped and the singing began, "Carmelita-aaaa… hold me *tighter* I think I'm sinking down. And I'm all strung out on heroin. On the outskirts of town."

"He damn well better not be," Steward said as he got up from the table just as Doctor Mason came into view outside the glass. He was…strolling…down the hallway, head tossed back, singing to the tune on his iPod as though he didn't have a care in the world.

"Well, I'm sittin' here playing solitaire with my pearl-handled deck . The county won't give me no more methadone and they cut off your welfare check." Whistling once more he opened the door, turned to his team, smiled and said; "Good morning."

"Awww, crap," Wylds bitched tossing her hands in the air, "what are you on now?"

"High on life," Doctor Mason retorted. "Disappointed?"

"No, I just don't believe you that's all."

"Too bad," he chimed, "got anything interesting or are we all just sitting around on our butts today?"

There wasn't anything that was really going to peek Doctor Mason's interest at the moment but that didn't mean their skills couldn't be put to use. "Forty year old male," Wylds began.

"Not interested," Doctor Mason dismissed it. "go on."

"Don't you want to hear the symptoms?" She asked.

"Maybe later. Who's next?"

"Twenty-one year old female," she started, paused, and then continued when he didn't tell her to stop. It figured he'd go for the young woman over the middle-aged man. "Presents with severe dry mouth, double and blurred vision—she can hardly read the eye chart at all—labored breathing and vomiting."

"Hung over?"

"Tox-screen said no and her sister, who brought her in and is twenty-three in case you're interested, said they went to some new horror movie last night and then went home." She tossed the folder across the table. "Anyway, she's negative for alcohol which should still be showing up if she was drunk last night."

"Any other illicit drugs?"

"Pot," Wylds shrugged her shoulders. "She says she been feeling bad for a few days, felt a little better yesterday so she went to the movie but this morning she had trouble standing up when she got out of bed."

"Could be Guillian-Barre syndrome," Steward suggested without much interest.

Well a little round of Who's Right and Who's Wrong was always fun. "Could be Myasthenia Gravis," Doctor Mason countered. "Let's get to work."

The rest of the day went just as well as any other day but the pretty little twenty-one year patient kept getting worse. That wasn't anything new. They often got worse before they got better. Around noon Doctor Spaulding walked into the office.

"You know, I heard the strangest thing earlier today," he commented," it sounded like, like, you were singing." Mason just sat there staring at him. "Others heard it too and they've said they didn't know you had such a lovely voice," he teased. "The nurses actually had nice things to say about you today." The tone of his voice grew slightly. "What's going on, Mason? What new drug are you on?"

"Gee, one good day and everyone thinks I'm on heroin or something." He complained. "What? I can't have a good day? That's not allowed?"

Spaulding stood there staring at his old friend who was bright eyed, not pale in the slightest, wasn't shaking or scratching himself and just genuinely seemed... "This isn't you, Mason, you actually look...dare I say it...giddy?" He leaned in closer. "Who's the new hooker?" That made Mason smile wide and give a chuckle. "Ah, that is it. So who she is? Care to share her number? I could use it."

"I know you could but sorry, she's not a hooker," Mason said as he got up and came out from behind the desk.

"You mean to tell me you had a *real date* with a real woman? One you didn't pay for?" To Spaulding that was astounding. As far as he knew Mason hadn't been on an actual date since the breakup of his fourth and last marriage nearly five years ago. Scotch, Internet Porn and the occasional hooker had become Mason's sexual relief of choice since then.

"Sort of."

"Well, who she is? What's her name?" Spaulding asked excitedly. This was big news and he was a bit miffed that Rick had been able to keep it from him. Now that he knew, he wanted to hear every detail.

What's her name? Small sticking point. "No idea."

Spaulding groaned. "Oh, I see you had random sex with some woman you picked up in a bar? Typical."

"Nope, with some random woman who picked *me* up in a bar." Rick corrected. "Again," he grinned slyly.

"Well, at least you didn't have to pay for it." Spaulding held his hand out. "Oh, wait, was it the woman you told me about over the summer?"

"Yep." He said happily. "Ran into her Saturday night, I left her hotel room on Sunday night."

"Good for you." Spaulding complimented. "I didn't know you still had it in ya, you old dog."

"Actually....'it' was in her." Rick crooned.

"Crude, but ok." Spaulding agreed with a smile. "And you don't know her name? Are you going to see her again? She must be really something, huh?"

Before Rick could reply, Wylds ran into the office to tell them that the patient was now experiencing a degree of paralysis. The three of them rushed off toward her room.

II

Sad and lonely she sat by the bed holding his still warm hand. It was always still. He never curled his fingers around hers anymore. Never opened his eyes. Never smiled for her or told her that he loved her. Yet she still sat here almost every day, holding his hand, talking to him, reading to him, hoping that one day he would wake up. There was no hope of that. For the last two years, he laid here in this bed never moving or making a sound. The doctors said he wasn't in any pain and that he could go on this way another five or ten years, maybe even more. Wiping a tear away from her pale eyes she drew in a deep breath. "Tommy made the football team, Craig. First string." She said trying to keep her voice light. "I know how much you'd love to see him play. He's so proud. He's good too, the coach says he's first rate. He misses you, I know he doesn't come often but he's just a kid, you have to forgive him." She patted his hand and then brought it to her lips.

"She's getting worse because it's not Guillian-Barre it's Myasthenia gravis and your treatment is making her worse!"

The voice was a way down the hall yet but it was growing louder. She looked down at the diamond watch on her wrist, a wedding present from Craig just four years ago. It was past noon and usually by now The Doc was down in the cafeteria having his lunch. Not today.

"It's not Myasthenia,"

30

Another voice and it was joined by a third telling the other two to calm down this wasn't helping the patient any.

The blinds of the glass wall behind her were open. She doubted she had enough to time to get up and close them before he came into view. She turned her back fully to the windowed wall and held her breath.

Doctors Mason, Steward and Spaulding were walking quickly down the hall passing the coma ward as they argued. Mason was almost past it when the woman inside caught his attention or rather the strawberry color of her hair did. It was pulled back in a ponytail, she was wearing a white fisherman's sweater and faded blue jeans as she sat on the bed holding the hand of the man in the bed.

"Look, Mason, it's Guillian-Barre, it fits perfectly...."

"If it fit at all the treatment would be working," Mason interjected trying to keep one eye on Steward and one on the woman in the room. Was she purposefully turning away from him? Trying to hide her face. That was the way that it seemed, the closer he got to where she sat, the more she turned her head in the other direction casting it toward the floor. What was so interesting on the floor that she just couldn't take her eyes off of it? If she was hoping to hide her face, it wasn't working for her because He thought he knew the back of that head all too well. There should be a large bruise on the side of her...

As he looked for it, she brought her hand up to her neck as though it ached and rubbed it. Was she trying to cover the bruise his teeth left? Was it really her?

As he hurried down the hall, he couldn't help strain his neck to look back only to see that she turned in the other direction. Still even facing away from him and unable to get a look at that pretty face he knew it was her.

"Mason!" Steward demanded. "What are you looking at?"

"I'm coming, leave the old gimp alone." He wanted to break off from the little group and walk into the room, wanting to grab her by the chin and turn her face to look at him so he could know for sure. Right now, he had to tend to the patient. "You're supposed to be kind to veterans, you know." On his way back he'd get a better look at her.

For twenty minutes, they went back and forth over the diagnosis but in the end, when the tests came back they were both wrong. The patient had botulism. Twenty-one and she'd gone to some non-board certified plastic surgeon and gotten tainted BoTox injections two weeks before. What was the world coming to when a woman who was barely old enough to drink was putting her life on the line to rid her face of non-existent wrinkles?

"You wanna get some lunch?" Spaulding asked but Mason stopped in front of the coma ward. "You can tell me more about your mystery woman...much more." He coached cheerily.

Mason walked into the room now devoid of anything but the patients and their monitors. He walked over to the third bed, the one in the middle of the room, the one where the woman had been sitting. It could just be his imagination but was that the scent of cinnamon hanging in the air? Looking down he picked up the chart; Craig Miller, aged 39, and resident of the Mountainside's Coma Ward for the last two years. Emergency contact; Wife, Juliette Miller. "A rose by any other name," he mumbled. "Slick. But I got you now."

"Mace?" Spaulding asked from the doorway. "Lunch? I'm buying...as usual."

Mason put the chart back. "Can't." He said. "Got a date."

"With the mystery woman?"

"Nope, with Emma in Medical Records."

"Emma?" Spaulding asked in disgust. She was a lovely woman but she was over sixty, she was as grouchy as Rick and, word was...a lesbian. "Oh, you're pulling my leg, right?"

"Nope." He looked at Spaulding. "Catch you tomorrow."

"Tomorrow? It's only 12:30."

"Really? Seems later." He wandered off to the Records Department.

III

Being one-third owner of The Mountainside had its advantages such as the Records Secretary not giving Mason any crap when he asked for the file on Mr. Miller in the Coma Ward. Sitting there with the thick file on his lap, Mason quickly read it over.

Craig Miller, architect, business owner, avid tennis player and golfer...hit by a bus at the tender of age 37 and never woke up. Looking at his medical records, Mason had no idea why the man wasn't dead. He should be. Be better for him and obviously a lot better for Rosie...Juliette. Craig wasn't even on a respirator and his brainwaves were too small to matter except in the eyes of the law. With no plug to pull, Craig's body kept breathing, his heart kept beating, and the only thing truly keeping him alive was the feeding tube down his throat.

Mason couldn't help but think of how hard that must be on Rosie, but of course, her name wasn't Rosie.

33

He kept reading the file.

Juliette Miller, aged 38, married to Craig 2 years before the accident. No kids. She was a teacher at the Williams School. The records provided him with her home phone number, work phone number, cell number, and home address, which was not exactly in the poor section of Willington, in fact it wasn't in Willington at all. Juliette lived in Killingly which was a quiet town full of big houses and old money. "Swank." He mused as he read understanding that Juliette didn't like to shit where she ate so she came over to Willington to go slumming, pick up a few guys, and have a little fun while her husband laid comatose blissfully unaware of what his beautiful wife was up to. Of course, the administrators at the Williams School were also unaware because if those stuffed shirts found out what she was doing they'd fire her for sure probably based upon some Morals Clause in her contract with the fancy Boys Prep School.

Mason thought that building buildings must have been paying off pretty well before Craig had the misfortune of stepping off the curb at the wrong time. It certainly helped explain how she could afford to keep a hotel room on a permanent reservation. Then again, her paycheck probably wasn't anything to sneeze at either.

Thanking Emma for her help, Mason went back to the Coma Ward and inquired about the patient in the middle bed. "Does he get a lot of visitors? Who are his family members?"

Nurse Ratchet stood behind the station desk looking keenly at Doctor Mason who always had something up his sleeve. "Why?"

Mason never liked being questioned but knew he might have to come up with a good excuse for checking on the records of a coma patient, "I'm thinking about taking on his case."

"What for?" The nurse asked. "He's hopeless. Even you can't cure him, Doctor Mason. He's broccoli."

"Visitors?" He asked becoming annoyed.

"Mostly it's just his wife, Juliette." She told him and then stopped. "Very pretty, isn't she? Is that what this is about? You want me to tell you about her so you can manipulate the poor woman? Into what? Your bed or letting you perform some wacked-out experiment on her husband?" She huffed. Doctor Mason didn't answer her but he did stand there staring at her with very cold eyes. Nurse Ratchet tried to dial it back a bit, after all, technically Doctor Mason was her boss. "She comes at least five days a week, usually in the afternoon, on her lunch break I think, she stays an hour or so. Sometimes she comes back at night. She sits with him, talks to him, reads to him, tells him about her day."

"She's done that for two years?"

"Yes."

Two years.

How many times had he passed her in the hallways? How many times had he passed by that room and seen her sitting there but never noticed her? That wasn't like him, he always noticed a beautiful woman and hardly ever let the same slip by without some type of comment, usually crass. She noticed him that was obvious. She knew exactly who he was before he even walked into the bar last August. He'd accused her of not being very discriminating but it seemed he was wrong, she didn't get into bed with just anybody. So why was that what she wanted him to think? Why her deep need for anonymity? It wasn't like her husband was going to care that she was sleeping around or that there was even the slightest risk of her being caught. Ros—Juliette, could bring any man she wanted right back to her own place and screw them until their eyeballs fell out. So why didn't she?

The answer was simple; Hannah. He'd been so involved with his newly discovered sister that he hadn't noticed much of anything else for the last two years. Hannah needed him, he hadn't wanted her around at first, but she needed him and, as it all turned out, he needed her just as much. She'd consumed his entire world, turned it inside out and upside down, and in the process made him all the better for it. Mason hadn't even thought much about sex since Hannah came to live with him or since she left four months ago to start living the life that had been so brutally ripped away from her thirty years ago.

Maybe now it was his turn. After all, his baby sister was always the one telling him to take a chance on love. Mason looked up at the nurse, "Anyone else come to see him?

Nurse Ratchet thought for a moment. "Occasionally, a young man comes to visit, he looks like Mr. Miller, maybe he's a younger brother or a nephew. I think his name's Timmy or Tommy, something like that. Other than him, it's just her."

Where was his family? Mother? Father? If he had a nephew where was the brother or sister? Friends? What about them? What about her family? Who was there for her?

The men in the bar.

Mason left The Mountainside for the day wondering what his next move should be. He could call her or just show up at her house but she'd consider that an intrusion and he really didn't want to blow...whatever this was...with her. Maybe he'd just take a swing by, just to check out her place. What was the harm in just taking a drive by and getting a peek?

Around seven o'clock that evening he got up the nerve to do just that. He got in his car, drove two towns over to Killingly and found Chapman Lane. Number 12 was a particularly nice old Victorian with its exterior lovingly restored to all of its former grandeur. It had a large wrap-around porch, a huge yard just waiting for a family to enjoy a game of Frisbee or Hide n Go Seek. Summer dinners out there would be delightful. It was a damn big house for a single woman, he could imagine her rattling around in there at night, lonely and sad. Juliette and Craig must have purchased the house with the intention of filling it with a happy family. That never happened. Now all she had was a big empty house full of broken promises. On the nights when the house got too quiet or the loneliness too heavy, Juliette headed for Tony's Bar.

Nights like tonight?

The lights were out. The driveway empty. Just to be sure no one was home, he got out of the car and walked up to porch to peer inside. He couldn't see much, just the front entryway which looked inviting. When he heard a dog begin to bark inside, he backed away from the house and waited to see if a light would come on but it did not.

She wasn't here.

Was she at the bar?

By the time he got back to Willington it would be just after eight. Maybe he'd run into her there.

Luck was not with him.

Making the drive back to Willington he parked in front of his own house to make the walk to the bar where there was no handicapped parking. As was his custom, when he arrived across the street from the El Royale Hotel he looked up to the window.

The light was on.

There were people up there. A man and a woman...Juliette. He was too late. She'd already mined her quarry for the night. Silhouetted in the window he turned her to the street, she put her hands against the glass, and he just knew that lucky bastard was getting her from behind the way he did yesterday and the day before.

Were her eyes open?

Did she see him standing here?

He didn't know.

Feeling much less giddy than he did earlier in the day, he turned up his collar against the crisp wind and wound his way home alone.

Chapter Three

Rick spent the remainder of the night brooding and drinking before climbing into the bed where he tossed and turned in frustration. He just couldn't get the sight of her with him, whoever the hell he was, out of his head. When he closed his eyes, the image was even clearer. He could almost hear her moaning and sighing as that...that...guy...moved in and out of her. He shouldn't have gone there last night, he didn't need the headache. Didn't need the hassle of dealing with some wacked out nymphomaniac no matter how pretty or pleasurable she was.

Doctor Richard Mason went into work more out of sorts than usual and made his entire team miserable for the day. Wylds wondered if Mason was bi-polar, he was so up yesterday, and today he was down as dirt. Worse yet, they didn't have a patient to take Mason's mind off his current troubles. The old guy just sat there grumbling, bitching, and being a general pain in the ass to anyone unlucky enough to get within earshot.

All day he sat in his office doing almost exactly the same thing he'd done last night after he got home except them he'd had a bottle of scotch to keep him company. He sat here scowling, tossing his ball against the wall and when that got boring he turned to the TV and ESPN, which was running a Monster Truck Marathon. Watching the cars crushed by the huge trucks didn't do the trick either. Popping an Oxy, he told himself (for the thousandth time) that he wasn't going to get involved. He was better off without the crazy bitch.

That may be true but, still, even here in the sanctity of his office; Rick couldn't get the image of her in the window out of his head. Naked body pressed to the glass, hot breath steaming up the glass, while, whoever he was, worked behind her. Couldn't help but feel—no matter how irrationally-that was HIS place. That other guy, well, Rick wouldn't mind if a house fell on him on his way home. Maybe he'd get hit by a bus and end up next to Craig then Juliette could visit them both.

"I'm probably going to regret this since you're in such a foul mood today but you want to get some lunch?" Spaulding asked stepping into the office with caution.

Lunch? He looked down at his watch to see that it was nearly 1:00. Was she up there in the Coma Ward at this very moment? Sitting there holding the hand of her comatose husband and pretending to be the Good Wife all the while waiting to turn into the Bad Wife when night fell. "Sure."

In the elevator, Mason pushed to go up instead of...

"The cafeteria's downstairs." Spaulding said in a puzzled voice and pushed the correct button. Too late, the elevator already started its ascent. When the doors opened, he stepped off without a word. "Where are you going?"

Mason didn't say anything as he looked back and he hoped Spaulding wouldn't say his name. If she was there then there was no sense in letting her know he was coming. Stealthily making his way down the hall he strained his neck to see into the Coma Ward before anyone inside might see him. It was empty except for the patients. She wasn't here today.

"You have a patient in the Coma Ward?" Spaulding stuttered.

"No." Feeling disappointed, he stepped inside and took a breath; nothing but antiseptic covering the scents of human waste and the stench of near death. She hadn't been here. Confirmation was always nice. Mason wandered to the Nurses' Station. "Mrs. Miller been in today?"

"Not today, Doctor Mason." Nurse Ratchet informed him.

Spaulding and Mason walked back to the elevator with Mason more convinced than ever than Juliette Miller and Rosie were one in the same. She saw him yesterday, knew he'd recognize her, tried to hide her face from him, and then changed her visiting schedule with that vegetable still passing for her husband so she wouldn't risk running into him today. "Do you want to tell me what that was all about? Since when do you care about coma patients unless you're ducking work by using their TVs to watch your soaps?"

"No." The doors opened and they rode down to the cafeteria. Looking down at the chicken salad sandwich that he'd only taken a single bite from he suddenly said, "That's her."

Spaulding looked around the cafeteria. "Where? Who's who?"

"Not here," He said grumpily, "in the Coma Ward. There's a woman whose husband has been there for two years...."

"Mrs. Miller?"

Mason dropped the sandwich he just picked up. "You know her?"

"Well, no, not really. I pass her in the hall sometimes, say hello, stuff like that. She seems like a nice woman."

"Oh, she's a *very* nice woman." Mason said slyly.

Spaulding wasn't paying very much attention, "Yes, she is she's..." he looked up at the expression on Mason's face.

"What?" He thought about what Mason just said and put it together with the sly expression. Spaulding leaned across the table. "Mrs. Miller is your Mystery Woman? The one who picked you up in the bar?"

"One in the same."

"Are you sure about this? Really, I mean it, you're absolutely positive they're the same woman?" Even as he watched Mason nod, Spaulding found it was very hard to believe. Admittedly, he didn't know her very well, but to him Mrs. Miller seemed a shy, even timid woman who hardly spoke two words. Yet, according to Spaulding's own mother, it was the quiet ones you had to look out for; they were always up to something. Mrs. Miller was a beautiful woman and almost exactly as Mason had described her to him. "That's why we stopped up there? You were looking for her?"

"Not exactly." Mason told him about yesterday and last night. "What do you think? I think the chick's got problems. Issues, ya know? Big ones."

"I'm sure she does," Spaulding murmured. How could she not have issues? Her husband went to work one morning, stepped off the curb, got smacked by a bus, and there went the rest of her life.

"Why doesn't she just divorce him?" Mason said quickly as he leaned over the table. "It's not like he'd even know."

"Why don't you ask her that? And, by the way, why do you care? I thought you were just in this to get your rocks off. From your history, I'd say that conscious husbands aren't exactly a problem for you, are you going to tell me that a comatose husband is a moral issue?"

"Thanks," He sniped grabbing a French fry off Spaulding's plate. "Why do you think she does it?"

"Me? What do I know?" Spaulding asked. "Maybe she's lonely; I would certainly imagine that she is after all this time."

"So she just goes around picking up random men in bars and having sex with them?" He was lonely too, but at least he had the good sense to hire a hooker. Maybe Rosie didn't know she could get a good-looking stud for hire.

"Have you stopped to think that, at least in your case, it wasn't exactly random? She's probably seen you around here."

"Of course." So she knew who he was before she bedded him, so what? What about the others? Did she know them too? Was she stalking all of them? What about Spaulding? Why didn't she go after him? If he talked to her and knew who she was then why not make him as an easy mark? Had to be that anonymity thing she had going for herself.

"You're just pissed because she was with someone else last night." Spaulding popped the last French fry into his mouth and looked down at his watch; he had a patient he had to attend. "I'd watch that if I were you, never know where it might lead."

"Where what might lead?"

"Jealousy." Spaulding said and left the table.

"I'm not jealous."

That was bullshit, he was jealous as hell.

"There you are," Sinclair said exasperated, "I have been looking everywhere for you."

Mason looked up coming out of his daze. "What?"

Sinclair, also one-third owner on The Mountainside and Chief of Staff, slammed a small stack of files onto the table making the remainder of his chicken salad sandwich jump off the plate. "You owe me sixteen clinic hours and I want them...starting now." She ordered.

Oh, crap. "Nah," Mason picked up his mangled sandwich, popped the rest of it into his mouth. "I got a patient—"

"No you don't," she put her hand on her hip, "I checked. You don't have a single case or anything that even looks interesting and the Clinic is backed up. Go. Now." She pointed toward the door.

With a long snarl, he picked up the files and leered at her. "I hate you."

"So what?"

He pushed past her. "Skirt makes your ass look big."

Sinclair smiled and sighed. "Nice to know you're still looking at my ass, Mason." She called after him as she waved.

Sinclair was right. The Clinic was packed. Where did they all come from? "Was there an accident?" Mason groused to the closest nurse.

"Nope," she said in a frazzled voice, "it's just mid-November and it's been raining the last week."

"And?"

"And they've all got the flu," you idiot, she wanted to add but refrained. "Hear the chorus?"

The what? He turned around and heard the chorus of coughs the nurse was referring to, most of them were low, deep and congested as hell. He was going to spend the next two hours writing out prescriptions for antibiotics and cough syrup while he exposed himself to the bug. Just friggin' lovely. "Crap. Anybody here that actually *needs* a doctor?"

There were a few and one woman in particular had been waiting a rather long time. It was faster to get those bogged down with the flu or similar virus in and out. But if she were honest with herself, it was because no doctor wanted to deal with that woman. "Exam Room 2." She handed over a file.

"What is it?"

"Small head laceration. She's not too bad but she's been in there a while. Probably needs a few stitches and some painkillers, you're perfect for the job." She said in a cocky tone still holding the file.

Well it was better than being coughed and sneezed upon; He took the file and headed down the hall giving the hackers a wide berth. Head hung low and dragging his feet, he made his way down the end of the hall to Exam Room 2 looking at her chart and the highlighted words; abusive patient. "Hi, I'm Doctor Mason," he sighed as he struggled to sound pleasant, "sorry to keep you waiting...Miss..." he looked at the chart, "Montague."

Rose Montague.

Mason looked up to take in the woman sitting on the table, "Rosie?"

Of all the bad luck in the world. Juliette waited to come to the clinic until she thought that he'd probably gone home for the day. She shifted on the exam table until she was sitting on her hands. "Hello, Doc."

45

"What'd you do to your head?"

"Slipped."

"And fell on what? A razor blade?" Mason asked as he walked over to her and began to examine the cut over her right eye. "When did you do this?" With his thumbs, he poked and applied pressure to the area trying to determine if she'd cracked her skull. Rosie let out little cries of pain and winced as he worked. The bone didn't appear fractured but it was best to get an x-ray just to be sure.

"Last night, I thought it would be fine but it just won't really stop bleeding. I think it needs a stitch or two."

"Or four." He countered. "Maybe five. What's wrong with your voice?" She sounded raspy and she was almost whispering.

"Getting a cold," she explained through tight lips, "it's nothing."

"Did you pass out? Do you feel dizzy? Any double or blurred vision? Vomiting?"

Well, she did pass out but it wasn't from the cut on her head and while she felt a little lightheaded today, it wasn't much to complain about. She did throw up but that was from the booze. "No."

Admittedly, he didn't know her very well but, Mason had the sneaking suspicion that she was lying to him. Why? "Any other wounds?"

"No," she said softly. "Just this."

Something started to creep around at the back of head and told him she might be lying. "I'll take a look at it when I 'm done. I think we should get an x-ray. Any objections?"

Yes, she had many objections. She objected to being here. She objected to being treated by him and she objected to being subjected to unnecessary tests! Her heart was starting to race and her breath becoming shallow as the panic attack threatened to hit full bore. Hold it together, she thought as she stared at him, just hold it together Julie-Baby. "Whatever you think best, Doc."

Oh, well, in that case...I think it would be best if you got up, dropped your jeans, and bent over the exam table for me. I got a special tool I want to use to examine you very closely. He actually bit the tip of his tongue to keep the words from slipping out of his mouth. This was awkward; did he tell her he saw her here in the hospital yesterday? Did he wait for her to say whether or not she saw him outside the window last night? He didn't know. One thing was fairly certain, he couldn't blow anything if he just kept his mouth shut and played Doctor. All he had to do was clean her up, numb her up, and then stitch her up. If she didn't say anything then maybe he shouldn't either. "Tilt your head back," with an antiseptic wipe he cleaned off the wound and removed tiny bits of broken glass from it. "How did you do this?"

"Hit my head on the cabinet."

He stopped cleaning the wound and took half a step back, "I thought you said you slipped."

Juliette thought about it for a second, "Yes, I did. I slipped and hit my head on the open kitchen cabinet." She offered. "I was getting the cleaner out from under the sink, the floor was wet and I slipped."

What a really terrific liar she was! Excellent! If he hadn't slept with her, he would have bought that in a heartbeat. "Glass cabinet? Under the sink?"

47

"Yes."

"Well, now you know my name," he led, "I'm thinking yours isn't Rose Montague."

"Perhaps not Rose," she offered without saying anything more.

"There's no 'perhaps' about it and it's not Montague either." Mason countered. "Stay still, this is going to sting, but once the Lidocaine takes effect I'll be able to stitch you up." He thought about that for a second. "Would you rather a plastic surgeon did it? This is going to leave a scar."

"That's all right, Doc, I trust you." She held onto the sides of the exam table while he poked the needle through her skin and injected the numbing agent. When the syringe was empty, instead of taking a step backward and away from her to put it temporarily on the counter, Mason turned at the waist and reached behind him instead. When he turned back, she had her legs wrapped around his waist. "Not too bad, right?" She was looking at him with smoky eyes.

"Not too good either but you'll live." Mason said as he looked down, the last time those legs had been so snuggly encircling his waist there hadn't been any bothersome clothing between them. The woman on the exam table, the one with the minor head injury, tucked her fingers under the hem of his shirt to run them along his warm skin as they made their way upward to his chest. "This is a hospital," he said without much strength. How many times had he wanted to grab a nurse or Sinclair—oh yeah Sinclair—and just give her what for right here in one of these rooms?

"There's no one here but us, Doc." She whispered.

"Yeah, for now and those doors don't lock."

"So then they can join us or just watch, which would you prefer?" With one hand under his shirt roaming over his chest, the free one found the space between his legs and gave a good grope. He was halfway to hard already. "Maybe it doesn't matter to you? I don't mind being watched."

"I noticed," He pulled her hands away and then sat down on the stool and waited for the injection to take effect. "About that name, Rosie?" He leaned forward. "I'm Rick," he looked toward the door, "you heard me when I came in, right? Doctor Richard Mason."

"Who cares?" She sighed in annoyance as she let his first comment slip by, "but, yes, I heard you."

"You don't? You don't like to know who you're screwing?" She didn't answer him and that was the second or third time she'd refused to take the bait. He stood up and poked her wound harshly with his index finger. She didn't say 'ow'. "Looks numb to me." He said slyly. Taking a suture kit from the cabinet he began to stitch. "So you heard me, did you see me last night, is that why you let him get you in the window? You wanted me to watch? So, did you see me or were you too into it to open your eyes?" He let out a chuckle as he worked, "'Cause you looked pretty...deep into it to me, or should I say he looked really deep into it?" She started to pull away from him. "I wouldn't move right now if I were you, not unless you wanna leave here looking like Frankenstein's Monster."

Yes, she'd seen him under the street light all right. "I knew I shouldn't have come here."

"Oh come on, you knew I'd be here, didn't ya Rosie? That's why you waited so long. What's the matter? The guy sucked—he didn't, ahh, *measure up*— so you came around looking for a little of the good stuff?"

"I waited so long because the service in this place *blows*," she said angrily, "as a matter of fact...*Doctor Mason*....I was hoping *not* to run into you during my visit." Eye to eye, she added coolly, "Just because you fucked me, don't think you own me."

"Believe me lady; I'm aware that nobody owns you." He did not care for the way she said 'Doctor Mason' in the slightest. Much less seductive than 'Do-c'. "Except maybe the guy in the coma upstairs."

Juliette, taken by surprise, in shock and in anger, pulled all the way away from him. The suture went with her and henceforth through her skin making the wound larger. "Ow! Damn!"

"I told you not to move." Mason railed. "Now look what you've made me do."

"What I made you do?" She held her hand to head to catch the new blood dripping there. "Who the hell do you think you are, Doc?" Juliette stomped around the exam table to the counter where the suture kit lay and she picked up the scissors.

"What are you doing? Get back up there." Mason ordered as he watched her cut the silk thread and then toss it at him. "You can't walk out, you're bleeding."

"Watch me." She gave the door a hard yank only to have it shoved closed by the bottom of his cane. "Get out of my way, Doc."

"No." He asserted. "Get that cute little butt back on that table and let me finish stitching you up." She stood there with a gaze of defiance the likes of which he had never seen. "Right now. Get up there."

Juliette had a good mind to shove him to the ground but she waited over two hours. What was she going to do? Drive two towns over to the next clinic and wait another two hours? "Fine." She got back on the table. "I don't owe you any explanations, Doc, so don't go around thinking that I do. You got what you wanted..."

"I think we both did."

"Just do your job and then let me out of here."

"That's not what you were getting at a few minutes ago, but, sure, right away, Mrs. Miller." He agreed haughtily. "Got a hot date?"

"Not with you."

Fifteen completely silent minutes later, Juliette was stitched and bandaged and on her way out of the exam room. "So I suppose this means I won't be seeing you again?" He asked.

"I wouldn't think so. I thought you were different, Doc, but I was wrong. You're just like all the rest." With that, she left. He stepped out in the hall to watch that fine ass wiggle its way down the hall, through the doors and out of his life.

Chapter Four

The night was long, crisp, and damp, however, that didn't stop Mason from walking down to the bar around 8 o'clock. He looked up to the window to find it dark...and broken. Looked like someone hit it with a rock or maybe a tennis ball. Not hard enough to smash the glass but more than enough to crack it into a spider's web. Maybe one of her jilted lovers had been trying to get her attention. Mason walked into the bar to find it nearly empty. "She been in tonight?" Rick asked the bartender as Tony put a scotch in front of him.

"Not tonight, Doc."

He downed the scotch as he cursed himself for chasing this woman before he made his way home, the damp crisp air of his earlier walk having turned to a deep chill with sprinkles of rain. The window was still dark. Maybe she was at home like a Good Little Wifey.

What did it matter if she was?

Maybe she would change her hunting ground now that he discovered her secret. If that were the case then his chances of running into her at an...opportune moment...would be severely lessened. Wouldn't that be a pity? Yes, yes, indeed it would. Then again, what was she doing here anyway? He was no slouch in the paycheck department but Juliette's neighborhood consisted of bankers, stockbrokers, other Wall Street types, and those in the high end of the construction business. Average pay there, he would guess was around three-quarters of a million a year. Slightly less than his income by about, oh, two-hundred thousand dollars give or take. It was one thing to go slumming— even fun from time to time—it was another thing all together when it turned out *you* are the slums. Educated at Johns Hopkins, known the world over for his diagnostic skills and talents, Doctor Mason didn't think he'd ever be considered 'the slums' and he found it most insulting.

Back at home, frustrated and brooding once more, he picked up the phone, punched six buttons and hung up. If he screwed up over the phone—probably even worse than he had this afternoon-- she'd change her number and he was likely to screw this up no matter what he did, that included sitting here fondling his Oxy bottle.

"Fuck it," he grumbled, grabbed his coat, snatched up his keys, and made the twenty-five mile drive from his front door to that of one Juliette Miller. In the pouring rain, Chapman Lane was very quiet this time of night and his was nearly the only car moving as he slowly passed her house. The lights weren't exactly on, the house wasn't lit up, but there appeared to be several candles in the front room which provided him enough light to see her moving around in there. Passing by before he garnered any unwanted attention, he drove to the end of the street, turned around, and then parked across the way from her house. Killing the engine and the lights, he sat there wondering why he was chasing her and just who the stalker was now as he watched her. In the house, she called the dog up to the couch, a white American Yorkshire Terrier, better known as a Pit Bull. In the driveway was a silver Lexus, he'd have to look for that outside the bar and the hotel from now on. It was the only car in the driveway and he didn't see any signs of anyone else in the house.

His own car was rapidly cooling now that the engine was off taking the heat with it and the windows were beginning to fog over as Rick started to shiver. "This is ridiculous," he admonished himself, reached for the key to turn the ignition and then looked back at the house. He didn't come here to walk away at the last second, did he?

Juliette was sitting on the couch in her living room with her dog, Max, absently watching TV and drinking her fourth gin martini for the night when Max jumped off the couch and began to bark. A few moments later, there was a knock at the door. "Who could that be?" She wondered aloud as she made her way to the front door to see a familiar and very unexpected figure standing there. "Doc? Isn't a little late for a house call?"

"Hi ya...Rosie." There was the strong smell of alcohol on her breath and her eyes told him she was a little further than only three sheets to the wind. She was wasted.

"What are you doing here? Haven't you done enough?"

"How's your head?" The dog barked at him ferociously, annoyed with the new intruder who was obviously making his mistress uncomfortable. "It's raining, you going to let me in?"

"Max, stop it!" Juliette told the dog. "Go!" Giving Rick a menacing look the dog stopped barking, went back in the house and sat in the front hall behind her ready to pounce on him should make the slightest mis-step. "What do you want, Doc?" She asked not stepping aside to allow him entry.

"Kinda obvious, isn't it?"

"I'm not in the bar tonight," she said coldly. "I don't appreciate you coming here."

"Ok, I figured as much." Rick mumbled.

Juliette leaned against the doorjamb and crossed her arms over her chest. "I told you, I don't owe you anything. Go home, Doc." Juliette uncrossed her arms and turned to go back inside. "There's nothing for you here."

Before she could get the door closed, Rick shoved the cane into it blocking it open. In bed at least, she liked being the submissive, he thought he'd assert himself a little as he did this afternoon to get her stay in the exam room long enough to let him tend to her medical needs. "Let me in," He demanded and the tone of his voice set off Max, the dog came running, barking, snapping, and snarling. Max knocked his mistress to the ground and out of harm's way, the door opened and the dog attacked. Before Juliette could get to her feet, Max had The Doc on the ground and a firm hold around his arm with its teeth. "Get this beast off me!"

Juliette had a good mind to let Max go on and do what he was doing but there were lights coming in the houses next door and across the way. "Max! Namaste! Namaste!" The dog, still with its teeth around Rick's forearm, looked up at his mistress. "Now, Max." With a whimper of dissatisfaction the dog let go and went back into the house.

On the porch, The Doc cradled his arm. "Gonna let me in now? I'm injured here."

"Physician Heal Thyself," Juliette crooned as she watched him stumble to his feet. "I'm sure you'll be fine."

"I'm *bleeding*."

"How's it feel?" She mocked. "It's your own fault." She huffed and then capitulated. "All right fine, come in, use the bathroom, bandage yourself up and then go." Juliette stepped aside to let him into the house. "Go, Max." The dog wandered off to the living room.

Neither of them noticed the non-descript car parked across the street or the occupant watching them.

Holding his wounded arm, Rick followed her as she lead the way through her home to a bathroom on the first floor just off the kitchen. From what he could see the majority of the house was painted white; front foyer, staircase leading to the second floor, living room, small room off to the other side, front hall, and even the bathroom on the first floor was white. Flat white. Juliette and Craig must have been in the middle of interior renovations when Fate struck, she never finished them. She just lived with the white walls although she probably had colorful cans of satin and gloss finish in the basement or garage. In the living room she had more than a dozen candles going along with the fireplace, there was carpeting in there; white matching the walls and the furniture. On the coffee table was a bottle of gin and a martini glass. In the room off to the right, there was a very large wood drafting table that looked very old and very expensive. Rick thought that was going to be Craig's room where he would make designs and plans for the buildings he created.

The kitchen, however, was a lemon yellow and looked as though it hadn't been painted in a good many years. At some pointed someone began the task of stripping the wood cabinets but never got around to completing the task. "I'd apologize but this is your fault, you provoked my dog and no one asked you to come here."

Richard Mason had gone a lot of places and felt unwelcome more times than he could count but this was the first time he truly felt that he'd invaded someone's inner sanctum. Coming here was a big mistake and if she hadn't changed her hunting ground already, she would now. He totally blew it this afternoon and then made matters worse by showing up on her doorstep tonight. Nevertheless, while he was here, he'd see what he could do about the situation. Hell, it couldn't get much worse, could it? "Ow," he cried as he took off the coat even though it didn't hurt very much and the wound wasn't likely to need much attention. "I didn't come here to upset you..."

"And I doubt that you came here to apologize, you must have come here hoping to get laid," she said through tight lips. "You're out of luck, Doc."

"My name's not Doc, its Rick and you know it, Juliette." He took off the sport coat and pushed up the sleeve of his shirt to see two deep puncture wounds.

"Whatever...*Rick*...you're still out of luck." She opened the medicine cabinet and threw a box of Band-Aids at him along with a tube of Neosporin. "I'm afraid I just don't do that here and by the looks of things I won't be doing them at the El Royale Hotel anymore either, strange but almost every time I look out the window I see you standing under the streetlight. I told you already; just because I fucked you doesn't mean you own me."

"Oh, yeah," Rick scoffed, "saw *that* for myself last night."

"I know. Did you enjoy it?" Juliette asked as she stepped toward the bathroom door. "You know where the front door is, you can show yourself out when you're done." She walked away from him without looking back.

In the bathroom, Mason washed the blood off his arm. Grabbing a towel from a nearby rack, he dried off the arm to see the wounds weren't very deep, a little anti-biotic ointment and a few Band-Aids would do the trick. Looking at his reflection and gathering up his nerve, Mason took a deep breath and exited the bathroom but she wasn't anywhere to be seen. He walked back the way he came and found her sitting on the couch with the dog at her feet. "The physician has healed himself," He announced and showed her his arm. "But I think you owe me a new coat." He picked it up and then put his fingers through the holes Max's teeth left behind. "I'll settle for a drink." He offered.

"I'll settle for an apology." She countered.

She was right. "Yeah, alright, you're right, you don't owe me anything. I just wanted to know who you are. I told you before, I like to know who I'm getting in bed with."

"Who you *had been* getting into bed with." Juliette corrected.

Mason felt deflated, he should have let her stay a fantasy, a Mystery Woman, but that just wasn't his style. If there was puzzle, a mystery, of any type he just had to solve it no matter the cost. "Yeah, about that drink?"

Why not? She could use another one. "Just one but then you have to go. You shouldn't be here."

Did she have plans for the night? No, not from looking at her, she wasn't dressed for a night out or even a hot night in. Worn, faded, and very comfortable looking blue jeans, a lavender turtleneck sweater—also well-worn-- and stocking feet. She wasn't wearing so much as lipstick on her face. She'd been sitting there on the couch, under the blanket, by the fire, drinking the night away when he showed up on her doorstep. "Why? Your boyfriend coming soon?"

Juliette gave him a wan smile. "You're the first man to enter this house since Craig left for work two years ago. One drink and then you have to go, Do-c."

She couldn't be serious. "First man?" He asked as he followed her back to the living room. "Cable guy? TV repair man? Mailman?"

"No, Doc."

What about the kid who came to visit Craig from time to time? Didn't he ever come by here to check on her? Maybe she just didn't consider him a man. Passing through the kitchen earlier something caught his eye; those cabinets. "Nice wood in the kitchen," he commented and pointed at them. "Old cabinets."

"I doubt it'll ever get finished," she said wistfully.

"I thought you said they were glass."

"I did? When?"

She was too wasted to think too quickly. "In the Clinic, you said you slipped and hit your head on a glass cabinet under the sink."

"I did," she said in the same wistful voice, "the upstairs bathroom has a glass cabinet."

Ahhh, but you said it happened in the kitchen. He could push that issue but it was probably better to let it rest for now, he was already skating on very thin ice. "How's your throat? Still sore?"

"A little."

"Want me to look at it now?"

Holding her hand to the turtleneck collar and fiddling with it a bit she tried to blow him off, "Don't worry about it, Do-c." She pulled a blanket over her legs. "I'm afraid I don't have any scotch, Doc, only gin in this house, will that do?"

"Fine by me." He agreed, he didn't get the feeling she'd like it too much if he sat on the couch with her so he took a seat in one of the Queen Anne style chairs facing it. The fire was warm; he glanced over it and the mantle above it. The candles' flames bounced off something up there, it was a silver picture frame and inside was a wedding picture of the Happy Couple Craig and Juliette Miller. "You wore a black wedding gown?"

Juliette looked up the picture as she poured two glasses of gin, handed him one. "Craig loves that dress." She picked up a pack of Newports, "No lectures, Doc," Juliette said as she lit the cigarette and blew the smoke rings into the air. "I'm already aware smoking is bad for my health and, yes, it's not going to do my sore throat any good." He was still looking at the photograph. He was nosey old man that much she knew as she'd often hear him in the halls going on about things he had no business going on about or even knowing about and thinking it was all just a hell of a good time. That was the side of The Doc she could do without. "My life isn't open to you, Doc, but if you must know, we had a 'Backwards' Wedding...he wore white and I wore black, see?"

Indeed. Craig looked dashing and ecstatic in his white tails and top hat with a radiant Juliette in the long black chiffon gown at his side. She had red roses and baby's breath in her hair. He was a very handsome man; Rick could see how easily Craig attracted the fair Juliette to his side with his dark wavy hair, bright green eyes, and Tom Cruise smile. They should have been a very happy couple for a very long time. The only other photograph in the room was one of Juliette that must have also been taken on her wedding day. In this photograph, she was in her black wedding dress, her fiery red hair hung down around her nearly bare shoulders as she twirled in the mist against a backdrop of barren trees.

"Big wedding?" He asked taking his first sip off the gin. He wasn't a big gin drinker and he was apt to nurse this a little. "When did you get married?"

"Hundred and seventy-five." She said as she took another drag and then a large sip from her glass. "We were married at the stroke of mid-night on New Year's Eve."

"I like that one," he pointed to the picture of her dancing in the mist.

60

"Craig took it; it's his favorite, that's why I've left it there." She admitted and then took a long sorrowful look at her company.

"It *was* his favorite picture. He lov*ed* the dress." Mason corrected knowing he was walking an incredibly thin line tonight, even sharper than the razor's edge of nights past. Sitting here looking at her and the photograph Mason could see why it had been one of Craig's favorite pictures of his Juliette, she looked so happy and free but not now. Now she was trapped nothing more than a bird in a cage of her own making.

"He's not dead."

"Not much difference in his case."

"Watch your step...Rick." She said in a low even chilly tone, "You know where the door is."

Oh yeah he knew where it was all right and had little doubt that he'd be walking through it soon if it was lucky, if not he'd be chased out by the mutt on her lap. "Do you think he'd approve of what you do?"

Juliette looked up at the wedding picture, "I don't really discuss it with him." She turned back to the living man sitting across from her.

"You're gonna get yourself killed, do you know that? One night you're gonna pick up the wrong guy and he's going to have his way with you and then he's going to kill you." He told her flatly and let the words echo in his head for a moment. "Or is that what you're after? Is that what you're hoping for? Then all of this..." he gestured to the house, "would be over?"

How many times had she heard that tone in his voice as he stood in the hallway, outside his office or a patient's room, trying to get his way? Trying to figure out the how and the why

61

of it all. "What is this, Doc? Am I one of your puzzles now? Is that what this is about? If it is, then I have to tell you, you'll go insane trying to figure me out so it's probably best if you just don't try."

"One of my puzzles? You've done more than just see me in the hallways occasionally."

"You're hard to ignore."

"Am I?"

"Oh please," she rolled her eyes and took another drink.

"Why me?"

"What?"

He leaned forward. "You knew who I was well before I walked into the bar that night. Why not Spaulding?"

"*Doctor* Spaulding?" She asked in surprise. "The nice man with the brown hair and soft brown eyes?"

Rick grinned, she noticed Spaulding all right, so why didn't she go for him? "That's the one and only Spaulding. What's wrong with him?"

Her mouth hung open a little. "Nothing...I guess." She stammered. "I just never thought about it until right now."

She didn't seem to be lying. "You know my staff, right?"

"Very well," she cooed in the candle light.

"Yeah, that one too." He agreed. "Back to the other staff, the people who follow me around all day like little kids...what about Steward? Not into black guys? What about Goodspeed? There, now, he's cute."

"The blonde man? Yes, he is very cute. Both of them have wives. I don't fuck married men." Juliette stated trying to keep her anger, her indignation at his intrusion into her inner sanctum but there were thoughts emerging in her head, ones she shouldn't be thinking. "What's wrong with you, Doc? Why *not* you?"

Back to playing head games. Instead of telling him she didn't owe him any explanations—which she didn't—or telling him to shut up or go away, Juliette was going to dance with him to distract him and turn his attention in a more interesting direction. Yes, this was going to be a lot of dancing, waltzing to be precise. Three steps up and two steps back, one step up and one to the right. "I'm a crabby gimp," he returned, "ask anyone who knows me. I'm a real prick."

"Oh, you got that right. No argument here."

The sultry tone of her voice made goose bumps rise on his arms. It seemed Juliette Miller was even more discriminating and particular then he'd given her credit for. She'd noticed all of the men around her but she picked him. He wouldn't pick him if he were her. "I'm arrogant, pushy, downright obnoxious most days. Spaulding or Goodspeed on the other hand, much more even-tempered, pussy cats even."

"Yes, well, if I ever want... a little pussy... cat I'll look them up."

Was it getting hot in here? Juliette didn't want a pussy cat, she wanted a tiger, and he knew it. For whatever reason, in her eyes, Rick fit the bill. He pulled at his collar as the image of her with him and another woman—Sinclair perhaps—heavily involved between the sheets danced behind his blue eyes. "You knew who I am but you let me believe...."

"Richard Edwin Mason," Juliette began easily, "born June 12, 1962 Osaka, Japan to Claire and General Edwin Mason. Schooled all over the world. Graduated St. Mark's High School in Victorville, Michigan in 1981, valedictorian. Attended the University of Pennsylvania and again graduated at the top of your class. Received a full ride to Johns Hopkins, graduated with no less than three degrees, again at the top of your class. Married four times, joined the military after the death of your first wife, Barbara that's where your hip was injured. You came home and recovered in a VA hospital. Today you're considered the premiere Exploratory Physician on the planet. How am I doin', doc?"

Mason's blue eyes narrowed on her until they were no more than slits, "Not bad. How did you..."

"You ever Google yourself? I learned everything there is to know about you in less than fifteen minutes." She drank the last of her glass and poured another while she waited for him to respond.

Pursing his lips and swallowing hard to keep his anger down he gazed at her with cold eyes, "Google doesn't know everything. Actually, I was born in Victorville to Adelaide Morgan and the son-of-a-bitch James Rice II. Recently discovered my adoption and my sister, Hannah."

Sipping on her gin to give herself a moment Juliette thought that was interesting. Hannah Rice made the local paper a few months ago along with Doctor Mason as the victims of an art thief who tried to steal an original Renoir from the small home they shared in Willington. The paper noted the woman as Rick's sister but Juliette thought that was a mistake as the Almighty Google listed him as an only child. Six months ago she read

64

Hannah Rice's wedding announcement in the same paper. One night as she sat here drinking, Juliette used Google to dig into the past of Hannah Rice but the woman didn't have a digital footprint. No website. No Facebook page. No LinkedIn. No Twitter. Nothing. All she could find was scant information on a horrific car crash in Victorville, Michigan over thirty years ago. "How's that going for ya?" She tried to sound casual even though she'd picked that night in August to strike because she knew Hannah was gone and Rick was lonely in her absence just as Juliette was in Craig's.

Mason wasn't going to sit here and discuss Hannah with a woman who refused to tell him anything about herself so he changed the subject as he glanced back to the picture of her twirling in the mist, "Your hair, why'd you color it...again?" Did she...shrink? Rick wondered as he stood there. He stood up straight and tried to gauge her height; he looked down to see she was barefoot. He hadn't realized the heels she wore were so high and must add at least four inches to her because in stocking feet the top of her head barely came to his chest.

"Isn't that why you noticed me yesterday? The darker hair? You like brunettes don't you, Doc? Or do you just only notice a woman after you've fucked her? You've seen me around that hospital a thousand times and never even said 'hello'."

"Blonde, brunette, redhead...bald...I don't really care." He had hoped the 'bald' comment would make her snicker, those translucent eyes sparkled a little, but that was it. "I like this color better, not that you care or that you should care what I think, I'm just sayin' I like it better." She didn't say a word and he couldn't keep his mouth shut. "Google tell you I like brunettes? Is that really what you do? You see a guy who catches your eye, you stalk him on the Internet, find out all about him, then strike?"

"I told you when we first met; I'm very discriminating."

It seemed she was after all, Juliette might be playing fast but she wasn't playing loose she only wanted him (and the other men) to think she was. "The mutt?" Rick asked pointing to the dog and taking another drink, "Trained guard dog?"

On the couch, perched with his paws hanging over his mistresses' curled legs, Max let out a growl. The Doc overstepped his bounds tonight and Juliette felt she'd done the same inquiring about Hannah so she went with the flow of the conversation. "That's right, Maxie, you tell him. I'm no mutt." She encouraged and pet the dog. "He's a wedding gift from Craig," she explained not wanting to talk about her husband any more than it seemed the Doc wanted to talk about Hannah, "For the most part, his job allowed him to work from home, but there were many times Craig had to go to New York City where his firm is located, sometimes he was gone for days," she sighed, "he didn't like the idea of my being here alone."

"Yeah, never know what your wife might get up to all alone out here in the suburbs while you're hard at work in the big bad city." He cracked. The crime rate around here had to be near zero. "Namaste?" Rick asked and watched the dog's ear prick up. Max heard the safety word for 'quit' but he doubted that's what the dog would do should he or anyone other than Juliette utter the command. "It means..."

"I know what it means, Doc." She interjected. "You think that an odd command word?"

"I think it's an odd word, period."

"Depends on who you are."

Finishing the glass, he poured another and then refilled hers although he thought she'd probably had enough. "You fill that prescription I gave you?"

"Yep."

"You take them?" As if he had to ask as he stared into those eyes both vacant and distant at the same time.

"Yep."

"How many drinks have you had?"

"Six."

He took the glass out of her hand. "This makes six?"

"Yep, give it back, Do-c."

"Nope." He put it on the floor next to his chair. "You eat?"

"Not today."

He hadn't either and she could use the carbs. Out here, he didn't think delivery was much of an option. "Wanna go out and grab a bite to eat?" He'd offer to cook but that wasn't his thing. She wasn't falling down drunk although she should be passed out, he could take her out in public and getting her out of the house to some place other than the bar, or the El Royale might be a good thing.

On the couch, Juliette leaned forward so that the candles illuminated her face and those haunting eyes. "Then what...Do-c?" She asked drawing in the smoke from the cigarette and letting it out slowly.

Rick felt a rush of heat as he cleared his throat. "I don't know, we'll see, maybe I'll return the favor and show you my place." He suggested.

"That would only be fair." She agreed.

"Or we could just go upstairs now." He ventured and almost winced at his own words. *She's gonna throw me out for sure.*

"Not here, Do-c, never here." After blowing out the candles and sliding closed the glass doors on the fireplace, Juliette locked up the house and followed the Doc out to his car. On the way out, passing through the front foyer and the large round table with its vase of flowers, his eyes caught on the mail sitting there. Several envelopes from different places including the electric company and her mortgage company. All of them were unopened. All marked 'FINAL NOTICE' in big red letters.

Juliette was losing this house. Not that it was any of his business but that was certainly something to be depressed about and depression could make people do any number of things from lazing around the house in a deep funk to looking for a little distraction in the arms of strangers on cold nights.

III

That guy last night. He'd been a real boar. Just another bully with a badge. Not like this one, not like The Doc. Now that they were away from the house and all of its restrictive ghosts, Juliette felt more at ease as she took off her coat and tossed it in the backseat. Fishing in her purse, she pulled out a cigarette pack before dumping the purse in the back as well. "Do you mind?" She asked holding up the pack.

"As a matter of fact, I do." Rick said as he rolled down the window. "But go ahead."

"Thanks, Doc." She cooed and pulled a joint from the pack. "Want some?" She asked as she kicked off her sneakers, tossed them in the back, and put her bare feet on the dashboard.

"What? You're not high enough?" He bitched taking in the sweet smoke.

"Can never be too high or too numb." She returned glumly and put the joint back to her lips since The Doc didn't seem to want to join her. "How many of those pills of yours do you pop in a day, Doc?"

"Touché," Rick returned unhappily.

Juliette turned up the radio and danced in the seat as she toked her joint. Bare feet on the dashboard her little butt ground round and round on the leather seat as her head rolled from side to side and she sang along with the Steve Miller Band's *Wild Mountain Honey.* She turned those wasted smoky eyes to him. "Turn down here, Doc." She said and pointed to a road off to the right.

Rick didn't know what was down this road that was so interesting, it certainly wasn't going to be a restaurant. "What's down here?" He asked as he slowed down, the pavement disappeared and in its place appeared a dirt road.

"Keep going," she cooed, "just a little further down."

"I don't know if you noticed but this car isn't four wheel drive," he groused.

"Just a little further, Doc. You'll see. You'll like it. I promise."

A little ways down the dirt road and Rick saw what she was after. A public boat launch site. It was vacant now in the dark of night with the cold rain falling on the river. He pulled into the parking lot and turned off the car. "What did you want to come down here for?"

"Is that a real question?" Juliette asked as she toked the last of the joint then tossed the lit roach down her throat. She sidled up next to him and put her hand on his crotch. "Come on, Doc, when's the last time you did it in the backseat?" She dared.

"Twenty years ago?" Rick answered as he tried to think not only of how they'd gotten to this point so quickly but if his leg would hold up for such a treat. If he sat on the seat and let her do the work, it would. No problems there. No problems anywhere, as she massaged him he stood at full attention. There was one problem; "I don't know about you but I don't have any protection."

"Didn't seem to bother you last time." She said in a sultry voice and began to lower his zipper and her head. "I don't think it bothers you now either." Juliette pulled the lever to raise the steering wheel so that it was out of her way before she finished her descent. Her lips closed down over his hard shaft. Rick let out a deep moan as her tongue danced around on him. Before he knew what hit him, his pants and her blue jeans were around their respective ankles, and she wasn't waiting for the backseat, she was climbing over him. Settling down on him, taking him inside that sweet warm place. "This what you came for, Doc?"

Damn straight it is. Rick planted his hand on the back of her head to bring her in for a kiss but she dodged him and nibbled at the nape of his neck instead. If she wasn't going to let him kiss her then he wanted to suck on that supple neck but the sweater was in his way. "Take this off." Rick tugged at it.

"Leave it, It's cold." She whispered against his neck.

Cold? Not from where he was sitting.

"Come on, Doc, fuck me." She begged.

Screw the sweater. Rick reached down and pushed the seat all the way back before grabbing her hips with both hands and pushing her further down on him.

IV

70

A few moments after Mason and Juliette pulled away from the curb across from her house, the non-descript car did the same leaving its headlights off for as long as it could so as not to be noticed. The well-lighted little suburban neighborhood gave way to darkened back streets as he followed them the driver had no choice but to turn on his lights. He hung back, far back, so that the good doctor wouldn't care about his presence. Five or six miles down the road the car in front of him turned onto a side street, he slowed down as it passed it and read the street signs; Winding Hollow and Dead End. He drove down the main road a little ways before turning around, killing the lights and parking within view of Mason's car. They were parked at a public boat launch that closed at sunset.

From his vantage point, only a few yards away, the occupant of the car watched the two lovers go at it like rabbits as the windows fogged over with their steamy breath. Before it could go too far he decided to interrupt and make his presence known. Reaching out to the dashboard, he wondered if he should flip on his headlights and the red and blue flashers. *Nah. Let them be surprised.* He climbed out of the car, smoothed his blonde hair back, and got his flashlight ready and walked up to the car. The couple inside were too busy to notice him standing outside the door watching them get it on, watching her grind on Mason's cock. No they didn't notice and that was only fair and right, after all, Mason got to watch them last night so why shouldn't he get to observe the good doctor's style in return? A few more seconds, the good doctor was groaning, he was right on the edge of climax and that's when he turned on the flashlight and banged on the car window.

"What the hell?" Rick said and grabbed hold of Juliette who latched onto him with fear as the light shined in his eyes.

"Police, roll down the window." Came the barked order.

71

"The cops?" *Oh sweet Jesus, Spaulding and Sinclair are gonna love this.* "It's ok, go on, get off." Juliette rolled to the other side of the seat, brought her knees up to her chest to cover herself as she wiggled the jeans back into place. "Evening officer," Rick said as he hoisted up his own pants and rolled down the window. "I know this looks bad but she's not a hooker or anything."

"Oh I know that, Doctor Mason."

The light flashed away from Mason's eyes. "Ritter?"

"Long time no see, huh, Doc?" The big blonde man crooned, savoring the moment and the look on Mason's face. "License and registration, please?" He shined the light into the car. "Evening, ma'am, can I see your ID, please?"

"We weren't doing anything wrong." Juliette stammered as she pretended to look around for her purse which was in the backseat. She didn't want to give him her ID and saw no reason to do so even if he was a cop. Rummaging around, she offered a sad smile, "I must have left it back at the house, officer."

Rick turned and gave her a sharp look. He just saw her dump the purse back there not ten minutes ago. He kept silent, it was Ritter after all. It all started three years ago when Trooper Ritter wandered into the clinic with the sniffles and a big case of Holier Than Thou. Ritter felt that Mason had been rude to him during the exam so Ritter decided to harass Mason on his way home. He busted Mason on a possession charge that almost cost Rick his career. Well, six full bottles of Oxies were a lot and the State of Vermont considered it Possession with Intent to Sell. Mason produced his prescriptions, Ritter said they were forged, then the bastard began investigating his patients. For nearly a year Ritter stalked and harassed Mason at every turn. The Trooper pulled him over for; drunk driving, reckless driving, a busted tail light (which Mason was positive Ritter busted just so he could pull him over), he even tried to arrest Mason for shoplifting….twice! To Mason, it seemed that every time he turned around there was State Trooper Ritter. Mason tried to take out a restraining order but they weren't easy to get against cops. At the end of his trial, when Mason was found innocent, the judge was very explicit in his desire for Trooper Ritter to quit playing games with Doctor Mason.

"Actually ma'am, it's Trooper…State Trooper Ritter. What's that smell? It wouldn't be marijuana, would it, Doctor Mason?" Ritter asked as he took Mason's license and registration. "Those Oxies just not enough for you these days? What with the rain and all?" He offered slyly. "Have you been drinking tonight, Doctor Mason?"

Yes, he had. He had a drink at the bar and two at Juliette's house there was no sense in lying about it since Ritter could probably smell the booze on his breath along with the pot in the car. Rick was sure he was taking a tiny detour downtown before the night was over. "I'm not drunk."

"I didn't say you were, I asked if you'd been drinking."

"Yes."

"Well then, I'll just run these to make sure they're still valid. You're not under suspension for DUI or anything."

"I'm not." Rick said angrily.

"Good, then if it all checks out I'll have to give you a breathalyzer, if you pass you can go back to doing whatever it was you were doing." Ritter said with a wicked little grin.

"This is harassment. The judge told you to leave me alone."

"You can lodge a formal complaint in the morning, Doctor Mason."

"Did you get your rocks off watching us?"

The wicked little grin on Ritter's face brightened as he looked past the good doctor to his companion, "Not tonight, Doctor Mason. Not tonight." Ritter said happily as he made his way back to his car and pretended to call in the information.

"You know him?" Juliette asked hoping to sound casually upset even though inside she was freaking out.

"Unfortunately." Rick said through tight lips. "Don't be surprised if he gives us an even harder time, he hates me."

"What did *you* do to *him*?"

"What? The Almighty Google didn't spit that one out for you?" Mason bitched and watched her flinch. "I stuck a thermometer up his ass, he didn't like that." He looked over at her and the shocked expression on her face. "What? I thought it would force out the stick!"

Juliette clasped her hand to her mouth to keep from laughing. Yes, Trooper Ritter did have a stick up his ass. A big one. No, Google hadn't told her about this, if it had she would have played her cards differently as this presented a sticky situation she wanted no part of.

"Everything checks out," Ritter said as he leaned into the open window and eyed Juliette.

"I told you it would. Can we go now?"

"Sure, right after you blow into this...Doc. Come on, get out of the car."

74

Jesus H. Christ. His cane was in the backseat and Rick didn't want to risk Ritter saying he was reaching for a dangerous weapon so he got out the car without it.

"I'm sure you remember how this goes, don'cha Doc?" Ritter said and held up the little gray machine. "Deep breath, blow until I tell you to stop."

Rick did as he was told, put his lips on the machine, and blew.

".06," Ritter mused looking at the read out.

"See, I'm not drunk. The legal limit is .08." Rick countered. "One more time, can we go now?"

"Well, now, fornicating in public is a misdemeanor and I could write you up for it." Ritter mused as he stood there in the rain. "You sure she's not a whore?"

"She's my date. I told you, she's not a pro."

"Sure?"

"Yes," Mason grumbled through tight teeth.

"All right then, I'll let it go, for now. For...old time's sake." He said still leering Juliette. "What do you say? That sound good?" Ritter pulled himself a little ways out of the window. "Doctor Mason?" He said as though trying to direct the already asked question to the driver.

"Mighty white of you."

"Good then, it's settled." Ritter patted the car door. "You two have a nice evening but take it to a more private location." He started to walk away but then turned back. "Oh, yeah, ya know,

I hear the El Royale Hotel is good for that." Before he could get back in the car, he heard Doctor Mason exclaiming;

"YOU and RITTER?"

The big burly cop chuckled and shook his head happily as he climbed into the car with a satisfied grin and drove off.

Chapter Five

"What are you so upset about?"

"What am I...Jesus Christ! RITTER?" Rick railed. "Did you let him do what you let me do, huh? Did you let him stick his naked dick in you?!"

"It's not like I did it on purpose, Doc. Not like I set out to buddyfuck you. I had no idea you even knew him." That was true; Juliette had no idea of the history between Doctor Mason and Detective Ritter. "I don't owe you any explanations."

"Was it him last night?" Rick asked through gritted teeth.

"I don't owe you..."

"Was it Ritter I saw fucking you in the window last night?!"

"Yes," she screeched back and then held a hand to her throat as it tightened. "It's not your concern but he's been after me for months so last night I let him. So what? I didn't do it to spite you, I didn't know about any of this."

"But you knew who he was, didn't you? Like you knew who I was."

"No," she admitted. Ritter tried to pick her up several times but she wasn't interested so she never Googled him. "I've seen him, he hangs out at the bar a lot, Doc. Even when you're there and it never seemed to bother you."

Rick couldn't remember ever seeing Ritter at the bar as he reached past her and opened the passenger door. "Get out."

"What?"

"Get out," he said again. "You don't owe me anything, fine. I can make decisions for myself, I'm not sharing a bed with Ritter, and I'm sure as hell not taking his *sloppy seconds* either. Get out."

"The least you could do is drive me home." She protested as she stared out at the cold rain.

"It's not that far," he countered, he didn't want to leave her here in the rain but he couldn't take looking at her either, not knowing she'd been with that bullying brute, she let him touch her and, "Did you?" He whispered and grabbed her wrist. "Did you let him ride bareback?"

Juliette had no idea of what she'd stepped into, all she knew was the big blonde man hung out at the bar often, he chatted her up from time to time or tried to anyway. She wasn't much interested in him but his interest in her was more than obvious. "It's none of your business."

"That's a 'yes', isn't it?" His grip on her wrist tightened.

"No," she tried to yell but it only came out in a raspy whisper. "Let go, Doc."

"Did he do it like I do it?" He whispered as he stared at her. "Huh? Was he better? Worse? What's his style?"

"Doc?" Juliette tried to pull away from him but he was stronger than he looked. "I didn't know, I'm sorry." Whatever really went on between Doctor Mason and Trooper Ritter it must have been something big and ugly, Doc was right pissed off over this. She didn't want to hurt The Doc; she'd just been spooked after he saw her and recognized her in the Coma Ward. When she ran into Ritter last night, even though he wasn't really her type, well, she'd just said 'yes'. She ended up sorry over it in more ways than one.

Instead of letting her go, he pulled her in closer and gave her an ultimatum. "Me or them." He spat and then let her go. "You either do this with me or you do this with men like Ritter, which is it going to be? You can't have both."

Juliette climbed out of the dry car and into the cold November rain. "Been nice knowin' ya, Doc."

"I thought so. Go on, you could use the shower." He sneered.

Juliette slammed the door shut.

Rick put his foot on the gas and tore out of there leaving her behind. Speeding up the hill he glanced in the rearview mirror to see her standing there watching him go. He had every right to be angry but he knew he shouldn't leave her out there in the rain, alone, out there at night. It was a good three miles back to her house. He was too wrapped up in his own anger to do the right thing and he just kept on driving. All the way home, the image of her in the rain haunted him.

Pulling into his driveway, he turned off the car and then reached into the backseat for his cane. Pulling it up it was heavier than usual, getting it to the front seat he saw Juliette's purse hanging from the crook. "Oh, shit." He murmured and turned around. There was her coat and her shoes. He left her standing there with nothing, not even the keys to get back into her house. "She's fine." Rick told himself. She'd be wet and cold when she got back to Chapman Lane but she'd be all right and surely she had a hide-a-key or a trusted neighbor with an extra key to let her into the big empty house.

Didn't she?

He brought the stuff into the house and glanced at his watch to see that he left her there nearly an hour ago. She was home by now. She was fine. Just fine. He didn't have to drive all the way back there to find out. A half-hour, two scotches and two Oxies later, the thoughts kept nagging at him until he picked up the phone and punched all seven buttons. It rang once, twice, three times and a male voice told him that Craig and Julie-Baby weren't home or they were busy, please leave a message and someone would call them back. His heart sunk as his stomach turned into a knot and he tried to tell himself that she was sitting there by the phone and warm by the fire looking at the Caller ID, she just decided not to take his call, that was all.

She was fine.

She was a big girl. She could take care of herself.

She was fine.

"Oh, goddamnit!" He yelled to the dark. Grabbing up his keys from the desk so he could make the drive back to her house he caught sight of a cab pulling up to the house. Someone got out; he couldn't see who it was. It was a little late for company for his neighbors and hardly anyone ever came to visit him. There was a small rap at the door, he opened it to see her standing there, dripping wet, cold, shaking, and barefoot. Then he remembered that her shoes were in the front seat of his car.

"You, Doc. It's you." Juliette whispered. "Now pay the man." She hitched a thumb toward the waiting cab. She'd walked almost six miles in the pouring rain and bare feet before she was able to flag him down and he'd been kind enough to accept her sad story of her argument with a boyfriend who left her on the side of the road.

"Me?" He asked not believing her. "For what? Tonight?"

"Maybe tomorrow night too, don't push it, Doc."

"Me or them and not just for tonight or you can get back in the cab and go home, Julie-Baby. My treat."

Julie-Baby. Only a handful of people ever called her that. The only way The Doc would know is if he called her house to check on her. He'd been worried about her and felt badly for leaving her the way he did. "You really want to spend the night without me?"

No, he didn't and he should consider himself damn lucky that she'd chased after him. "Wait here." Rick went outside and paid the cabbie. When he got back inside, she was already naked in his bed.

"Leave the light off, Doc." She whispered as he reached for it and redirected his hand from the lamp to her body. "We don't need it, do we?"

He did like looking at her and there wasn't much light coming in through the windows on this stormy night. If she wanted to leave it off then that would be all right. There was enough illumination from the streetlight to show him her silhouette and dimly light up her face. Her hair was wet and her skin was cold but it was soft and silky. "Why'd you come here?" He asked as he settled on the bed next to her and let her slide his hand down her thigh.

"For you. No one does it like you, Doc." No one did and she should know she'd been with a lot of them over the last year. "Don't you want me anymore?" She reached out to the place between his legs to find that wasn't the case at all.

The tone of her whisper tickled his ear and made the goose bumps return. "I want you." He bent his head to kiss her but she dodged him again and landed her lips on his neck but only for a moment. Rick grabbed her chin and pushed her away. "What's wrong, Julie-Baby? Won't kiss me anymore? I got too close, huh?"

"Far too close," she advised, "now come a little closer." She brushed her lips over his hoping that would satisfy him as she went for the neck again but he didn't let go of her jaw. Instead, he pushed her back against the pillows and the mattress and covered her lips with his. Warm moist tongue parted her lips as it searched around in her mouth.

There wasn't just heat between them anymore there was passion. Enough to last through and light up the night.

Chapter Six

With Mason's robe snug around her slender lithe body, Juliette stood in the bedroom doorway watching her Doc sleep as she held on to two steaming mugs of coffee. She wanted to go over there and wake up him properly but he was sleeping so peacefully she didn't want to spoil the moment. She liked Doc's house, it was small and cozy, well kept, nicely furnished with a mixture of American Comfortable and 18th Century Antique. Most of all, this place was quiet and still, there was serenity here. It seemed to her that even the air was lighter here. Back in her big empty and very lonely Victorian home the air was thick, as though it weren't air at all but lead turned to gas. It was always pushing, pushing, pushing, down upon her and, she feared, it would not be satisfied until she was crushed.

Julie thought that, if she let herself, she could stay right here for a nice long while just watching The Doc sleep.

No matter how much she would like to, she kept telling herself that she must not get caught up in this, not get caught up in him. "Mornin', Doc," she whispered sweetly as she walked to the bedside and held out a cup to him. "Sleep well?"

He took the coffee from her hand. She looked pretty in the morning, she looked pretty any time of day, but right now, she was beautiful. After such a hard night—figuratively and literally—he would have thought she'd sleep the day away. "Very." Taking a sip off the warm brew, he still felt a little guilty for leaving her in the rain, just peeling out of there like some half-crazed maniac and dumping her on the side of the road. He never should have done that, he never would have considered doing it to anyone else. It was only later, when he opened the door and saw her standing there dripping wet nose to toes, he realized he'd done the right thing...with her. Julie really did want a tiger, that was why she followed him home. If he had dropped her off at her door, she would never have given him another thought.

"Don't worry, I won't be staying long."

"Who's worried?" He looked over at the clock; it was past time to get ready for work. "I'm late, you must be too." He tossed the covers off and climbed out of the bed. "I like this way this looks on you." He kissed her cheek.

"Thanks."

"Why don't you take it off?"

"You're an animal," She cooed. "My clothes are in your dryer, they're almost done, and then I'll call a cab and be out of your hair."

"You're not in my hair. " He looked up at her unsure if he should say the words rolling around in his head, they came to him so rarely for one and, for two, tigers did not apologize, but he wasn't a tiger. "I'm sorry I left you there last night but I'm really glad you came here."

"It's ok, no big deal." She leaned in a little closer. "I honestly had no idea about you and..." Julie's voice trailed off for a moment, "that cop."

Rick didn't want to talk about Ritter, eventually they'd get into it, or so he imagined but not this morning, not after such a perfectly wonderful night. "What are you teaching today?"

"Hum?"

"You know I read...the file." He said carefully avoiding the use of her husband's name. "It said you're a teacher at the Williams School."

"Oh, not anymore." She said sadly and then went on to explain, "Budget cuts. Five teachers were let go over the summer and I

84

was one of them." Then she went on to give Mason a very abbreviated version of her life. A graduate of Yale with a Master's in English Literature, Julie had once been a professor at NYU helping young eager minds explore English Lit, and then she met and fell in love with Craig. There was a long and tumultuous courtship considering he was married to the fair Susan Miller when she met him and they had a son, Timmy.

Julie tried to stay away from Craig but Fate had other plans. As many times as she told him to go away, go home to his wife, he was right back on her doorstep. Nearly 5 years after meeting Craig Miller—three of which he had been officially divorced from Susan—Julie married him. He didn't want to raise a family in the City. She didn't think the long commute on a daily basis would do their relationship any favors and she was in love. They moved here. He kept his job with the New York City architecture firm and spent two or three days a week away from her while she gave up her professorship and took the job at the private prep school in hopes of one day having a family.

So much for that.

"Sorry, Julie." English Lit, that explained a lot about her and the fact that she lost her job over the summer, helped to explain all the Past Due notices she had sitting on the foyer table at home. Craig was just a lifeless, useless, lump now, nothing more than a huge economic drain who didn't have the good sense to just die. The medical bills must be staggering. If he had died then at least his life insurance would have paid off for her. If he was dead then maybe Julie could mourn his loss in a more constructive manner and then move on with her life. As it was, they were both stuck in limbo. It wasn't a good place to be and Rick would know. Death would have been kinder for husband and wife. Craig was hanging on somewhere between The Land of the Living and The Land of the Dead, he'd taken Julie with him. She was just like her house, so pretty and inviting on the outside, so empty and hollow on the inside.

"Me too," she said with a sigh. "I've been looking but all of the schools are slashing their budgets and there aren't many open positions for an English teacher, especially not one who specializes in Modern American Novels & Literature."

"I've got an open position for you."

She laughed a little. "I'm sure you do. I'll explore it later. Got a busy day ahead of you?"

"Dunno."

"Interesting job you have, Doc. You never know what you're going to do until you get there." She smiled for him.

"Your voice still sounds hoarse, gonna let me look at your throat now?" He put his hands on her hips. "I think I've looked at everything else." Rick winked.

Julie held the robe closed. "I'm fine, but thank you. Why don't you pop in the shower and I'll freshen up your coffee?"

"Oh, I thought I'd go in all funky and dirty," he smirked. "How's your head?"

"Stop fussing, Doc. I'm fine." She nuzzled the top of her head against his chest. "Just fine." *Yes, things might be all right now, Doc, if you just stay with me for a little while. Not long, I promise, just a little while.*

There was something to talk about and he wanted to be absolutely clear in this area. "So...where do we stand?" He asked. "Last night was fantastic as usual, but I mean it Julie, either it's you and me, or it's you and them." He felt a little guilty knowing he didn't have the right to make such demands on a woman he hardly knew but how was he going to get to know her better if she kept spending her time with other guys? If nothing else, he was worried about her. Last night he told her she was going to run into the wrong man some night, he meant it and it scared the hell out of him.

It was Julie's turn to smirk as she pulled away from him. "Are you asking me to...to go steady...Doc?" Her eyes sparkled. It had been a very long time since someone made her feel the way The Doc did, too long. For a reason she didn't comprehend, whenever Rick was around, the whole world simply stopped spinning. Everything fell quiet, there was room to breathe, and she felt alive again. For a while, perhaps, it might be good to stay here and play house with him. "Do you want me to wear your ring?"

"Would you?"

"Only if you still have your high school ring," she tittered.

"I'll look for it later. In the meantime, what do you say?" He asked trying to keep the annoying sound of hope out of his voice. "I'm not asking you to fall in love with me or to marry me..."

"That's good," The mood in the room as well as the tone of her voice turned serious. "Because I'm always going to be someone else's wife, Doc. Craig will always come before you."

Rick could say something here but it would be crude and it wouldn't get him the result he wanted so he settled on, "I'll share you with him but not with the rest of them."

"One day at a time but...alright. If you don't expect too much of me this will go easier." She invited.

"Dinner? Is that expecting too much?"

"I think that would be fine."

Oh, good. Well, while he was on a roll here; "You know, since you don't have anything to do," he put his hands on her hips, "you know, like work or anything, you could just stay here, and I could sneak home for a little nooner?"

That did sound very tempting. "I have to go home and take care of Max."

Damn dog. "Yeah, right. Or you could just not do that and you could be naked in my bed when I get back."

Also tempting but "I'm afraid not." Max would have to go outside by now, she didn't let him out last night and it was past time for him to go out this morning. He'd be looking for his breakfast and confused by her long absence. She'd be lucky if she didn't walk into piles of poop on bedroom floor and a urine soaked bed as that was Max's favorite way of showing his displeasure at such times. "But I'd love to meet you for dinner."

"I'll pick you up, around seven?"

Julie sighed and then smiled. "I guess it's a...date."

Half an hour later, feeling good, Rick was on his way into work leaving Julie at the house while her clothes finished drying. Stopping at the light near the El Royale Hotel, habit took over and he looked up to her window even though he knew Julie was still at his place. In the light of day, the crack in the window was easier to see, it looked like someone tossed a tennis ball at it or maybe....

In the middle of traffic, Rick pulled a three-point turn and headed back home. She wouldn't let him see her last night, insisted on making love with the lights out, she wouldn't let him look at her throat even though it obviously bothered her and now he knew why.

Julie was scared half out of her wits when the front door burst open. "Doc?" She'd just been taking her newly dried clothes from the dryer when it slammed against the front wall. "Did you forget something?" Julie stammered not liking the look in his eye. "What is it, Doc?" He just kept walking towards her without saying anything. "Doc?" Julie held her arms out in front of her in 'stop' motion. "Rick!"

"Take it off." Rick ordered.

"Wha—"

Rick reached out and grabbed her by the upper arms to repeat his demand but before he could do that, she cried out in fear and pain; she tried to pull away from him as he ripped the robe off her.

"No, please, don't...Doc...don't."

In the cold light of the autumn morning, she stood there in his kitchen naked and bruised. Her throat, her upper arms, her thighs, all covered with paw prints. Undoubtedly, some of the handy work on her thighs and hips was his but the rest was... "Ritter?" It had to be because Ritter was the only other guy to have her alone after him and the last time Rick saw her she was bruise free. "Did he slam your head into that window? Is that how you got cut? I know it wasn't on any glass cabinet, Julie-Baby. Although it was a valiant effort on your part." Grabbing her jaw, he pushed her head back to get a better look at the bruise that encircled her neck. "What'd he use? His BELT?" The bruise was too uniform for Ritter's bare hands. "Damn it! Tell me!"

"Yes," she stammered.

He thought he'd lose it. "You let that son of a BITCH put his BELT around your NECK? What the hell is WRONG with YOU?" He yelled at her. If that was what she was really into then she even crazier than he thought and he didn't want anything to do with her. Julie stood there, naked, quaking and looking very ashamed but she didn't answer him. She didn't have to the bruises spoke for themselves. Mason turned away from her and tried to get a hold of his anger before speaking again, he must have scared the shit out of her when he burst through the door to begin with. "Did you pass out?"

"Yes. "

Now he was even more concerned, "How long?" He didn't have to ask why she hadn't let him look at it in the clinic yesterday that was obvious. She hadn't waited all of that time for him, she waited all of that time for him *to leave*. In the end she only got half of the medical attention she needed when he walked through the door.

"I don't know. " Julie offered and reached for the robe on the floor afraid The Doc was going to kick it away but he didn't. He let her pick it up and hold it in front of her. "When I woke up he was gone." She was oh so glad that he was!

"Did he rape you?" Rick watched her flinch at the ugly word. "I'm not a cop, I don't give a damn if you actually said 'no' or not, because to tell you the truth, I don't think that's a word that comes out of your mouth too damn often except for, maybe, like this... oh, no, please don't stop." He mocked her passionate sighs.

"Well, and here I thought you liked that," she lobbed back. Legally, what Ritter did wasn't rape, maybe it was, she wasn't sure, "I don't owe—"

"Don't you dare stand there and tell me you don't owe me an explanation! If nothing else, I am a DOCTOR; you should have been honest with me yesterday!"

Yes, perhaps she should have; after all, her throat was the main thing that had forced her to go the clinic at all, not the wound on her head. When he walked into the Exam Room, she just couldn't do it. "It was just rough." That was all of the explaining The Doc was going to get out of her. Julie held her hand to her throat and then slipped back into the robe tying it tightly at her slim waist. It was rough. It was unpleasant. It was humiliating. She didn't want to fucking talk about it.

"Understatement of the *year*." Rick railed. A nasty thought struck him. "In the window, what was he doing when I saw you?" Had he misinterpreted what he was seeing? "Did he put your head into the glass?"

Two nights ago, Julie saw The Doc standing under the streetlight and so did Ritter, at that point as they were fucking, Ritter just lost it. At the time she didn't know why but she did now, she still didn't have any idea of what really happened between the two men, all she knew was that, somehow, she'd gotten caught in the crossfire. "Just as you walked away, yes." Julie had wanted to call out to him, do something, give him a sign, but she was so shocked and then embarrassed to have him standing there watching them all she could do was whisper his name. Even though the big brute was hurting her, she was glad when The Doc walked away. "It's just...an occupational hazard, Doc, that's all." Julie said in a raspy voice. "It's no big deal." She wasn't about to give him the gory details of her unfortunate evening with the big brute.

"It's a very big deal; you're going to charge him."

Julie's eyes went wide and she felt the blood drain from her face. "No, I'm not." She asserted in that same hoarse voice. "I'm not going to be a pawn in this rather twisted chess game the two of you are playing." *And I'm not going to have my very private life put on public display!*

Chess game? Mason hadn't seen Ritter in over, what? A year? Two? Not until last night. So, insofar as he knew, he wasn't playing any chess game. Was Ritter? "Did you tell him where you live?" That was a stupid question, of course, she hadn't she wouldn't even give the brute her ID when he asked for it. Julie probably never told any of the men where she lived or what her name was.

"No, Do-c. I never tell anyone that although you didn't seem to give a fuck."

"Neither did Ritter," He said more to himself then to her. Yes, Ritter knew, so either the cop followed him to Julie's or he was already there when Rick arrived. "You don't think that was just a coincidence last night, do you? If you do, I can assure you it wasn't." The wheels turned in his head. "When was he at the bar?"

"Monday?" Julie offered.

He shook his head, "No, you said he'd been in the bar when I was and I didn't care. That's because I didn't see him so, when? Did he see us together?"

Julie didn't understand but she thought about it anyway. Ritter, the Blonde Cop tended to hang out in the far corner of the bar by the dartboard when The Doc was around. Up until now she'd thought nothing of it but maybe it was because he didn't want The Doc to see him. "He was there that night last summer," she said thoughtfully, "he was there Saturday night, and he probably saw us leave together both times. What difference does it make?"

"He tried to pick you up before?"

Now she was getting annoyed. "Yes, I told you that."

So then, that meant that Ritter had to watch Mason score with her while he, himself, struck out. That must have pissed Ritter off but good. Ritter was a lot like Julie's dog, Max, once he got his teeth around something, he sunk in and didn't let go until someone made him.

The dryer went off; Julie opened it, fished her warm clothes from it, and then got dressed without taking off the robe. "I don't know what this is all about, Doc and I don't want to know.

What I do know is that...whatever it is...for me it's over, so are we still on for dinner tonight?"

"Seven o'clock." He agreed with a sigh. Was it over? Was Ritter satisfied after having broken off a hard piece of what Rick was getting? Even if Julie was telling the truth and she didn't want anything to do with Ritter that didn't mean the slime ball wouldn't insinuate himself into her life just to needle Mason. "Watch out for him, ok? Take my word for it, he's a psychopath." That was putting it mildly. "With a badge and a gun." He added for emphasis. Ritter must have seemed (almost) like the ideal playmate for Julie; big, strong, forceful, alpha-male all the way but Ritter wasn't too bright. He didn't understand Julie's game, hell; Ritter didn't understand that it *was* a game.

"I don't have any plans to see him." She offered. "Don't care to make any either." No, she thought it would be just fine if she never saw Ritter again. "You're late for work."

There was more going on here, Rick just knew it, he could feel it. He just couldn't figure out what it was but that was all right, for now, it would come to him.

Chapter Seven

A yellow cab pulled up outside Julie's home just a little after 9:30 am.

She went inside.

She came outside with that blasted dog on a leash. The dog didn't wait, it pulled her over to the nearest tree and gratefully did its business after being locked in the house alone all night. He'd known the dog was alone, he'd made the mistake of coming back here first instead of making the drive to Mason's abode last night. Ritter was sure Mason would dump her off here after he pulled them over but the good doctor didn't do that. Ritter sat here at least twenty minutes, in the rain, waiting for her to return, when she didn't he took a slow drive back to Willington. On the way, he passed her walking in the pouring rain, no coat, and no shoes. She was soaked to the bone. The first thought to enter his head was to offer her a ride, just pull up, roll down the window, smile and make the offer. But, no, she'd only turn him down so he decided to see where she was going. After all, if home was on her mind she was wandering in the completely opposite direction. Down around the bend about a quarter mile he pulled over and killed the lights. Ritter rolled down the window to keep the windshield from fogging over as he stared in the rearview mirror waiting for her to make it this far. Shortly after she came stumbling around the bend a set of headlights lit up her silhouette, she turned and began to wave. Ritter thought it was Mason coming back until he saw the cab. It pulled over, she stood outside the driver's window a moment or two and then climbed in back. He followed it all the way to Mason's door and parked across the street.

When it became clear that she wasn't going to exit anytime soon, Ritter got out of the car, crept around to the back of the house and peered through Mason's bedroom window. No light and he knew why but that was all right, even in the rain there was enough light from the streetlight to see inside and make out what they were doing if not the minute details thereof. The view wasn't as good as the one in room 406 of the El Royale but it would do for the night and any night hereafter especially once the rain subsided and the bruises he left on her faded. She'd turn the light on again then.

A few months ago, he'd taken to renting the room next to the suite that Julie kept on permanent reservation.

Being that he was no longer employed by The Vermont State Troopers and having been let go under less than valorous circumstances but with his pension along with a generous severance payment that came to him with the VSPs sincerest wishes for him to go away quietly, Ritter was forced to find another line of work. Like most any other ex-cop he had two choices; open a bar or get a PI license. Early last year he got his license and he opened his PI business.

Business was good even if it was generally boring cases concerning mundane people with mundane problems. Half the time he just went to Google and followed web links to in order to find whatever information he was being paid to find. It was steady but lacked the genuine thrill of police work. Then Susan Miller, ex-wife of Craig Miller, walked into his life and hired him to spy on the current Mrs. Miller, Juliette. Susan Miller wanted a bigger alimony check and child support check even though her ex-husband was in a coma. She swore that 'little whore', the current Mrs. Miller, was hiding a small fortune from the Court and she wanted it found.

The chick was a bitch, Ritter could see right off why any man might divorce her, but he took the case and half his payment upfront. The first thing he did was check into the Miller family's financial history and found it a fucking mess. If Susan Miller thought there was any money there she was out of her mind. Juliette, and by association, Craig was in debt up to her pretty translucent eyeballs. Craig's medical bills were staggering. At first, his medical bills were covered under the health insurance policy he had through his big shot job with the New York City architecture firm. Julie's job also had insurance so hers served as a backup but then his firm let him go. What choice did they have? The firm gave Juliette a tidy sum of money as a 'we're so terribly sorry' consolation but it didn't last long. Thirty thousand dollars a month in medical bills drowned a person rather quickly. Julie had to change insurance plans through her work to one that cost several hundred dollars more a month just in the hopes of breaking even. Then Julie lost her job at the private prep school. She danced as fast she could for months to pay for private insurance/ She let the mortgage lapse. He knew all about those PAST DUE notices that kept showing up in her mailbox causing her to frown and fret on her doorstep whenever she plucked the mail from the box. Any day now it wouldn't be PAST DUE or even FINAL NOTICE a Sheriff would show up on her doorstep and serve her with FORCLOSURE papers.

In light of that, Ritter didn't think she was hiding any money but he checked into Juliette's background trying to ascertain if she even had the wherewithal to hide large sums of money.

Juliette Mansfield was born October 31, 1974 in Castle Rock, ME. She was the only child of Michael Mansfield and his wife Miriam King. All in all she seemed to have a normal, if somewhat sheltered and slightly idyllic, childhood up until the age of 8 when she started having problems with, of all things, doctors. She was first sent home on the first day of elementary school that year after being called down to the nurse's office for a school physical. Little Juliette bit the school nurse hard enough to draw blood. Then she was kept out of elementary school for three months until she saw her own physician and was inoculated for re-entry. Juliette would not go to the doctor

96

so her good and concerned parents drugged her and, when Juliette regained her senses while the pediatrician was examining her, she grabbed the pen out of his pocket and stabbed him with it. Twice.

Afraid there was something terribly wrong with their precious little girl, her parents (and the school system) forced her to see a shrink who diagnosed her with Iatrophobia; an irrational fear of doctors. If he'd only known then what he knew now he would have laughed himself silly.

Other than that, Juliette Mansfield had a sparkling reputation up until her father died when she seemed to develop a nice little morphine addiction. That ended one night in a car accident that sent her to Court Ordered Rehab. While it was all mildly interesting there was nothing that pointed to an ability to embezzle or otherwise hide money. Even if she was capable of it, there still wasn't any money to hide. Being a very meticulous man, Ritter stayed on the case expecting to turn in a boring report to the ex-Mrs. Miller in a week or two.

Then he followed her to Tony's Bar one night where he watched her pick up a total stranger and take him to the El Royale Hotel. Three or four times a month she went to the bar, picked up a guy—any guy—and took him to the hotel. Telling himself it was part of the job, he had tried several times to pick her up. A few times she sat with him, bought him a drink, passed fifteen, or twenty minutes with him and a bit of chit-chat but that was as far as he got. She wouldn't tell him her name, what she did, where she lived, or even where she grew up. Julie never bought him a second drink or offered to sit with him through a second round, not even when he offered to buy. She was always polite and sweet even when she was telling him to bugger off. He would go back to the far corner with his tail between his legs and his cock tingling from the lustful thoughts coloring his mind. She was always off to the next prospect for the night. Most nights, even if she had to stay until midnight, she left with someone but other nights she left alone and that was by choice because any guy in there would have ecstatically escorted her to her door. Whether alone or with company, Julie always went to room 404 of the El Royale Hotel at the end of the night. Once he discovered that, he realized Julie was running away, problem was, she didn't have anywhere to go so she settled for a little escape and then returned to her prison come morning.

Ritter found that very interesting, so much so that, on his fourth stakeout, he went so far as to rent the room next door to hers and charge the ex-Mrs. Miller for the expense. PIs have such wonderful toys that they don't need warrants to use. Camera and microphones were his favorites and it didn't take much to drill a hole no bigger than a pencil through the crumbling plaster of the hotel. He drilled near the baseboard of the wall that a adjoined their rooms and had a perfect view of her bedroom. A few yards down he drilled another hole and had a lovely view of her sitting room. Ritter watched her with every single man she brought back to the hotel. He watched, he listened, and he taped the events.

Then, as Fate would have it, Richard Mason made his appearance on the scene last August. It was clear that Doctor Mason was smitten with the current Mrs. Miller. Ritter watched the tape of their first night together often it was definitely one hot summer night. Mason was priceless, at first he seemed so lost, like a fish out of water, but then he got the hang of it only to be let down spending the next three months in and out of the bar obviously hoping to run in to Julie. Last weekend, he finally got his wish. Mason put on one hell of a show, yes, the old dog did. Ritter never would have guessed that an old guy with a bum leg could still be so nimble.

How many tapes did he have of her fucking this guy or that guy? Including, of course, Doctor Richard Mason and himself. Ritter wasn't sure but he thought he could start a small Internet Porn Site with his collection and make a good bit of money, after all, Julie was exceptionally gifted at what she did. Men would pay a small fortune just to watch and a large one just to touch her.

Two months ago, he brought his dossier to the ex-Mrs. Miller who was unhappy at the poor financial news to say the least. Sitting there in her living room, he wondered what she'd say if he told her about the El Royale Hotel and all of the men the current Mrs. Miller was fucking. The information wasn't any good to her in court, she couldn't divorce Julie on Craig's behalf. Even if she could, what court wouldn't sympathize with the near-widow Miller? What court would look at her and force her to divorce a husband who could no longer keep up his end of the marriage contract because she was getting a good chunk on the side? So he kept it to himself as he tucked her $10,000.00 check into his breast pocket with a smile and a 'nice doing business with you'.

But he didn't give up his investigation.

Even though it poured last night, he didn't leave the window until near dawn as that seemed to be when the lovers inside finished. Soaking wet, shivering and cold, Ritter went back to his car but didn't abandon his stakeout until he saw her leave about a half hour ago. However, he did wonder what it had been that brought Mason back to the house so abruptly and in such a snit. Ritter watched him storm into the house and even from across the street he could hear the raised voices inside though he couldn't understand what they were saying with any real clarity. Fifteen minutes later—give or take a minute or two—Mason, in a much cheerier if still perplexed mood, came out of his front door, climbed in his car, and, Ritter assumed, finally made his way to work. Ten minutes after that, the cab pulled up and Julie climbed in.

Now here she was walking that viscous mutt of hers around the block. She'd be extra nice to the dog feeling guilty for having left it alone all night, chances were she'd take it on an extra long walk. Further chances were that she hadn't turned on the alarm, in fact, he didn't think she even took her keys. Looking out of all the car windows and in the rearview mirror to see the street quiet, Ritter crept from the car, crossed the street, glanced around again, then tried the knob to find it turned easily in his hand and the door opened. "Stupid woman," he muttered, "don't you know anyone can just walk in this way?"

He didn't have long, twenty minutes at the outside. This was the first time he'd actually been able to gain entry. He'd tried several times but the damn dog always got in the way. He'd have to shoot it to get past it.

Quickly making his way through the front he took in the shrine to Craig Miller on Julie's mantle, he'd seen it and the rest of the lower level through the windows over the last few months. The first floor didn't interest him, it was the second floor Ritter wanted to see and he nearly flew up the steps two and three at a time as he ascended. Reaching the landing he nearly sprinted down the hall to the master bedroom.

Julie's bedroom, the one she'd shared with Craig, was the only finished room in the house. It was a calming pale blue with eggshell accents. The master bed was of the four-poster variety complete with lacy romantic canopy. He looked through her drawers, fondled her clothes, and held her underwear to his face, burying his nose in them before stuffing them into his pocket. He sprayed the cinnamon perfume into the air and over the bed. Ritter ran his hand along the mattress and over the pillows picturing her laying here in the white satin nightgown lying there unused last night.

Time was not on his side, he couldn't stand around and daydream, he ducked into the master bathroom to look at and touch the things inside. There were a lot of pill bottles in the medicine cabinet, funny thing was, they were all full and the dates ranged from the pills Mason prescribed for her yesterday as far back as two years. She filled them all and never took them.

Those wouldn't do.

100

Back in the bedroom, he opened the nightstand to find an open carton of Newports. Perfect. Quickly dumping the remaining packs onto the bed he drew a syringe from his pocket and began poking each pack on the bottom, just once, and injecting some of the liquid into the cigarettes inside. He didn't want to rush things here, this way she would only smoke one—possibly two—tainted cigarettes per day depending upon how much she actually smoked. It would build up slowly in her system and be nearly unnoticeable except for some easily explained fatigue and some flu-like symptoms to start. When he was done he looked at his work. She'd never notice the pin pricks in the packs, he put them in the tax id stamps just to be extra cautious, and it wouldn't smell or taste bad, in fact she might even think them a little bit sweet. Carefully stuffing them back into the carton and making sure they were tightly packed together he put them back into the nightstand and rushed back down the stairs.

Ritter lost his job because he was rude, mouthy and a downright bully but he didn't see it that way at all. When Julie Miller and Richard Mason got together and sparks flew, Patrick Ritter found his opportunity to get even. Mason robbed him of something he loved and Ritter was going to repay him in kind.

On his way through the foyer, he saw the shrine once more and the bottle of gin on the coffee table. The syringe was still half-full and that would get her going good. With his heart racing as he ducked into the living room, Ritter unscrewed the cap, injected the last of the liquid and screwed it back on. "Time to find out just how good you are, Doctor Mason. Let's see you deal with this." He muttered as he made his way to the front door and then back to his car. Behind the wheel, he watched as Julie came around the corner with the dog, she was smiling and talking to it, the stupid mutt was waging its tail and almost smiling at her as it jumped around at her feet. She went inside and he drove off. He did have a client or two to work for, had to pay the bills and find the means to feed his little obsession somehow, didn't he?

Ritter would be back tonight and doubtlessly so would Mason.

Chapter Eight

Still cold and damp upon arriving home, Ritter stripped off the clothes that were sticking to him and caused his skin to prune. Wandering from the front door to the bathroom he left a trail behind him. Turning on the hot water, he still could not believe his luck where Richard Mason was concerned and the whore! Hooo! She made the pot even sweeter, didn't she? To Ritter it didn't matter if a woman got paid or not, if she did what Juliette Miller did then she was a whore and he didn't give a flying fuck why. Not even with poor Julie's reasons. Mason on the other hand, that man had to figure out everything and Juliette Miller currently resided at the top of his list.

Stepping under the hot jets to warm his clammy skin he could not help but wonder what she had told Mason this morning. He took a drive down the usual route on his way home, went past Mason's house and on down to the El Royale where he looked up to the window and saw the crack. Perhaps Mason saw it too and that's what sent him back home this morning. With all of the pills he took, Ritter was quite certain that Mason was insane. But he was sharp and that sharp mind worked in strange and fascinating ways that could be hard to keep up with. Ritter always did like a challenge and he hadn't had one like Richard Mason since, well, his last encounter with Richard Mason.

Julie, well, she seemed very attached to Mason. That surprised Ritter. Night after night, he watched her in the bar as he sat in the far corner by the dartboard. She was always dressed to the 9's in a very sophisticated, elegantly sexy fashion that put the goods on display without putting out the 50% Off Sign. He would watch her scope out the crowd until she found an interesting target; her targets had no rhyme or reason that he could see. She picked up this man and that man but passed on three times as many once she got them to sit down with her. Julie always paid for their drinks. Soaping up with a bar of Ivory he thought that was so she wouldn't feel quite so much like a whore when all was said and done and the sun rose once more. The night Richard Mason walked in her eyes lit up and she even blushed. Ritter looked toward the door to see what type of man could garner such a reason from the pretty little barfly and there was Richard Mason.

Saints be praised!

Rinsing the soap from his hair, Ritter smiled wide as he thought about this past weekend and the show Mason had put on for him. He had to give the good doctor his props, kudos even, for the way he handled Julie. Most of the other guys she took back to the hotel were bumbling idiots, they were too shy or too nervous or too freaked out by the simple fact that they were there with her to be useful to her. Now and then she got one who went for it with everything he had, sometimes they worked out and she had a good time. One thing about Julie, she never faked it, if you weren't doing a good job she wasn't going to stroke your ego. Nope, you were going to get shown the door five seconds after you came. Mason was not shown the door either time; in fact, the first time she slept with him was the first time Ritter witnessed her do such a thing. Julie never fell asleep with the Man-of-the-Night, even if all went well and a second round ensued, the man always left her there alone. When she curled up in Mason's arms on that first night Ritter was fairly certain she'd found something in Mason that she hadn't found in all of the others. Two hours later she left him there but that was another first, she never left the Man-of-the-Night alone in her room.

For a few months after she hooked up with Mason, Ritter made habit of getting to the bar early and taking his seat in the back. It wasn't long before he noticed that Doctor Mason started showing up three, four and even five times a week, asking the bartender; She been in tonight? Ritter knew he had a fish on the line. Seemed the good old doctor was just as smitten as

104

Julie was. He wanted to be there when they discovered that fact.

Last weekend the skies opened up, the seas parted, and God granted his wish. She did not just fall asleep in Mason's arms for a little catnap; she slept the rest of the night there with him just like a lover. The next morning they did it all over again.

Then Monday came.

Ritter had been working on another case that just so happened to center on a certain doctor at The Mountainside whose wife suspected he was sleeping with several of the nurses. She was right and Ritter didn't doubt she was about to take him for at least half of everything he had. Good for her. One of the nurses was a stone-cold bitch anyway. In disguise, he wandered through the hospital to the usual meeting place of the subject and one of his little tarts, got the photographs he was being paid to shoot and then, since he was so close, wandered down past the Coma Ward to see if Julie was sitting there with her husband. Ritter got there just as the elevator doors opened and Doctor Mason along with several other doctors hurriedly exited it. He waited to see if Mason would even notice her let alone recognize her—he hadn't in the past that was all right because Mason hadn't recognized Ritter hanging around the past three weeks either and that was fine with him. Standing on the other side of the Nurse's Station he watched Mason near the Coma Ward, he watched Julie as she stiffened at the sound of his voice, he could see part of her face and she wasn't blushing she was pale as a ghost. The closer Doctor Mason got the more she turned her head away from him, the more Doctor Mason tried to get a good view of her. Ritter was sure Mason recognized her, twenty minutes later Mason was back but Julie fled long before that. Didn't take a genius to figure out where she was going.

Ritter finished up at the hospital, ran home for a quick shower and change of clothes then headed to the bar. It was early but she would be in soon enough. Sure she would, Mason scared her this afternoon, spooked her good and she would be looking for a little comfort. Two hours later there she was. She'd made a stop at the salon and had her hair colored to the darker shade, Ritter liked the strawberry blonde better it made her look a little slutty. Moreover,...it was early. Pickings were slim. Ritter lucked out.

Ritter walked up to her, offered to buy her a drink, she bought him one, halfway through it she was running her barefoot up his pant leg. Less than five minutes after that they were in her hotel room and he put it to her until midnight, well past Mason seeing them in the window from the street below. What did she tell him? Ritter would have loved to be a fly on the wall during that conversation but he'd had to settle for spying from across the street. He took her to the window because he liked Mason's idea of putting her against the wall, yes, Ritter liked that very much and, in fact, he'd sat in room 406 with his cock in his hand stroking off as he watched them on his monitor. Being more of an exhibitionist than Mason, Ritter thought the window a better idea than the wall. She went along but not happily, she said if he wanted someone to watch he should have brought a friend.

"Next time." Ritter told her. He could see it in her eyes; *what next time?* If he wasn't going to get invited back then he might as well get everything he could out of tonight. So he did. From the angle of the camera, Ritter couldn't tell which hole Mason had been indulging in when he put her against the wall but Ritter knew which one he wanted with her against the window. He pushed her hard against the cold glass with one hand, grabbed her hip with the other, and sunk his hard cock deep in that fine ass with one thrust. Julie let out a harsh cry, told him to stop, don't do that, he was hurting her. She hardly ever said that to the others so Ritter knew it must be true and that turned him on even more. She reached back and tried to push him away, Ritter put her hands on the glass and told her to leave them there, or he'd get the cuffs. Then she was quiet. She

106

didn't make any fuss until she saw Mason across the street and realized he saw her as well. Julie probably never heard herself say it but Ritter heard it loud and clear even though it was really soft and muttered.

"Doc."

Why don't you stand there and watch this?

That was the thought that went through his head and he gave it all he had as he thrust in and out of that fine teardrop ass. He knew Mason could not see his face or hers so why not just dig in and go for it? Who was she going to tell? Mason? Not likely. Unless...for some reason or another...Mason were to find out on his own. That would just drive the old doc right up the nearest wall, wouldn't it? Sure, it would.

Mason stood there watching for a minute or two but then he wandered away. That pissed Ritter off. He wanted him to stand there and watch until he was done with her.

"Doc."

That set him off. "Shut up!" Ritter grabbed a handful of her hair, yanked it back, and then shoved it forward into the glass splitting it and her alabaster forehead. Her skull bounced off the glass and the strength went out of her knees, good thing he had that hard cock in her to keep her up or she might have fallen. He caught sight of the purple bruise on her neck and the teeth marks in the middle. Just a little harder and Mason would have ripped off a chunk of her flesh like a wolf taking his first bite of the night's prey. The hand that had been in her hair went to the other hip and clamped on without mercy as he pushed her down so he could thrust upward with more gusto. Her thighs were already covered in paw marks, some of from him this evening but most from Mason. Surging in and out of her with an ever-hardening cock, Julie began to weep. She didn't wail. She didn't cry or blubber or beg him to stop. With her face pressed to the glass, she just silently wept until he was done. The climax was spectacular and as hard as his cock, the kind that a man really has to reach down for to bring to fruition. The kind that leaves him shaking and weak in the knees.

Standing here in the shower, Ritter discovered he had a hard piece of wood just thinking about it. No sense in wasting the hot water and the silky suds as he let his mind wander down this enjoyable path with his cock in both hands stroking it hard.

After that, when Julie regained the strength to stand, she tried to throw him out. Ritter would not go. He wasn't done, the night was still young. When she started to tell him she was going to call the cops, he coldly told her that he was a cop.

"Go ahead, call." He dared. "I'm sure they'll love to help me with you, honey. How many of us can you take on at once? What do you think? Three? Four? The whole precinct?"

Julie put down the phone.

Ritter grabbed her by the upper arms, threw her down on the bed, she started to scream and he slapped her with an open hand across the face. "Shut...up." His slacks were on the bed next to her; he saw the belt, snatched it out of the loops, and fastened it around her neck before she could protest. He might not be invited back but it would be a night Juliette Miller would never forget.

In the shower, his cock let go of its load to the demand of his own soapy hand.

It was quite the night.

When he finally hoisted up his hungry cock and left the room, Julie was passed out and in need of medical attention. Ritter thought that maybe she would run into her Doc. Maybe she would have to explain to him how she got so fucked up.

She went to The Mountainside Clinic, what other choice did she have? They billed on a sliding scale and Julie didn't have any health insurance. He sat amongst the flu infested in a baseball cap and sunglasses behind a newspaper. They took Julie back and two hours went by! The woman could have bled to DEATH by the time someone even looked in on her. Good thing he didn't do more damage to her than he had. But, then, sure enough, as though Fate itself decided Juliette Miller and Richard Mason were star-crossed lovers, Mason walked into her exam room. The fur started to fly. Ritter listened outside the door.

When she left in a huff and Mason stood there in the doorway of the exam room looking after her with that dejected expression like a lost puppy, it was all so delicious. He had to run outside to laugh long and hard.

Shutting off the water, he put a towel around his waist and wandered into his bedroom to change into fresh dry clothes. Sliding, commando, into a pair of jeans, he gave himself kudos for pulling them over last night. Ritter had Julie's phone bugged for months and it was easy since he did not have to actually get into the house to bug a cordless phone, all he had to do was search for the proper frequency and then listen in. He should have bugged the interior today but hadn't brought the proper materials with him. The thing about cordless phones is people so often forget to hang them up. Julie Miller was one such person. When Mason arrived at her apartment and the phone was sitting on the coffee table, he heard everything they said. He even heard them when they were (probably) in the front hall near the kitchen. She did not intend to tell Mason about her evening with Ritter so he came up with the spur of the moment plan to force her hand. He just wanted to see how Mason would react. That's all.

Ritter let out a hearty laugh as he slipped a sweatshirt over his dry head. "YOU and RITTER?" He said mocking Mason in between bouts of laughter. "Poor bastard." Unfortunately for Ritter, Mason always did hang up his phone so he hadn't been able to hear any of the conversation once she arrived there last night. He didn't listen to Mason's phone conversations much anyway, just a bunch of medical talk and the occasional call to the local Sex Chat Line and Escort Service. He should bust Mason for solicitation, then again, he wasn't a real cop any longer, and everything he was doing was completely illegal. Even if he still had his job with the State Troopers, Attempted Murder still wouldn't be legal. Ritter kept telling himself that he wasn't trying to kill Julie, if it happened it happened—it would be Mason's fault for not being as smart as the old bastard thought he was— but killing her wasn't the goal. Just a possible side effect. That's why he was taking the slow and steady approach. Mason wouldn't think of it at first, neither would Julie, they would just think she had the same flu everyone else was spreading around. Soon after—hopefully soon after anyway, it'd be a bitch if Mason caught on too late—he'd figure there was something seriously wrong with his new girlfriend's health. Then Ritter would stand back and watch Doctor Mason run himself into the ground trying to save her life.

If he were as smart as he thought he was then Julie would live.

If he wasn't...well...thems was da breaks.

Hey, if nothing else, Ritter could take solace in the fact that, should Julie die, he would have ended her pain in a way Mason never could. After all, wasn't she already one of the Walking Dead? Oh, no, she didn't look like she was straight out of *Dawn Of The Dead* to be sure but, when you thought about it, what was the big difference between her and those mindless zombies? (Other than outrageously hot sex, of course.)

Yes, for Julie, it might just be a mercy killing.

Chapter Nine

The house felt strange when Julie came back from walking Max, even the dog seemed to notice it. He barked, yipped, and wandered around smelling the floor as though he were following a scent trail. She looked around, nothing was missing as far as she could tell, and nothing looked disturbed or rifled through. Must just be her imagination. Wandering into the kitchen, she made her second pot of coffee for the day but this one was just for her, The Doc wouldn't be having any. Feeding the dog and taking in the aroma of the brewing coffee she smiled to herself as she thought about him and the way he made her feel.

"What's wrong with me, Max, huh?" Julie asked the dog. Max couldn't be bothered to look up from his kibble, it had been a long lonely night for Max, and he was starving. "Why am I doing this?"

Coffee ready, Julie took it into what had been Craig's office for a short time. She sat down at the computer, and then looked around for a cigarette. She'd smoked the last one in her pack last night in The Doc's car. "Crap." She muttered as she put in the password and then hurried upstairs to the nightstand and the half-carton of Newports there. Reaching into the carton, she pulled out a fresh pack, unwrapped it, and threw away the silver liner. "You know," she told her reflection, "if you're actually going to hang out with a doctor, which is a sucky idea to begin with, you should probably quit smoking before he rides the hell out of you over it."

Yeah, well, The Doc wasn't here right now so....screw it.

Stuffing the remainder of the carton back into the nightstand, she caught sight of her bed. The coverlet was messy and it looked as though someone had been sitting on it. "Max, were on the bed last night?" The dog looked up at her with guilty eyes. The dog knew he wasn't allowed on the bed if she wasn't in it. "Well, at least you didn't pee on it." Although he did poop in the kitchen, scratch up the already beleaguered kitchen cabinets and ripped one of her nice couch pillows to shreds. "Come on, Max, you know what time it is, let's go."

Julie waited until she was back at the computer before lighting the cigarette. First stop on the Information Super Highway; Monster.com. Since August, Julie spent two hours (or more) per day online tracking down new employment. She'd go to Monster first then HotJobs, then CraigsList and a half a dozen other employments sites before hitting the local papers online. Times were tough, friends and neighbors, yes they were. It seemed everyone was beating feet on the street looking for work. Teaching positions were hard to come by and lately Julie started applying for jobs that didn't require a degree such as those in the Food Service Industry. By early afternoon, she'd gone through a pot and a half of coffee, half of the fresh pack of cigarettes and she'd submitted nearly a dozen resumes online, printed out four more and sent them out with the morning mail. Incoming in the morning mail was her weekly unemployment check in the grand amount of $350.00, a far cry from the figure she'd been bringing home. At least it was something since her kitchen cupboards were nearly empty, as they almost always were these days. It was a good thing she didn't eat much and only had Max to look out for in that department, Julie and Max took a quick trip to the bank and then the grocery store.

Home by 3pm and putting her packages away, Julie started to feel tired and a little achy. She held a hand to her forehead to feel if she had a fever but couldn't detect one. "The last thing I need is the damn flu." She cursed. She'd sat in the clinic for hours among the coughing, sneezing and wheezing, she'd probably picked it up too. Perhaps a hot bath would make her feel better and, God knew, she could use it after last night.

Pouring the water into the cast iron tub, Julie gathered her favorite bath items. It was still early in the day and she always preferred to bathe in the evening so she could slip into a nightgown or t-shirt and be lazy if she planned to stay home for the night. By now, it was nearly 4 o'clock, three hours until The Doc was supposed to pick her up. As the tub filled, Julie went back downstairs to retrieve her bottle of Beefeaters. It was almost past four so taking a drink or two would be just fine, she wouldn't have to consider herself an alcoholic or anything like that. Adding lavender scented salts to the hot water, she put the bottle on the floor with a clean glass, ashtray, and her half-empty pack of Newports. In her bedroom, she took off the clothes from last night, tossed them into the pile in the corner for later washing, and then slipped into the warm silky water.

Max stood next to the tub with his chin resting on the rim as he stared at her as though he were asking her; What are you doing?

"I don't know, Max." Julie sighed and patted the Pit Bull's head. "Give us a kiss." The dog licked her face and wagged his tail. "That's a good boy." Reaching over the side of the tub, she poured a shot of gin and lit a cigarette. Relaxing in the warm water, she drank down the clear alcohol and smoked as she asked herself over and over again; What the hell am I doing?

Sleeping with oodles of men nearly indiscriminately was one thing but she could fall for The Doc and she knew it. That made him dangerous. She took another drink and the glass was almost empty, she made a strange face and licked her lips. "Does that taste funny to you?" She held the glass out to the dog that sniffed it and backed away. That wasn't anything new; Max wasn't a real big fan of alcohol to begin with. Max wrinkled his nose and gave a whimper as he looked at the glass. Julie finished it off before putting it down on the tiled bathroom floor and finishing her cigarette. "Well, let's hope one of those resumes pays off, huh, boy? We'll be starvin' in the street pretty soon." Julie had a plan for that, the mortgage company kept calling and calling and calling. She sent them money every single week but it wasn't enough. She sold the stocks she and Craig owned over a year ago, the bank account was down to a grand $68.00. It was a good thing she owned the car outright. When the mortgage company finally decided they were going to kick her and Max out of their home, Julie thought she'd move into her room at the El Royale. The manager said that since she'd been such a good customer over the last year and a half or so, they would let the dog come with her. At $400.00 a month, it was a lot cheaper and easier to keep than the house at $1,700.00 each month. Her unemployment checks would cover the cost of the room, she'd have no utilities to pay, the rest could just go to groceries and assorted items necessary to keep living on planet Earth. However long that lasted. Before The Doc came along Julie had seriously been contemplating suicide, not just contemplating, researching. She scoured the Internet looking for the most efficient and painless ways for one to off themselves. She discovered she had the perfect solution in her medicine cabinet and all those little amber bottles within.

Neat.

Quick.

Clean.

Painless.

If it weren't for Max, who'd end up in a shelter and probably be killed just for being a trained guard dog and a Pit Bull, she would have ended it all when she was fired over the summer. Her job and the kids were the only things that were truly keeping her going anyway and they were gone. What was left? Nothing. What was the point in sticking around? There wasn't one. If it hadn't been for the dog, her stupid, wonderful, always-there-for-her dog, Julie would have ended it all quite a while ago. If it hadn't been for Max, she never would have made it through August at all, she never would have been there the night The

Doc walked into the bar, and something in her life changed. For better or for worse she couldn't really say but she was willing to stick around a little longer to find out. In the end, nearly doubtless, it would all be for the worse. Sooner or later—probably sooner—The Doc would have his fill of her, he'd be off on his way and she on hers. When that happened, Julie still had that plan to fall back on.

Dunking down below the water to wet her hair she heard the phone ringing when she emerged. "Be a really good boy and get the phone, Max."

The dog's ears pricked up but he was soon off to the bedroom and then back at tub-side with the cordless phone between his teeth. "Good boy, Maxie, you're the best doggie in the whole world, yes you are." She complimented and took the phone from his mouth even though it was covered in dog drool. Julie looked at the caller ID to see the call was coming from Willington-Middleboro, perhaps Doc was calling to cancel their date. "Hello?"

"What are you wearing?"

Julie snickered. "Absolutely nothing, Doc."

"You're lying." Rick said hopeful that she wasn't.

"Nope, honest, Doc. I'm in the tub. Naked."

"Yeah?" Yes, maybe she was in the tub, maybe there was a bit of an echo on the line as though she were in a bathroom. "Splash the water." He dared. Through the phone line he heard a great splash of water as Julie kicked her little feet and slapped the warm tub water with her free hand. "Hot damn! Have I got good timing or what?" Rick complimented himself as the image of her in a steaming tub of water danced through his mind. "Stay there I can be at your door in twenty minutes."

"You won't get in, I'm afraid.   The doors are locked. What's up, Doc?"

"Just calling to make sure we're still on for tonight. You know, no other guy's come along already and stolen you away from me."

"No other men, Rick." She said with a sad smile as she thought about Craig. "Where are we going tonight?"

"It's a surprise." Rick teased.

"That's not fair, how will I know how to dress for you if you don't tell me where we're going."

"You're going to dress for me?" Rick thought about it. "How about you just undress for me? I like that idea better."

"Shall I do a little striptease for you? Would you like that...Doc?"

On the other end of the line, Rick swallowed hard. Thoughts of Julie naked in the tub went to thoughts of Julie naked dancing on a stage with a silver pole, but, of course, he was the only one in the audience. "Why, yes, yes, I would."

"If you tell me where we're going, I'll see what I can do about that." She coached. It had been a very long time since she'd been a real date, Julie was almost certain she'd forgotten how it went and what she was supposed to do but dressing for her evening's escort was one thing she still knew how to do. "Fancy? Casual? Steak? Burgers? What?" She continued when he didn't answer.

"Yes."

"Oh, you're such a big help, Rick." She said in a mildly exasperated tone. "Come on, give me a hint. Shall I wear slacks? A blouse? A dress?"

"I like dresses."

"A dress. What kind? Long? Short?"

"In the middle." He liked short dresses but didn't want any prying eyes during dinner. Rick didn't want to have to keep one eye on his date and the other on every other man in the restaurant. Although, that was bound to happen no matter what Julie wore. "I like those green heels. You know, just in case you were interested."

Julie snickered again. "Don't you have a life to save or something, Doc?"

"I'm working on it, geez." He huffed happily.

"Still seven?"

"I'll be there. You get good and clean now so I can get you good and dirty later."

"See you soon, Doc." Julie clicked off the line. "Hummm...can you put it back?" She asked the dog. Max just stood there looking at her as if to say; *Wasn't bringing it to you enough*? "Oh, that's all right. What about that?" She pointed to the empty glass. "Can you fill that?" Of course he could, Julie taught him how to do it months ago and she watched Max as he gripped the neck of the bottle with his teeth, backed up a step, looked at the glass on the floor, then used his powerful jaws to tilt the bottle sideways. He stopped just as the glass began to overflow. "Love ya, boy, I knew there was a reason I keep you around. You get an extra treat tonight." Max's ears went up again at the word 'treat'. She gave him a pat and picked up the glass. She took a sip but put the glass down with a sigh and then rubbed her aching shoulders, she felt tired and rundown. Maybe she could talk Doc into giving her a little massage tonight then again, "I really don't feel very well, maybe I should call him back and cancel?" She asked the dog. "No," she sighed, "he'll just want to know what's wrong and I could tell him I'm coming down with the flu but he won't be satisfied unless I let him check me out...not in the good way," she said to Max. "You know how much I hate doctors...so...you know...again...why the hell am I doing this? What the hell am I doing? I don't even know anymore." That was true, Julie hated them...all doctors everywhere were lower than dirt in her eyes and they had been for years upon years. They were all so smug and condescending—just like The Doc, he was no exception to that rule. They were rude and pushy and again The Doc was no exception. All of them suffered from the most morose affliction; The God Complex. There, however, The Doc might be slightly different from his peers but she couldn't be sure. In any event, Juliette Miller wasn't Richard Mason's patient so she didn't have to take any shit from him if she didn't want to. "I hate them," she muttered to no one, not even the dog.

All of her adult life Julie staunchly refused to go to a doctor for any reason...she had to be puking up blood for days before she'd ever consider walking into a clinic or an ER. Even then, she wouldn't stay in the hospital, always refused to be allowed to be admitted even when the doctors were pulling their hair out, she never took a single prescription they gave her. She got them filled because they'd know if she didn't but that was it. She got them home, lined them up in the medicine cabinet and there they stayed. Julie didn't even take the Percocet The Doc gave her, she lied to him last night, mostly out of habit. The Doctor always asked; *Are you taking your medication?* The proper answer was always; *Oh, yes, doctor*. End of story.

As with anyone who isn't immortal, during the course of her natural every-day life, several events came along which forced her to deal with the medical community; she seemed to hate them all, it wasn't reserved strictly for doctors, nurses, receptionists, PAs, MAs...they were all the same in her eyes. Rationally or irrationally, they could go to hell as far as she was concerned.

When she was 22 her father was diagnosed with Alzheimer's Disease, she was still in college not far from graduating from the University of Maine at Orono with a Master's in English Literature.

Understandably, things got a little tight at home and Julie had to take a full time job to finish paying off the last semester. When she was 24 her mother was diagnosed with terminal ovarian cancer, her father was in a nursing home by that time as he'd become too much for her mother to handle. Julie, who'd just gotten a sweet job at a local preparatory school and was working on obtaining her Doctorate at Yale University moved from her home in New Haven, Connecticut to be near her mother in Castle Rock, Maine. It was a long grueling year and in the end Mother and Father, Husband and Wife, died within six months of each other. Her father never understood why Miriam stopped coming to visit him that was all right because most days he didn't remember her anyway. That was ok too because by the time she put her father in the ground, Juliette Mansfield couldn't remember her own name on most days as she was too strung out from a nasty morphine addiction—her mother died with a whole pharmacy at her bed side including an amber bottle of truly kickass little blue pills that did nothing for the penis but much for the mind-- she was keeping a secret from those few remaining friends and relatives surrounding her and offering words of comfort and wisdom.

What a joke.

Soon after the funeral, Julie sold her ancestral home and moved to New York where she began work at NYU. To this day, Julie couldn't remember much of her life between the ages of 24 and 27. It was all just a blur that ended with forced rehabilitation in a State run facility after she ran into a local donut shop that didn't have any aspirations of being a drive thru. Not a good scene.

Wouldn't The Doc and his ever-present stash of Oxycodone just love that story?

It was soon after she got out and returned to her job at NYU—from which she'd taken an extended leave of absence at the request of the State of New York—she met Craig Miller. When she went back to work at the start of the second semester, the school was undergoing extensive renovations, he wandered up to her one day and asked where the Administration Building was located. She thought he was just one of the crew in his blue jeans, yellow hardhat, and tool belt hanging from his rather attractive waist.

Seven years later, he walked off the curb of Lexington and Park at the wrong time and the doctors came back but Craig did not.

At first, Craig was in the Lagone Medical Center in New York there were so many doctors, they all blurred and ran together in her head. She couldn't keep any of their names straight. Julie muddled through it the best she could, even when she wanted to start tearing their eyeballs out for no apparent reason she held herself in place and kept her mouth shut. Then, when it became clear the facility could do nothing more for Craig she investigated The Mountainside Wellness & Research Center to find it had a cutting-edge Coma Ward. It was close to home and away from the noise of the city. Against the protests of his ex-wife, Juliette moved Craig back to Vermont. Now there were only a few doctor's names to remember like Dr. Anaballini who was Craig's attending physician. She didn't see him very much anymore, just once every other month so they could get together and chat about Craig's unchanged condition.

Soaking in the tub, she laughed a little at the thought of The Doc being clued in to any of this and how much more of an interesting puzzle she'd be to him if that happened. No one was more surprised by her desire for the Good Doctor than Julie herself.

With Max standing guard at the side of the tub, Julie scrubbed up and rinsed off before climbing out and deciding a small nap might be a good idea. Perhaps she would feel better when she woke. Afraid that once she fell asleep she'd stay that way, after all she was exhausted from the evening's festivities, she set her alarm clock to wake her at 5:30 so she could get dressed for dinner and be ready when Rick arrived. "Come on," she said to the dog and Max jumped up on the bed as she slipped under the covers. He looked at her quizzically as if to say; *The sun is still out, why are we in bed?*

Julie put her wet head on the pillow and was out like a light.

II

The alarm went off; Julie reached out and slapped it with a heavy hand. She tried to get up but she felt so sore and achy. Even worse than when she lay down. She let out a groan. "Come on, can't be sick, have to get up." She opened her eyes to see the dog staring back at her with an anxious look in his eyes. "Gotta pee?"

Max jumped off the bed, wandered around in circles waiting for her.

"I'm coming, I'm coming." She said groggily and shook her head in an attempt to clear it. "Oh if I get this flu that'll really suck." Julie complained tossing off the covers and planting her bare feet on the cold hardwood floor. That was helpful. Not much but a little, that was until she stood up. The world started to fade away for a moment and Julie felt a warm wave wash over her and a warmer bead of sweat break out on her forehead. "Oh crap." She mumbled and sat back down at the bed much to the dismay of poor Max and his overfilled bladder. Catching her breath as the world began to come back into focus she caught sight of the red light flashing on the cordless. It took her a moment or two to recognize that meant she had a message. Julie couldn't remember seeing the light flashing when she

121

came home from the grocery store. "I slept through a ringing phone?" She asked herself as she picked it up and stared at it as though it were a foreign object. That wasn't like her at all; Julie always woke up when the phone rang if she was sleeping at all. She had a medicine cabinet full of Lunesta and Ambien and even Halcion, of course she never took any of them, if she couldn't knock herself out with gin and pot then there just wasn't any sleeping that night. Then again, she wasn't feeling that well and The Doc had done a good job working her over last night, there wasn't much sleep to be had between five and eight am. At her feet, Max whimpered and gave her an urgent look. "Oh, all right." Getting up slower this time the world still threatened to go gray but she held on and the feeling of vertigo soon passed. Slipping into her robe she held onto the rail as she made her way down the stairs with Max in front of her and looking back every few steps to make sure she was still there. Through the kitchen to the backdoor that lead to the fenced in doggie yard, she opened the door and Max ran out into his pen. Standing there in the doorway with the late day sun fading and the breeze blowing across her, she felt a little better as she looked down at the phone in her hand. She listened to the message;

"Professor Miller, this is Professor Ethan Collins, I'm the Head of the English Department at Willington Community College and I am in receipt of your resume. Very impressive. I'd like you to come in for an interview, we're starting them on Monday. Please give me a call back at your earliest convenience at 609-555-3456 extension 2345. I look forward to meeting you."

Julie leaned heavily against the doorjamb. She sent that off on a lark, they couldn't be serious.

The Doc.

If he interfered, if he got this interview for her she'd be steaming.

"Are you done?" She called after the dog. "Or do you want to stay out there?" Max scratched around in the dirt in answer to her query. "Fine." Julie shut the door leaving the dog outside in his pen while she went back upstairs to get dressed for the evening.

It took her over 45 minutes to decide what to wear. She tore everything out of her closet all the while asking herself what the hell she was doing??? She was going on a DATE? She was a MARRIED WOMAN, she couldn't go off on a DATE let alone get all gussied up for it! Hook ups were one thing but this was quite different. The Doc had been right in the elevator that first night; he was a dangerous man. She couldn't seem to get enough of him.

In the end, she opted for a green dress, to go with the green shoes The Doc requested, but not the sweater dress she'd been wearing over the weekend. Julie opted for a lacy number that hung just below her knees. The best thing about it was the green lace collar that closed high around her throat hiding the ugly bruise from Ritter's belt.

Sitting at her vanity staring at her reflection in the mirror and thinking she must be out of her mind she put her hair up and did her make-up. The bottle of gin was sitting on the nightstand next to her pack of Newports. Just one drink and one cigarette, it was getting late and he'd be here soon. Julie downed a shot and half straight out of the bottle and then sat before the mirror smoking her cigarette. It tasted a little strange, almost like the gin, a little sweet, but maybe that was because of the shot she just took. She'd take the cigarettes with her along with a bottle of body spray and pack of Altoids, if she had to she'd duck outside and have a smoke. Couldn't smoke in restaurants anymore and she'd do her best to refrain from smoking in his car. If they were taking her car it might be another story.

Her joints seemed to ache something awful, Julie told herself she was getting older, and even though it had been sunny today, it had been raining the last week and the damp weather wasn't good for her joints. Although she had many pills that stronger than mere aspirin by far, Julie opted for the bottle of Bayer and took two along with another small swallow of gin. She capped the bottle, crushed the remnants of the cigarette that really wasn't anything more than the filter and then went into the bathroom to brush her teeth. Whatever she was coming down with, she sincerely hoped it was over and done with by Monday. It wouldn't do her much good to show up at the interview with the flu.

Just before seven o'clock her doorbell rang, she opened it to see The Doc standing there. "My, don't you look handsome tonight, Do-c." She complimented with a smile as she took in the sight of him standing there, wrinkle free for once, in dark blue suit with light blue shirt that set off his eyes. "Come in." She stood back to let him into the house.

"For you."

"Thank you," Julie blushed as she took the bouquet of flowers from his hand. "They're beautiful."

Mason was relieved. He thought maybe she'd think that the flowers were hokey but, to him anyway, she seemed like the kind of girl that really dug flowers. He was glad to see that he was right. "You don't look so bad yourself." He liked the dress and the hair she even put on the heels he'd asked for. She looked so picture perfect and pretty that he couldn't wait to take it all off and mess her up. "Ready?"

"One moment, let me put them in water." She went off toward the kitchen. "How was your day? Did you save that life?"

"Yeah, he's gonna live." Rick started to follow Julie but Max was sitting on the floor between the foyer and the kitchen. The dog was staring at him in a strange way that uneased Rick. "What's with the dog tonight?"

124

Julie came back into the foyer with the flowers he gave her in a vase of water. "Hum?" She looked down at Max. "Oh, I see." She said to the dog. "Well, in that case." Putting the vase down on the table in the foyer, she looked over at Doc. "Come here."

"Ah, I don't know. He's not going to leap at me or something is he?"

"Just come here." Julie said again. Rick walked over to where she and the dog were. "Put your hand out and tell him he's a good dog."

"Yeah, ya know, I'm a Doctor and I play piano too, did you see the baby grand in my living room?" He held up his hands and looked at his fingers. "Kinda partial to these."

"Chicken," she huffed. "Just do it."

"Chicken? Chicken?" Ready to lose a digit or two, Rick took in a breath and slowly extended his hand to the dog that attacked him just the night before. "Good, good dog, Max, good dog." The dog didn't growl, he just sat there waiting for Rick to pet him and when his hand got within petting distance the dog started to sniff it and then the dog licked it. "Good dog." He said again.

"That's right, Max, he's a friend." Julie said softly. "See, didn't hurt did it?" She said to him. "He's recognized you as not being a threat to me."

"Now he wants to be friends?"

"Exactly. You've been Max Approved. You should feel honored and proud." She tittered. Then looked back down at the dog. "You be a good boy, Max."

"Yeah, I'll have her home...tomorrow. No pissin' on the floor in the meantime." He told the dog. "You let him out?"

"Just a few minutes ago, let's go, Doc." She looped her arm through his as they made their way to the door with the dog looking longingly after them. "So, where are we going?"

"To dinner."

Julie set the alarm before they went out for the night.

Dinner turned out to be a rather fancy affair, Rick made reservations at a local, rather exclusive, bistro. Plates began at a price she couldn't afford in a long time and they shared a bottle of red wine over candle light. "You ok?" He asked. "You look a little pale even for you."

"I think I'm coming down with the flu," she admitted. "Being around all those sick people so long..."

"Yeah, they suck don't they?" He cracked and she laughed but when he reached out to her, mostly out of force of habit, to touch her forehead she pulled her head away from him. "Something wrong?"

"No," she muttered. "I don't have a fever." Julie didn't know if she did or not but she knew she didn't want him turning into Doctor Mason here in this romantic setting. "I have some good news," she ventured. "I have an interview on Monday."

"Really?" He asked not liking the sudden change of subject. "Where?"

She looked directly at him and smiled. "Willington Community College."

"That's great." He agreed and it was he who leaned back when she leaned forward with those nearly colorless eyes seeming to stare through him.

"You wouldn't know anything about that, would you, Doc?" She said in an accusatory tone.

"Me?" He looked around a bit, he felt as though someone was watching them and Rick had been very careful about driving here tonight, he checked the rearview mirror often and took a roundabout way as he looked for any sign of Ritter. "No, why would I know anything about it? I didn't get you this interview, Julie-Baby, you got it on your own. Good luck and congrats."

She thought he was telling the truth. *On my own? Wow.* The thought struck her like a ton of bricks. *And, in that case, did Professor King really say that MY resume was impressive? Whoo-Hoo.* This interview was a very big deal and not just someone doing a favor for a friend. "Sorry, I just thought the timing was a bit convenient."

Over dinner they made conversation ranging from where they grew up or in Rick's case the places he'd lived as he was growing up. Julie said that Rick being a Military Brat explained a lot about him, he asked her to explain, she told him that in her experience Military Brats never learned how to put down roots. They were always searching for something they'd never find. They never learned how to form relationships with people because they were always moving, they never invested in the people around them. They were always either trying to live up to some outrageously unattainable ideal of perfection or they shunned such a concept altogether and just stopped trying at some point. "What is it...Do-c?" She cooed as she finished the pasta primavera. "Is it my turn to get too close?" She reached for his hand over the table as he stared at her with a dumbfounded, nearly blank expression. "Rick?"

He cleared his throat. "Got a lot of experience with Military Brats?"

"Nope." Julie said with a smile. The waiter came over to clear the dishes and ask if they'd like desert. She looked to him for the answer. He was paying the bill. The Doc said they'd have two cups of coffee, he'd take a slice of the apple pie and then looked to Julie. "Two, please." She told him. Julie felt the nagging craving of nicotine fit, she'd been fighting it, trying to sit through it, but the ride to the restaurant had been longer than she'd thought. "Would you excuse me a moment, Rick?" She stood up purse in hand and Doc stood up with her. "I'll be right back."

"You should quit."

"I'm not your patient, Do-c." She said with a smile and then made her way to the door to have a cigarette outside in the crisp night air. Vowing to only indulge in a few drags, just enough to take the edge off the craving. Julie stood there until it was nearly gone, staring up at the stars and wondering what she was doing here in this place with this man. Crushing the butt under the heel of her green stiletto, she sprayed herself with White Shoulders, popped an Altoid into her mouth, and went back inside. Coffee and pie were waiting on the table.

"All better?" He asked.

"Much." Julie agreed. "Don't start."

"I won't." He held up a hand in surrender then he lowered it. "If you answer one question for me."

"What?"

"Ritter—"

"Oh, Doc!" Julie folded her arms across her chest as she sat back in the chair. "I thought we were done with this."

"Just one question," He reiterated, "just one."

"It better be the last one."

Maybe. Maybe not. "Ok," He muttered. "He tried to pick you up before and you didn't let him. Why Monday?"

"It was his lucky day." Julie huffed.

128

"Let me rephrase. Why NOT all the other times? Everything else aside, he sort of seems like your type." Rick ventured.

"My type. I see."

"I don't mean to piss you off, I just want to know why you said no all the other times."

Julie tried to let go of her sudden anger. It wasn't too hard to do. "I don't know, he just, he just, he has a bad vibe, Do-c. I know you probably think that's funny but he's got bad juju." Ritter wasn't her type, he was far too large for her, 6'5 and 250 pounds of sheer muscle. Normally, as a cautionary rule, she stayed away from men so physically powerful. Besides that, when it came to Ritter, he was just too anxious on the occasions he sat and had a drink with her. But she was spiraling downward fast that last night in the bar and when Ritter walked up to her, Julie was ready for whatever punishment he could dole out. At least she thought she was.

Mason sat on the other side of the table thinking that to her Ritter had bad vibes, bad juju and bad mojo, at least she got that much right but it still wasn't an explanation, "Monday his juju was better?"

"You said that was the last question."

"Part B?" He offered and watched her hang her head.

"Aww, Doc. You don't want the answer. Stop asking."

"Me?" He asked. "I freaked you out when I recognized you at the hospital, is that it?" He knew he should have gone to the bar instead of scoping out her house. If he had, he would have run into her before Ritter could get to her. "I drove you to him."

"It's not your fault, Do-c."

Yeah, then why does it feel like it is? Why are you calling me Do-c? Sitting there trying to gauge her over the candle light he reached into his pocket and popped a Oxycodone. He noticed everything and since last night Julie had taken to calling him three separate, but equal, names; Doc, Rick and her ever popular Do-c. Doc was ok, she was being playful, or maybe she was frustrated with him. Rick was good since this morning—last night not so good--, she was being serious and maybe playful. Do-c, that almost sinful way she said it and had been saying it again and again in his head since August that was a warning not a come-on. "I didn't say it was."

"Then can we just drop this?"

"Sure," He said wanting to say anything but that, "I'm an ass, I told you that. I didn't mean to upset you." He reached for her hand across the table and she let him take it. "No more questions about him, I swear."

"It's over? Done? A dead issue?"

"All of the above." He agreed.

In that case. "Let's get out of here."

"Where shall we go?" He asked as he rose from the table and held out his arm for hers.

"I was hoping your place."

"What a coincidence. So was I."

Chapter Ten

Julie and Rick didn't make it back to the house, not right away. Driving down the dark winding road it wasn't long before she was sidling up next to him, blowing in his ear and fondling his crotch. "Come on, Doc, let's finish what we started last night, pull over."

That was very inviting and there weren't any headlights in his rearview mirror for the last couple of miles. "Why don't you get me started?" He returned and tilted up the steering wheel. Just down the road a small piece there was an abandoned Drive-In Movie Theatre, between here and there she could just get his juices flowing. Like they weren't already but a little more coaxing never hurt.

She let out a little 'hum' sound and smiled when he tilted up the wheel just before she lowered her head between his legs and began pulling down his zipper. Her silky hand worked its way inside. "Keep your eyes on the road," she advised in a whisper as she pulled out his hardening cock and slipped it into her mouth.

Behind the wheel, Rick sucked in a deep breath and tried to keep his eyes on the road lest they roll back in his head. One hand on the wheel and the other on the back of her head, "I've been thinking about you all day," he said in a lustful voice and pushed her head a little further down. Seems she'd forgive him for his questions regarding Ritter.

Julie hardly heard him, his voice tickled her ears but his words were muddled as she lay there on the front seat giving him head. Her nose buried deep into material of his slacks preventing her from nuzzling the soft patch of hair below. It was frustrating not to be able to smell him but rather taking in the scent of his fabric softener, she couldn't wait to get these pants off of him. Couldn't wait to get him inside of her in a more satisfactory fashion.

The turn-off for the old Drive-In was overgrown with brush, no one came down here anymore, he had to keep his eyes open and sharp so that he didn't miss it. Keeping both hands on the wheel as he took the turn down the rutted road, she looked up at him with a mouthful of his cock. "Soon," he said, "we'll be there soon."

The massive silver-screen that once dominated the place was nothing more than a skeleton of rusted iron bars. The parking lot which had once held happy families and clandestine lovers on Friday and Saturday nights was nothing more than an empty space of pitted asphalt. He had to be careful not to run into the speaker stands that still stood here hidden by the thick growth of brush. Little less than halfway in, Rick put the car in park, turned off the headlights, killed the engine but turned the key to leave the radio running. He didn't know why she wanted to have sex in the car but he was glad for it just the same, it made him feel like a naughty teenager again, especially being here in the Drive-In. Reaching down, he pulled the pins from her hair to let it spill around her shoulders.

Now that they reached their destination, she went to work on the belt and clasp at his waist. With them undone, she pulled them down and he offered no resistance but instead raised his ass from the seat at the appropriate moment to give her a hand with the task. She'd get them all the way off him soon but right now this was good. She could smell him now, his heat and his sex and she wanted all of it.

Rick sat behind the wheel, blue eyes closed, completely immersed in the gratification she was giving him. He wasn't lying, he had thought about her constantly all day long. Even as they struggled to diagnosis a new patient who quickly went from mild to moderate breathing problems to stroke and then heart attack, all he could think about was getting his hands on

Julie again tonight. As usual, Rick pulled his and the patient's ass out of the fire at the last minute but that was because of her too, if he hadn't been thinking about how delightfully she sucked on his cock he wouldn't have come up with odd notion of a parasite which might be sucking the life out of his new patient. Much the way she was sucking the life-force from him now but a lot less pleasurably. No matter what he tried he couldn't get her out of his head, it seemed she was buried as deeply in his mind as he was in her mouth at the moment. One arm wrapped behind him, pulling him closer to her, the other hand cupping his balls while she extended that long, lovely index finger backward to press against and tease the sensitive place that waited, and usually went ignored and unloved. Not by her. The windows began to steam over while her tongue wound around his hard shaft, licking up, down, and all around.

**

Ritter was forced to wait outside of the old Drive-In and he wasn't happy about that...not one little bit. He couldn't drive in there without his headlights and not drive into a small tree or one of those old speaker stands that dotted the place. Headlights would surely give him away. He couldn't even walk in there without a flashlight and that too might give him away even though it would be much less noticeable than the headlights. Either Mason knew he was being followed or he just liked to fuck in strange places, then again, that was probably Julie. For the next half hour or so all he could do was sit behind the wheel, his own windows steaming over with a different kind of passion and wait for them to come out.

**

The climax was so hard that Rick's body stiffened nose to toes as he came up off the seat, one hand gripping the back of her head and the other white-knuckling the steering wheel while his foot pressed the accelerator to the floor. Looking up at him slyly from between his legs, Julie licked her lips, gave him a heated grin and then pushed up the material of the dress shirt so she could nuzzle her face against his heaving chest and listen to his racing heart. "Thanks for dinner." She whispered licking the last of him from her lips. "It was delicious."

Rick grunted and then laughed as he struggled to catch his breath. "I bought desert too, what do I get for that?" Julie slid her arm out from behind him and he reached down to bring her up close to him. "I haven't gotten a kiss yet."

Even though she'd like nothing better he wasn't going to get one now. "How's the back seat looking to you? Think you're up for it or, ah, am I asking too much?"

"Question is; are you up for it?"

"Oh?" She said and batted her eyelashes at him. "Why is that, Doc?"

"They make these wonderful little blue pills," he held his thumb and forefinger an quarter inch apart to shower her the size, "great for blood flow. Problem is you can only get 'em by prescription, good thing I'm a doctor."

"You're not serious," she said but the thought was intriguing and she brought her fingertip to her lips to bite down on the nail.

Even in the pale moonlight of the crisp November night he could see her blush. "Get in the back seat and find out."

"There's a warning on those things, you know." She advised. "If it lasts more than four hours you have to go see a doctor."

"I'll consult myself, don't you worry."

"How's your heart, Doc?" Julie teased. "I hear..."

"My heart's just fine, Julie-Baby" He tossed his head toward the backseat. "Now who's chicken?" Julie gave him a smoky stare then he watched her climb over the seat. He couldn't manage that trick on his best day but that didn't stop him from enjoying the sight of her ass as it went past his face, he just wanted to bite it so he did, just a little. She let out a little yelp as she tumbled over the seat.

"Fresh."

"You ain't seen nothing yet." Rick opened the door, pulled the front seat all the way up as he climbed out of the car and then climbed into the back seat with her. "You're overdressed."

"Am I?"

"Um-hum," he reached down to run his hand along the length of her calf and bring her foot up to him so he could start with the shoes he liked so much. "Let's get rid of these, they must be uncomfortable," he tossed them into the front seat before running his thumb along the arch of her foot. Julie let out a long sigh. "Why do women torture themselves with these things?"

"Because men love them so."

"True dat." He returned with both of her silky legs across his bare lap. Slowly he pushed the dress up a little further taking in a long look at those incredible legs in their black stockings and wondered if she was wearing thigh highs again? Then he wondered what else she was wearing under there? "You know what else we like?"

"Tell me."

Rick pushed up the hem of the dress past those thighs and those hips. "Oh, God, I think I love you." He exclaimed as his mouth began watering at the sight of, not thigh highs, but actual black silk stocking with a black garter belt and no panties.

She giggled, covering her face with her hand but not her eyes and they were smiling as she watched him look down at her. "Am I still overdressed?"

"Let's find out." The lacy dark green dress had buttons up the front, it also had a stiff high lace collar that had been elegantly hiding the discolored ring around her neck. Those smiling eyes stopped smiling when he reached for the top button. Last night they did this and he didn't know what had happened to her, Rick felt sick about it all day. Not tonight. He knew those bruises were there and she knew he knew so there was no reason to hide. Two buttons down. Three. Was she trembling? Yes, she was. With firm but gentle hands he pushed the top if the dress apart, the collar fell to both sides of her neck and, no, she wasn't wearing a bra or a slip. Except for a bite mark or two—that could have been his handy work—those pert little tits were in fine condition. That neck, not so much. Rick felt sorry for her and he felt angry but neither of those canceled out or overrode the desire taking over and filling his mind with all sorts of good ideas. He bent toward her and Julie turned her face away, instead of pushing the point Rick put one hand on either side of her neck, just his fingers, he ran them along the bruise with a gentle pressure.

At first it hurt, just for a moment, but then his touch felt good. It made the ache go away, she let out a little cry.

"I know, Julie-Baby, I know. Shhhh." He wanted to comfort her and make her pain go away but he also wanted to get a good feel of that neck and it seemed the only way she was going to let him do that was if she didn't know he was doing it at all. He'd prefer a more comprehensive picture of her neck but this would have to do. Nothing felt out of place or damaged but it was ugly and it hurt like hell. It was hard for her to swallow, Julie tried to eat her dinner, but she winced every time she tried to swallow anything larger than a dime. Impromptu exam over, his curiosity satisfied (mostly) it was time to get back to business. The buttons stopped at her waist, he undid each one

136

and then slid the sleeves down over her arms to see where Ritter had grabbed her—probably in order to throw her on the bed or the floor. Rick didn't want to toss the pretty dress in a ball onto the floor of the car once he got it off of her, he put it on the front seat.

"What do you want from me, Rick? Why are you looking at me like that?"

"I'm going to kiss you now and you're going to let me." He didn't wait for a reply he just went in for the kiss but she turned away and gave him her cheek. He wasn't going to settle for that and instead planted kissed along the bruise on her neck. He knew how sensitive the area was, just touching it caused a strange mixture of pleasure and pain. Julie sucked in a deep breath. "I don't pity you."

She wished that were true, wanted to believe that with all her being. "No? But I think you do."

"Don't mistake concern for pity." He advised. "I'm not allowed to be concerned about you? Is that it?"

"I'm not your mother, Do-c, I don't 'allow' you to do anything."

"No, you just disallow it." He countered. "If you didn't then I could do this..." he went for the kiss one more time, Julie hesitated. She turned away too late when his lips brushed over hers she stopped turning away and started turning back towards him. Her arms wrapped around his back and pulled him closer.

Oh, God, what the hell am I doing? She didn't know. Didn't really care. It just felt so damn good, she wanted as much of him as she could get before he went off on his way. Enough to last through whatever cold lonely nights in the El Royale were to come. "I want you." She whispered.

"Come here," he pulled back and pulled her up. He was standing at full attention but even though the front seat was all the way forward he could get down on the one knee position, she'd have to do the work. "Show me how much you want me."

Julie let out a long low growl as she straddled him. "Aren't you forgetting something?"

No, he wasn't forgetting anything, it was in his wallet, he knew she wouldn't bring them with her. Although he couldn't prove it, Rick was damn sure you wouldn't find a condom anywhere in Julie Miller's house. His pants were in the front seat and it wouldn't be the first time, he was getting used to riding her bareback. And he wasn't really taking any chances anyway. And that was because, well, no matter how hard he tried, he would always be Richard Mason. In between bouts of arguing over the patient, he'd done something very unethical. Rose Montague came into the Willington-Middleboro Clinic once every six months, her chart said she was 'a very difficult patient', it was full of notes about her being 'abrupt' and even 'abusive', he thought that very odd. Rose Montague came in every six months to get tested for STDs. The last time she was in was just two weeks ago and she was clean as a whistle. "No." He laced his hands behind her back. "Come on, Rosie, ride me."

"If you insist." No condom. That was so good. And it was *so bad*. And she let him do it so often, she really shouldn't do that. None of that kept her from sliding down on him. Didn't keep her from grinding on him. Kissing him. Wanting more. "Fill me, Doc."

**

Out on the street, Ritter sat in the car growing more irate by the moment. He was missing all the action, they were fucking in there, he just knew it. He had hoped this was just a little quickie pit stop on the way to the Main Event but, they'd been in there almost forty-five minutes. "Fuck it." He opened the door, turned his collar against the night air as he made his way into the thicket.

**

Inside the old Drive-In, Rick and Julie were lost to each other and the night. There was nothing else. Maybe tomorrow there would be telephones and faxes and patients and job searches once more but right now none of that mattered. The weight of all that lifted giving Aphrodite room to work Her way in and work Her magick on the lovers.

Julie's lips locked to his, her hands against his chest for leverage as she pushed, ground and thrust herself upon him in the backseat. Her fingers started to bend and flex, bend and flex against his chest and she pushed down slower and took longer to drag herself back upward. "Come on, Rick, cum with me, cum with me...please." She begged her breath hot in his ear. The air was hot and heavy, it was getting hard to breath and she couldn't stop doing what she was doing if someone threatened her life. "Please?"

Rick helped her out with those long, slow, thrusts, by putting his hands on her hips. Such lovely hips as they ground around and up and down on him. He could hold on to these babies for many nights to come, that would be just fine. If she'd keep doing this then that would just wonderful. Julie's fingers bent and stayed that way, they dug into his chest as her body stiffened and she couldn't hold it back any longer. He looked up to see her face in the moonlight, those translucent eyes closed, she bit down on her lips and let out a low slow moan. "That's so beautiful," he whispered. She looked like a Goddess, a very sexy, sensual, and satisfied Goddess as she rode on him. Those eyes opened, they locked to his, called to something deep inside his soul and he couldn't help but surrender willingly.

When it was over she collapsed against him, with her arms around his neck and her face buried deep in the nape. "I can't breathe."

"Yeah," Rick agreed in the same breathless tone. The car was hot, it was steaming, he reached over and opened the door to let in the chilly night air. "That's because we sucked up all the oxygen in here." He used the free hand to wave in the air. "Take a deep breath, Rosie, you'll be all right."

In the not too far distance Ritter saw the dome light of Mason's car come on and stopped in his tracks. He could hear them, they were laughing as they panted for air, and he swore he could see steam wafting out of the backseat. Must have been some show, he was sorry he missed it.

"How's your heart now, Doc?"

"Better than ever." He wrapped her up in his armed and buried his face in her hair. "Wanna go home with me?"

"Yes. I think we're just getting started."

That was good news and it made the grumpy Trooper smile as he turned back the way he came so he could beat them to Mason's apartment. No sense in waiting for them to finish up and listen to them tell each other what great fucks they were. That part wasn't very interesting. This way he'd be in position and all set to go when the show resumed.

**

Neither Rick nor Julie noticed anything out of place when they pulled up to his house but then again they were distracted by each other as they stumbled the short distance from the street to the door. Both of them were barely dressed having haphazardly tossed on their clothes for the ride. Hardly inside

140

the apartment and said clothes were already hitting the floor before the door could be shut and locked. "You do it on the piano?" She asked as she tugged at his pants for the last time that night.

"No," Rick said as he looked over at it. "No."

"Awww, c'mon, Rick, why not? Afraid I'll...break your instrument?"

"Funny, no." The idea was appealing, however if they did break it and they just might it was very expensive to fix. He loved that piano. "I got a better idea." As Ritter had done earlier in the day, Rick and Julie left a trail of clothes from the front door to the bathroom. "You need a shower."

"So do you."

"Perfect." He turned on the water.

**

Ritter was already in the yard, thankful there weren't any motion detecting lights and blessing Fate for a clear night. He saw them in the hall then watched them go into the bathroom. There were no windows in Rick's bathroom but soon he saw steam wafting through the open door. "Get the bitch clean." He muttered unhappy with having to wait once more.

**

In the hot steamy shower, Rick was sorry he didn't have a bottle of one of those fancy soaps women seemed to like so much. All he had was a bar of Irish Spring and it would have to do, he worked a up a thick lather between his hands.

"What are you gonna do with that?"

"You know what I'm gonna do with it." Under the hot jets, Rick leaned in, she let him kiss her and those legs parted as he slipped his soapy hand between them.

She bit down on his lower lip. "Got plans?"

"Several."

"I knew there was a reason I like you." She sighed as his lathered hand slipped around between that bald patch between her legs. Julie let her own hand slid down over his then past it to touch herself before taking the bar from his hand but he didn't seem to want to let it go. "You're are going to let me return the favor, aren't you? You're just as dirty as I am, Do-c." Her upper lip curled in a wayward little grin. He let go of the soap, she turned the bar around in her hand and brought the sensual lather to his balls. "So dirty, Do-c."

"Another reason why you like me."

The slightest touch and he was near hard again. "Did you really take one of those pills?" She asked still intrigued as she soaped him tip to balls and then behind. "Did you?"

"Why? Why so interested, Rosie?"

Julie didn't really know and she shrugged her shoulders as they stood in the shower each with their hand between the other's legs. "Why would you do that?"

"To keep up with you. In case no one's told you, Julie-Baby, you're insatiable." She always wanted more, no matter how much he gave her she always wanted just one more. He was starting to wonder if she was a sex addict and not merely a nymphomaniac. He took a closer look at the way she was staring at him. "It's not going to harm me. It's just a pill."

"If you say so, Do-c." Julie gave him a little shove until they were both standing under the running water letting it wash away the sudsy lather. "All clean now?"

"Not even close," he smirked and turned her toward the shower wall. "I'm going to get you dirty, then I'm going to get you clean, then I'm going to take you out of here and get you filthy." He whispered in her ear as he put her hands high on the wall covering them with his own. "It's going to be a long night."

She looked back at him. "That's your plan?" He nodded. "I like it."

"Knew you would." He slid into her from behind.

"Oh the things you do to me," she moaned.

On the downward part of the thrust he bent deeply at the knee so that upward produced that long slow intoxicating sigh from her that turned him on so much. "Yeah, you like them too, I know."

"You don't know, Do-c, you dunno." Julie's back arched in greeting of his next surge. "Don't stop."

He liked that too. Definitely two of his most favorite words in all of the English language when they slipped out of her mouth like that. He was sorry that he'd mocked her with it this morning and glad to see his sarcasm wasn't getting in their way tonight. "Don't you worry, Julie-Baby, I won't stop." At the sound of his words some of the strength went out of her knees and he tightened on his grip on her hands, pulled her upward, to keep her from sinking down.

There they stayed, deep in the clutches of passion, far into that euphoria where the world fades away and there's nothing but the heat and connectedness of two intertwined souls enjoying the comforts and pleasures of their equally intertwined bodies. That rush of endorphins and adrenaline and every other clinical element he could name involved in the sex act but did not care to took over and was not interrupted by things like driving home.

**

Growing impatient once more with the uncooperative lustful couple inside, Ritter began to pace around the yard in the shadows grateful none of the neighbors had a dog to give him away. "What the hell is up with those two? They fuck like rabbits." He groused. Then there was a shadow against the far wall and the happy couple soon followed, wet, and naked they went from the bathroom to the bedroom. "Hallelujah!" At least the night wouldn't be a total waste.

From the yard, he watched as Julie laid down on Mason's bed and Mason went to the closet. He came back with two neckties. "You old dog." Sure enough, Mason tied Julie to the bed with them. She didn't seem to mind.

**

"Stay there."

"Where are you going?"

"Ugh," he tossed his head, "just stay there."

She looked at the neckties on her wrists. "Yep, I'll just hang out here, seems I'm all tied up at the moment anyway." She called as she watched him leave the bedroom. He came back with a pint of ice cream in one hand and a pint of whipped cream in the other. "What'cha gonna do with the whipped cream?"

"Ahh, you should be more concerned with what I'm going to do with the ice cream." Rick taunted as he made his way back to the bed. He opened the container and showed it to her. "Butter Crunch, want some?" Before she could answer him, he scooped out a teaspoonful and put it in her mouth. "Tasty, isn't it?"

"Cold." Julie returned but it was sweet and it was tasty.

"Cold? Hummm, imagine that. Ice cream...is cold. Who knew?" He stuck the spoon into the ice cream and picked up the can of whipped cream. "This stuff, on the other hand, is...well, compared to the ice cream, it's...chilly. Right?" He tipped the can upside down and squirted out a dollop onto her breast. "My tongue, on yet another hand," he stuck out the tip of it for it, "is...warm." Rick bent down and took that small whipped cream breast into his warm mouth and licked it clean. "That's tasty too."

"Are you giving me a science lesson, Doc?"

"Yep and we're not done yet, so pay attention, there'll be a test later." Putting down the whipped cream, he stood up and waved his free hand at her nearly closed legs.

"Doc?"

"Gonna make me pry 'em apart?" He dared.

"Would you?"

"Is that a real question?"

Julie tittered, yes they both knew the answer to that. Depending on how far she let the game go he'd be happy to take it all the way if that was what she wanted.

"I'm waiting."

"You're an ass."

"We knew that already." He paused. "Still waiting."

"Whatever you want, Do-c." Julie's legs spread apart, he made his way between them, scooped out some more of the ice cream with the spoon and popped it into his mouth. The cold of the ice cream and the heat of his tongue met her lower lips.

"Ahhh." She sat up halfway as her hands strained against the ties at her wrists. "Doc," she moaned and heard as well as felt him laugh. "Oh, Rick, what are you doing to me?" she panted and the world around her seemed to spin. The ice cream began to melt, it turned warm and sticky, his tongue pushed not around her but inside of her. Then pulled it back out again.

Holy shit! Oh, I have to stop doing this with him, I have to stop this, I have to....oh for Gods' sake that feels sooo good.

"I told you, you should have been more worried about the ice cream."

**

With the light on and the shade up, Rick and the Fair Juliette went at it until nearly 2am. There was something different about it now, something...intimate. They weren't just two people scratching an itch any longer, if he could see and even feel that from out here surely they felt it inside. "Enjoy her while you can, my friend, it won't be too much longer now."

**

When they were done Julie laid in Rick's arms for a while but soon that old urge took over. "I'll be back."

"I'll let you smoke in here in you want, it's cold out there."

"Thanks, that's ok. I know, I'm a Second Class Citizen, I'm used to it." Julie wrapped his robe around her and made her way out to the living room looking on the ground for her purse, she found it on the couch. Opening it, she saw the pack was empty, she went through an entire pack today so she opened the new one she brought with her, slipped one out and took it out to the front yard. Weak-kneed and her head spinning she stood out there smoking the cigarette grateful for the quiet and solace of the night. She didn't notice Ritter standing by the near corner of the house. In the dark, he crept from the back window to the

146

front, he was so close her smoke was wafting into his face. "I've got to break this off," Julie muttered to herself. "I can't fall in love with him."

It was too late. She was over her head and she knew it.

Julie raised her eyes to the night sky. "Why him?"

Standing just on the other side of the corner of the house listening to her talking to herself, Ritter put his hand over his mouth to stifle the chuckle.

"This is insane. Just crazy."

Her cigarette done and God not answering tonight she crushed the butt, tossed it out into the street and made her way back inside to find Doc waiting for her. He was propped up on one elbow as he lay in the bed. Crossing the short distance to him something on the nightstand glimmered and caught her eye.

That hadn't been there before, had it?

She took a step closer and looked from the shiny silver item on the nightstand to the man in the bed then back again. "Is that?"

He reached over and picked it up. "My high school ring? Yep." He pulled the covers back and waited for her to climb in next to him before he put it in her hand.

Julie looked down at it in her palm; St. Mark's High School, it read on the outside around a rather large pearl, and on the inside was engraved; Richard Mason. All these years, he kept his high school ring. "You knew where it was the whole time."

"I'm a packrat, I never throw anything out."

"You're a sentimental old fool is what you are, Rick. Very charming though you hide it well."

"Does that mean you'll wear it?" He asked pushing a strand of hair away from her face. "I got this to go with it." Opening his other hand he produced a gleaming silver chain. "What do you say? Be my girl?" He opened the clasp and slipped the ring onto the chain.

Before she could stop herself, Julie found the words; "I'd love to," falling out of her mouth. He put the necklace around her neck and she held onto the ring. "Your birthday's in June?" She asked still staring at the ring and doubting that the pearl was the school stone.

"Sure is. When's yours?" He'd seen her keychain which proclaimed she was a Libra.

"Opal," Julie answered, "October. Halloween." She looked up at him. "Does this mean you're going to take me to the prom?"

"If you're lucky."

"How about if I'm very good?" She offered.

"How about if you're very bad." He countered with a grin.

Julie looked at him a little guiltily, "I think you've worn me out for the night." She rubbed her shoulder and then her chest.

"Still not feeling well?" Not that he could tell it by the way she made love with him tonight.

"Just achy, I wish whatever this is would just come on already and get it over with."

"By tomorrow you'll probably get your wish and be miserable." He offered cheerily. "Stay with me tonight?"

Yes, she'd like that. "Turn out the light." She let the robe fall to the flood as she crawled under the covers with him. He opened his arms to hold her. "No, you come here tonight." In the dark he hesitated a moment, it was traditional for the woman to curl

148

up in the man's arms and not the other way around but he laid his head on her breast and wrapped his arm around her. Julie held him close. "That's good, isn't it?"

Oh yeah, that was good. He threw a leg over her as though she were a full-body pillow as he listened to the sound of her heart; nice, steady, strong and her lungs; clear, no congestion, she wasn't feverish either. For someone coming down with the flu she didn't seem to have many symptoms. By tomorrow that would change. He started to dose off, sleep began to wash over him when that pumping little heart which should have been slowing down and settling in for a nice long sleep began to speed up. "Julie? You all right?"

"Do you see him?" She whispered in the dark. "Or is it just me?" She'd been laying here reveling in the warmth and weight of him in her arms, wanting to just hold him like this forever and knowing that wasn't possible no matter what the ring around her neck might have to say. She was about to close her eyes and try to sleep when the wind blew a branch out there and below it appeared the figure of a man. She laid here, not moving, hardly breathing, watching, watching, watching, to see if the figure moved or if it went away when the wind blew again. It did neither of those things.

"See who?"

"Don't get up." She hissed. "Just look with your eyes because I think he's looking at us. Do you see him? Over there, off to the left of the big tree?"

He saw a figure, something, maybe someone standing there by the tree, almost blending in with the trunk. "Stay here."

Julie's arms clamped around him. "Don't go out there, Rick."

He pried her arms off him. "You...stay here." He slipped into his own robe and thought about closing the shade but that would tip him off so he left it open. He went out to the living room and the front windows to gaze out at the dark quiet street looking for an unfamiliar car. "Is he still out there?" He called back to the bedroom.

Julie stopped looking out the window when she watched him walk out of the bedroom. She turned back to it now and didn't see the figure standing there. "No, I think he's gone."

A few doors down the street someone emerged from a front yard which was easily accessible through his own. They stayed out of the streetlights, wandered down a way, got into a car and took off.

"Rick?" Julie asked from the doorway of the bedroom.

"It's all right, he's gone." He pulled the shades and made his way back to her. "You ok?"

"You don't think it was..."

"I know it was." He answered.

"How long do you think he stood there?"

Knowing that bastard all fucking night. "I don't know." He said.

Pulling the blankets tighter around her she looked up at him with those unearthly eyes, "What does he want? Why does he keep following you?"

Coming back to the bed and taking her up in his arms, Mason wondered if she was wrong. He hadn't seen hide nor hair of Ritter in over a year. What would have set the lunatic off now? Maybe it was Julie Ritter was after and Mason was a happy accident. Then again, who could truly know the thoughts of a power-tripping bully with a badge? "I don't know." Holding her a little tighter he offered, "Maybe we should call the cops?"

Julie snorted involuntarily, "What? The two people Willington has that call themselves the local police? Yeah, they're asleep now and besides, Ritter's a State Trooper." If he hadn't been, if he hadn't flashed that badge as he buckled his belt the morning he left her sore and sorry, Julie would have reported him to the local authorities. As it stood now, she just tried to forget him but it seemed he wouldn't go away.

Running his fingertips down her spine Mason nodded, "Yeah." He tried for months to get the two local cops to take him seriously and to lodge formal complaints against Patrick Ritter but all they ever said was that Mason didn't have enough evidence. He was probably imagining things. "He's gone now. It's all right, Julie-Baby, we're safe in here."

Chapter Eleven

Rick was torn between wanting Julie to stay at his place and taking her home the next morning. He'd gotten up several times during the night, waking her in the process, to get up and check the windows, the doors, the street and just to see if anyone was around. He did not like the idea of leaving here alone all day any more than he liked the idea of taking her home. At least at her house there was an alarm system and Max, Ritter would have a hard time getting past the dog.

She looked paler than yesterday and she looked weary but he'd done a good job on getting her that way last night. "Still not feeling well?"

"Headache," she complained lightly, "achy all over and tired, that's your fault." She said with a painful smile. "Do you have any aspirin?"

Aspirin? Who took aspirin anymore unless it was low-dose and they had a heart condition? "Nope, but I got plenty of other stuff," he started toward the bathroom.

"That's all right, Do-c, don't worry. I'll just take some when I get home."

"Just hold on a second, I got lots of great stuff in there..."

"No!" She said more forcefully then she'd meant to and it didn't do her throat any favors. "Sorry, haven't had my coffee yet. I'm a real bitch first thing in the morning." Julie weaved an unsteady path toward the couch almost as though she were drunk. He knew she was sober, unless she'd managed to get his bottle of scotch out from under the bed in the night.

"Got a fever?"

"No."

"How do you know?" He countered and finished making his way to the bathroom only to come back with a thermometer. "Open up."

Julie sat there on the couch with her mouth clamped shut and shaking her head.

"What's with you?" He asked. "Just open your mouth, you didn't have a problem with that last night." He encouraged hoping to make her laugh but she just sat there staring at him with cold eyes. "Julie, it's just a thermometer." She held up her hand and waved it away. "Ok, you made me." He sighed before he reached out and pinched her nose shut. He sat there staring at her and her at him. "You gotta breathe some time. Since you smoke I'm betting it's gonna be much sooner rather than later."

Julie staunchly held her breath and kept his lips shut tight.

He waited.

She turned a little red.

He waited.

She turned a little redder.

"Open up."

Julie shook her head. She wanted to scream at him; LEAVE ME ALONE!, She wanted to kick him, bite him, do whatever it took just to get him away from her. But he was the same man who'd been spending so much quality time with her lately and it was hard to justify the two but she was working on it.

"You're gonna pass out soon." He warned. "I'm not letting go. If you pass out you won't give me any trouble. OR....I can do this the old fashioned way." His eyes glanced down to her ass. "Humm, would you like that?"

No, she wouldn't like that and he was apt to get a good old-fashioned Mule Kick right in the teeth if he tried it.

"What is with you?" He asked still holding her nose closed and watching as her face went from light red to crimson. "You'll let me tie you to the bed, you'll suck my cock, let me put it in your ass—which I *really* like, by the way—but you won't let me put this thermometer in your mouth? C'mon, it's smaller." He said with a grin hoping to coax her into doing things his way. Then he got a big surprise.

Julie didn't open her mouth, just her lips to bare her teeth at him and through those gritted teeth she said; "Not by much."

Geez, and here he thought he did a bang up job last night. "Ouch." His jaw dropped before he could stop it. "Ok, that's it. Open up!" He used the palm of his hand to cover her pretty mouth. That would force her to open it to breathe and when she did, the thermometer was going in. "What goes on in that pretty little head of yours, huh, Julie-Baby?"

My parents used to do this to me! This very same thing! Do you know what I did to them???? I'm going to slap you silly, Do-c! I'm going to slap you sooo hard and you're not going to like it! I'm going to knock you on your ass if you don't let go!

That wouldn't be good and Julie forced herself to sit on her hands.

Julie's crossed legs were jumping up and down nervously and she was starting to shake as she stared at him from behind unblinking eyes. To him it looked like she was about to scream and he thought about those notes in Rose Montague's chart, how she was 'difficult', 'abusive' and 'abrupt'. "If you don't like doctors, what are you doing with me?" She didn't answer him. "You know, Rosie, the good part about dating or, in our case at least, fucking a doctor, is you get free medical care. Most people would consider that a pretty good benefit." In those nearly colorless eyes, he plainly saw that Julie did not consider this a benefit.

Rick's willpower was stronger than her smoker's lungpower. Just before she went from crimson to blue and he was starting to wonder if he'd have to do mouth-to-mouth on her, below his hand, Julie's mouth opened. He pulled his hand away as he pulled in a big breath of air along with the thermometer. "Don't you bite it," He warned. "Don't you spit it out. If all my patients were like you I'd quit."

"Mmbe u shud." She mumbled.

"Maybe I should? Humm, yeah, well, wouldn't be the first time I changed jobs." The thermometer started to come out of her mouth. "Don't you dare. Don't make me tie you down." But she might do just that, so he held the thermometer in her mouth for her and swore for half a second that she was going to bite him. Not those sweet nibbles that he liked either.

The stupid thing in her mouth beeped and she spit it at him before she got off the couch.

He picked it up. "98.6, no fever."

"I told you that, Do-c." Julie said coldly. "If you do that again, you can kiss my ass good-bye. I am not...repeat...*NOT...your fucking **patient**!*" By the time she got to the end of the sentence she was screaming at him.

"Julie, what the hell..." he got up and tried to walk over to her.

"Get away from me!" She hissed as she put her hands up to block him. "Don't you touch me!"

He didn't know what was going on but she looked like she was ready to spit nails at him. They'd be more painful than the thermometer to be sure but less harsh than the comment regarding size that he was still choking down. Again, looking at her face, an outsider might have thought that he'd burned her with a lit cigarette instead of trying to take her temperature. "Julie?"

"I mean it, Do-c, just step the fuck off, and don't come any closer."

"I can see you mean it, what I don't know is why. What did I do?"

"You're a fucking doctor, isn't that enough?"

Oh God! Oh shut up, Julie! Shut up! Shut up! Shut up! Don't do this! Not NOW! For God's sake, girl...GET A GRIP! This is the same guy you couldn't take your hands off last night! So just **GET A MOTHERFUCKING GRIP!**

That was so hard to do because everything was spinning and it was covered in red. Spinning, spinning, spinning, all around while she stood still and watched its rosy hue turn into a running blur. Her heart was racing and she tried to breath, she tried to think about anything other doctors and pills and needles and white coats and stereoscopes and that polite 'we're-so-sorry-but voice. The smugness in their eyes and the arrogance in their voice and

GET A FUCKING GRIP, BITCH!

"You knew that before you slept with me," he countered. "Or is this just more of you being bitchy because you haven't had your coffee?"

She didn't like the way he was looking at her but who could blame him for it? The last thing she wanted was to lose him over this irrational and nearly debilitating fear. If she just stood here hissing at him....well, like it or not, her new beau did have the power to have her locked up for 72 hours of 'observation'.

156

Didn't THAT make the motherfucker an even MORE dangerous man! "I...I..."

"You what?"

Julie took a few more steps away from him along with a deep breath.

Stop spinning! Stop spinning! I demand that you stop spinning right now!

Her jaw was set so tightly her teeth hurt; they felt like they were going shatter under the pressure if she didn't find a way to relieve it soon.

His name is Rick, yes, yes he's a doctor, but he's a man, and his name is Rick.

"I-atro-phobia." She muttered. The world didn't stop spinning but it seemed to slow down and there seemed to be the possibility that she might obtain the ever-elusive grip on reality that she so desperately needed.

"You're *afraid* of doctors?!" Yes, she was, of course she was. Right now, standing here in his living room, she was terrified of him and all over a stupid thermometer. That explained her behavior in the Clinic the other day, how she ran hot—way hot—one moment and then colder than ice the next. Explained why Rose Montague's chart said all those nasty things about her. "This an actual diagnosis or something you got off the Internet?" He asked skeptically.

"Like Coke, it's the real thing."

"How long have you had it?"

"Since I was very small." Julie admitted but refrained from telling him colorful stories of early childhood doctor visits.

He had read articles about Iatrophobics but he'd never met one in the flesh let alone been on such an intimate basis with them. "Why in the world did you pick *me*?" It didn't make any sense. If she hated doctors, why would she go out of her way to meet him? Bed him?

"I have no idea." She whispered but that wasn't exactly true, she did have an idea or two, but the one that came to her head was just silly it was just....

"I don't wear a white coat, is that it?" He asked in a sly voice and knew he was right, probably only partially so, but right was right and he was it. "Steward, Goodspeed and even Spaulding with the brown eyes you like, they all wear white coats but I don't."

Yes, as stupid and irrational as it was, Julie thought his lack of a white lab coat had quite a bit to do with it all. "Are you a mind reader, Do-c?"

"Close." He agreed.

"Look, if you just stop being Doctor Mason we'll be fine."

"I'm afraid I can't do that, I AM Doctor Mason. There's only one of me and that's good because the world can't handle two. I didn't ask you to stop being who you are, did I?"

"No?" Julie looked down at the ring around her neck. "Then what's this?" She looked up at him with sad eyes and he didn't answer her. She looked toward the door. "I don't know what to tell you."

Ok, he asked her to stop sleeping around, but he intended to do the same—not that it was any big sacrifice on his part—he didn't ask her to give up her livelihood for him. Maybe she wasn't asking him to do that now. "How about if I stop trying to doctor *you*?" He wasn't sure he could do that but he knew he could sneak around it if he had to like last night in the car when he examined her neck without her knowing it. A lover's touch. A doctor's touch. In the end, there wasn't that much difference.

"Good idea. I know I'm a bitch, Rick. I know it's irrational but I can't help it."

"That's why it's a phobia, it's irrational." He said and then sighed. "You're not a bitch. Before you start yelling...."

"Humm, lemme guess....you have just one question."

"You're good." He complimented. "When was the last time you actually went to a doctor for an exam? I don't mean your trip to the clinic," he paused and then quickly added, "or any trips to a clinic."

"Grade school." She answered flatly. "If you don't count rehab."

"Rehab?"

"It was several years ago."

"For what?"

"Not little white pills," she pointed to his pocket, "they were blue, actually, but not the kind you took last night."

"Morphine?! You got hooked on *morphine*?"

"I said it was a while ago. I've been clean for years, Do-c. I don't take pills anymore, nothing stronger than Bayer aspirin or Tums. If I can't get it over-the-counter, I don't take it."

"Can't get pot over-the-counter in Vermont but you smoke that."

"It's a natural substance...."

"So's cyanide," he cracked. "You filled the prescription for Percocet that I gave you. I know because..."

"You get them all back," she said softly. "Every filled prescription comes back to the doctor for his log."

"How did you know that?"

She just smiled. "It's important to keep the doctor happy."

"Do... *what*?" He shook his head, fished in the pocket of his slacks to pull out his ever-present amber bottle and popped a Oxy, then another as he felt a migraine coming on. Maybe it was an aneurysm.

Julie felt that grip getting a little tighter and her thoughts and words sounding more insane. "Irrational," she pointed to herself, "got it?"

"Got it."

"When the doctor writes a prescription he knows if you fill it or not so you should always fill it that way he can log it and be happy."

"He won't ride you about why aren't you taking your pills, that it? So you take the 'script, you fill it, you..." she didn't dump it in the trash because she wouldn't want just anyone to find it and get their hands on it. "You bring it... home," he paused again. What did she do with them? Flush them? That would be rational, almost. What would be irrational would be if she... He blinked and shook his head. "You put them in the medicine cabinet and just *leave them there*, don't you? The doctor never knows that so he's happy."

"Congrats, Do-c. You did figured it out."

"Wow," he was staggered. Clearly, he didn't know this woman at all. Going back a bit, she said she'd been addicted to morphine. "Heroin?"

"Never. I'm terrified of needles."

160

Yeah, of course she was. How did she sit there while he stitched her up? Oh, that was right, she didn't. She jumped off the table and tore the needle out of her head. She must loathe going to the hospital to sit with Craig. It must make her feel like she wanted to slit her skin and jump out of it.

"Just the morphine," she looked at him closely, "that's, what, one, two steps up from those." She looked toward his pocket and the bottle hidden within. "How many of those do you take?"

"I'm a doctor, trust me, I know what I'm doing."

"That's what they all say." She whispered.

"Watch it, Rosie."

"My bad." Too close. Not nice. She was calming down and seeing him as Rick once more, just The Doc, the one she loved to fuck, but between here and there lie Catty and Bitchy. They were fading.

"What do you do if you get sick, Rosie?" He asked in a serious voice. "Really sick? What would you do?"

"Die."

Without his conscious permission, Mason's fists balled at his sides, "Not acceptable."

"Look, it's not like I haven't been to a doctor, Craig always made me go and he always made me take whatever pills they gave me, even if he had to hold my nose to do it, just like you just did." She said in a testy tone. "He'd throw me over his shoulder and carry me in if he had to..."

"He's not doing much of that anymore is he?"

Julie wanted to slap him, how dare he say such a thing to her? Except that, of course, he was a doctor. "The point is, I have been. Here and there." She muttered thinking of her medicine cabinet of prescription pills. How did he know that? How could he possibly know about her pile of old pills?

Mason hung his head and thought of those wonderful eyes of hers and her silky smooth alabaster skin that seemed to glow in moonlight turning her into some fantastical ethereal creature from heaven. But she wasn't, she was just a woman with a very rare medical condition. "What about eye doctors? Do you see anyone for your ocular albinism?" Keeping his head down he looked at her with just his eyes and knew she didn't. "You're more likely to go blind, you know that? You're more susceptible to melanoma, did you know that?"

Julie gave him a little smirk as she'd been wondering when he'd get around to mentioning her ocular condition, "Yes, Do-c, I did."

She should be on medication to strengthen her eyes, she should have special glasses to help her deal with her low vision problems. She probably couldn't see two feet in front of her at night yet she walked six miles in the rain, in the dark of night, barefoot, to get to him, "You're crazy, you know *that*?"

"I've been told." Julie agreed. "This isn't your fault, I'm fucked up, I tried to tell you that. Don't take it personally, ok? We're all fucked up and damaged and lost, Doc, even you, it's just a matter of degree, that's all. So please, just drop this."

"I'm a doctor, how the hell am I supposed to do that?"

"I don't know," she said sadly, "but like everything else you do, I'm sure you'll figure it out."

Mason thought that could be true but the physician in him wouldn't quit, "What color's your hair? The real color."

Julie sighed and then let out a huff of air that turned to a chuckle, "The lightest red you've ever seen, as though someone

162

threw a cherry snow-cone into the snow." She smiled as she tilted her head to the side, "I know what you're thinking and you got it right, Do-c, I'm not a full albino, close but not close enough." She pointed a stern but teasing finger at him, "if you start asking me about sunscreen and wearing long sleeves, we'll really have a problem."

Albinism was exceedingly rare in females, if she were his patient he'd subject her to a battery of tests that would make her pretty head spin but that probably wasn't necessary and may have even contributed to hatred of doctors, "Heard it all before, huh?"

"More than you can imagine."

No, it wasn't more than he could imagine but it was probably close enough. None of the previous doctors who lectured her had the privilege of sleeping with her, "Fine. Uncle. I give. For now."

**

Not long after they were pulling up in front of Julie's house. "Have a good day, all right, Rick?"

"I'm coming in with you." He had expected their conversation this morning to center around Ritter but got thrown a curveball and he still couldn't believe that a woman who had actually been diagnosed with Iatrophobia would consider dating, and sleeping with, a doctor. The whole ride over here he silently flattered himself by telling himself there must be something very special about him if Julie could get past her phobia enough to take him to bed or maybe it was something else about him that attracted her. He thought of the tiger that she wanted and the one he wanted to be for her, "I'm going to check the house."

Julie looked to the front door. "You don't think...oh come on, Max is in there. He'd never get past my dog."

"Not unless Ritter shot Max."

"Doc!"

"Sorry," He muttered. "You don't know him like I do."

Inside, the house looked fine. The door was good, the alarm was still on, Max whimpered that he had to go out and Julie went to the back door to let the dog into the pen. He followed her. Back door looked fine too. "You lock your windows?"

"On the first floor, yes."

"Not on the second floor?"

"Not always," she admitted. "How's anyone going to get up there?"

"Like cats, people can climb and you have that big elm tree on the side of the house right next to a window."

"Oh that thing doesn't open. I wish it did, I could get some air in the upstairs hall at night. It's painted shut or something, I've never be able to get it to rise."

"I want to see it."

"The window?"

"Your stash of pills."

"Oh for God's sake!" Julie cried and raised her hands in the air only to bring them down at her sides sharply.

"Humor me." He encouraged.

"They're upstairs, I'm sure you don't want to climb all the way up there. You'll need another pill or something."

"If you think I can't climb up a set of stairs you're crazier than I thought."

"You're exasperating."

"Right back at'cha. After you."

Julie led the way upstairs giving her hips a little extra angry swish knowing he was behind her. She led him to the master bedroom without a thought for Craig then sat down on the bed. "Well, go on, satisfy your curiosity." Julie pointed toward the open bathroom door.

"Where are they?"

"Oh, Do-c, I'm sure you'll find them."

He wandered into the bathroom and opened the medicine cabinet over the sink. It was chockfull of prescription bottles. "Jesus H. Christ!"

In the bedroom, she snickered as she waited for the other shoe to drop.

He stumbled out of the bathroom with a handful of amber bottles. "Do you have any idea how old some of these are?"

"Oh, sure." She muttered. "Keep going, Do-c."

He looked behind him and saw a large chest hanging on the wall near the tub. "You're kidding."

She didn't say anything.

Making his way to the chest he opened it, it had to be three feet long by three feet high, it had two sides with four shelves each. The right side was actually reserved for towels and bed linens but the left side was nothing but prescription bottles. He quickly realized that those in the medicine cabinet were her most recent acquisitions. Those in here dated back nearly 25 years. There wasn't a single bottle dated for the three years in which she was married to a still walking around Craig Miller. She didn't lie about that, come hell or high water, Craig made her take the pills. Vegetable in the Coma Ward or not, Mason's opinion of Craig Miller just went up ten points. "Where's the garbage?"

In the bedroom, she nearly panicked, "Oh no, don't throw them out."

"Why not?" He asked coming back to the door but she just glared at him causing Mason to feel an icy chill skip down his spine. "What do you do? Pack them up and move them with you *wherever you go*?"

"Yep."

"Do you have any idea how many thousands and thousands of dollars of medicine you have in here? And it's wasted! It's all wasted!" He railed. "Other people could have USED these. Other people WOULD HAVE used these!"

"Want your ring back now?"

No, he didn't. The sex was too good to quit now and she was crazy but baffling. "You have to get rid of these, Julie. They're way past their expiration dates; some of these are dangerous when they get old."

"Are they going to explode or something?"

I'm going to choke you, woman! I swear, I'm gonna choke you! Why? Why? Why is it that the pretty ones are ALWAYS crazy and they are ALWAYS the best in bed?! Why? What is this? Mother Nature's little way of getting back at Father Nature? "No, they're not going to explode," he sighed looking down at a bottle marked Amoxicillin and dated 1997. "Why didn't you take them? You were sick. You hate doctors but you managed to force yourself to them here and there. They gave you something to help you. What is this?"

166

"I told you already, I don't like pills and I don't trust doctors...present company excepted, of course."

"Not really," he corrected. "How did you get rid of the infection?"

"Most things just go away on their own," she said wistfully, "give them enough time and they...poof...disappear."

"If that were true I wouldn't have a job and there wouldn't be so many hospitals dotting the land scape." He couldn't stop himself. "And Craig would be here instead of me. Or are you hoping that he's just going to wake up one day, smile, take you in his arms, and be the same man you married? If that's the case, Julie-Baby, I gotta tell ya, it ain't gonna happen."

"It could happen."

"No it can't." He asserted. "Hate me all you want because I'm a doctor or for whatever other reason you want, no matter how irrational it is. But I'm telling you...as a doctor and one of the best in my field...Craig is never going to wake up. Never."

"You...you don't know that." She whispered.

How many times had she already had this talk and with how many of Craig's doctors? Yet it didn't sink in. "Yes, I do. I'm tops in my field, remember, so take my expert opinion. Even if he woke up, which he never will," Rick took her hands, "you know how much brain damage he's suffered. He will never be the same man you knew, he can't. He's gone. It's over. You can let go of that hope because it's killing you." He stopped and waited for the; *get the fuck out, Do-c! Don't you ever come back here!*

That didn't happen.

Julie's shoulders slumped forward and she hung her head. Suddenly the back of his hand was wet as a tear fell on it. "It's not fair."

"No, Julie-Baby, it isn't." Rick wrapped his arm around her shoulders and brought her in close. "But that's the way it is and we can't change it." He took a deep breath and ventured a bit further, "That's why you're saving all of those pills, isn't it? It's not why you started doing it but it's why you do it now. You're gonna use them to check out when this all gets too much for you, aren't you? When the bar and the booze and the men don't kill the pain anymore you're just gonna take a big old handful of old pills."

Julie started to cry harder though she tried to hold it back, "It's not fair," she whimpered.

"You think that's what he'd want for you?"

"No...I don't know."

"If he loved you, and I think he really did, that's not what he'd want. He'd want you to be happy even if you have to be happy without him."

"I don't know how, Doc."

Rick thumbed the tears away from her cheeks, "As long as you're alive you can learn how but you can't do that if you're dead." He sat there with her on the bed holding her close for a good long while as she wept.

Chapter Twelve

Mason left Julie in a light sleep, he checked the house twice including all of the windows before letting himself out and setting the alarm. He could have guessed the code but Julie gave it to him readily; 01-01-11, her wedding anniversary. In no mood for something as mundane as patients, he cornered Spaulding in his office and told him about Ritter.

"What do I do?" Mason asked seriously. "I wanted to call the cops last night when we got back in bed but she said no, she said he's a cop so what are they going to do? And she's right."

Cops were a lot like doctors, as much as one of them might like to on a moral level, it was hard to get them turn on each other when it came down to the crunch. The police might send someone out to investigate a regular prowler but if Mason said it was Ritter, well, everyone knew the history there; they might just disregard it altogether. "It doesn't give him free license to do whatever he wants."

"Shouldn't anyway." Mason popped a Oxy into his mouth and frowned deeply. "I hated leaving her in her own house even with an alarm system and a guard dog."

"You don't think he'd try to break in."

"With that dog," Mason snorted, "I wouldn't."

"Why do you think he's following you?"

That was Julie's assumption as well, that Ritter was following Mason trying to get some dirt on him but what if that wasn't the case. "That's just it, I don't think he's following *me*, I think he's following *her*." What if it was Mason who stumbled into the middle of something and not Julie? What if Ritter had been watching her in the bar, obsessing over her, in the same way he did to Mason two years ago, night after night watching her walk out of the bar with another man, any man but him. Maybe his obsession grew it turned dark and angry. When one night, voila...Richard Mason walks onto the scene and all hell breaks loose. "I think he's been following her and I just happened to show up."

Spaulding thought about that. "That would be, almost, convenient for Ritter."

"Convenient or infuriating?" Mason countered. "You've seen her, granted you haven't seen her all dolled up, let me tell you she looks even better when she isn't wearing anything at all, yep that's when I like her best." Mason couldn't hide the smile but then it faded. "He stood there and watched us, that's sick."

"You're worried about her. I mean, you're really worried about her."

"It's Ritter." He said sharply. "Did I forget to mention that?"

"Point taken. " Spaulding leaned forward across the desk. "You like her, don't you? More than just the great sex you've been having and which by the way has made you a lot more livable lately."

"She's crazy. Out of her mind."

"That doesn't answer my question. Besides, you tend to like and attract crazy."

"Do you know what an Iatrophobic is?"

"Someone who's afraid of doctors?" Spaulding offered thinking that Mason had a different definition in mind.

"Yep and she sleeps with me." He twirled his finer in the air by the side of his head. "Crazy."

"Mrs. Miller...Julie...is Iatrophobic?" Spaulding asked then listened while Mason related the story of his morning with her. "All over a thermometer? What'd you do with the pills?"

"They're still there. Silly me, I said she should throw them out and she said no she'd rather just lug 'em around with her the rest of her life."

"You do get the most interesting cases." Spaulding mused.

"Jealous?"

"Of the sex, yes, the rest of it, that's ok, you keep it." He leaned back. "She's likely to get over the phobia the longer she's with you, she'll get accustomed to it."

"One day she'll be fine?"

"No." Spaulding said slightly exasperated. "She'll be better and she won't freak out if you try to put a thermometer in her mouth. Most psychologists recommend a good stiff dose of what ails you when it comes to phobias like this. Once people are forced to confront the irrational fear it loses its power."

"I'll check her into the hospital for shits and giggles, see how she handles that." Mason cracked.

Spaulding let it go. "As for Ritter," he shook his head. "I think you've got something to be worried about. Why don't you call that PI friend of yours see if he can help."

"Lucas?" That wasn't a bad idea.

"Need a loan?"

"I got this one. Thanks." Mason got up and let himself out of Spaulding's office to go make a phone call to his old buddy PI Lucas Buck.

**

Julie didn't sleep long after Doc left, she dragged herself from the bed and into a hot shower. She felt like shit but she hadn't gone to see Craig yesterday and she didn't want to start skipping days because one lead to another and then pretty soon she wouldn't be going at all. Julie didn't want Craig to be lonely. Sitting at her vanity brushing her wet hair, Julie took Doc's ring from around her neck and placed it on the tabletop. She opened the front drawer, took out a white jeweler's box, and opened it. Inside were her wedding and engagement rings. She'd started taking them off when she started frequenting the bar but only for the night, she always put them back on when she returned home. Then the day came when she didn't put on the rings on, she left them in the box and only wore them when she went to visit Craig.

There they sat on her tabletop side by side, almost mocking her. One with its shiny golden past that should have been a shiny golden future. The other with its perfect pearl, which reminded her of the calm blue ocean and then of Rick's eyes. Did she see a bright blue future there or was that just a delusion? How would she know the difference?

"One ring to rule them all, one ring to find them, one ring to bring them all and in the darkness bind them." Julie said aloud and gave a bitter smile. *Lord of the Rings* had been one of Craig's favorite series, they owned all of them in the extended versions. She looked down to see the dog looking up at her as he sat on the floor beside her. "Pick one, Maxie," Julie encouraged, "go on, just pick one and that's the one we'll go with, what do you say?" The bitter smile turned into a bitter laugh. If only it were that simple. She slipped the diamond and the gold band onto her finger. "Wanna go for a ride?" Julie wasn't an idiot, just because she didn't talk about Ritter with Rick this morning didn't mean he wasn't on her mind. She'd feel safer if Max accompanied her to the hospital today. Getting to her feet, maybe too quickly, the world gave a great twirl and her stomach a great heave. She couldn't control either, fell to her knees and vomited onto the floor. She hadn't had anything to

172

eat today except a cup of coffee the two of them grabbed on the way to her house, that was over two hours ago. All that came out was dark bile. It smelled oddly sweet and it looked horrible. Bile was green or yellow, she knew that because she'd spent enough mornings heaving into the toilet after a late night but this was...different...it was dark, almost red, or black even. It had that strange sweet aroma beneath the acidic one. "Must have been something I ate last night," she mumbled herself ignoring the sudden splitting headache and the little voice that said; *maybe you want to tell Rick about this tonight.* Grabbing the towel she'd used to dry herself off, Julie cleaned up the hardwood floor, waited for the world to completely stop spinning before she used the bed to pull herself to her feet and pitch the dirty towel into the hamper.

Julie sat at the vanity for a few moments to catch her breath while she fumbled with the bottles of Bayer aspirin and Tums. Her hands didn't seem to want to grasp them at first but they soon bent to her will and she popped two of each into her mouth one at a time. She'd get a glass of milk down in the kitchen to help settle her stomach, right after she brushed her teeth again. That would be in another moment or two just as soon as her breath returned. "Oh, when this finally hits it's going to be some bout." She grumbled to her reflection. Before it debilitated her for a few days, she wanted to see her husband.

Breathing returning to normal, Julie did what any good nicotine addict does and got a fresh pack out of the nightstand along with her sunglasses. It seemed particularly bright today and she was supposed to wear these stupid things whenever she went outside. She hated them; no matter what style she picked out, she always thought they were pretentious.

Holding onto the railing a little tighter than usual and walking a little slower than normal with Max beside her she went into the kitchen for that glass of milk and the leash. She set the alarm before climbing in the car and driving off, lighting a Newport as she backed out of the driveway.

On the way, Julie stopped for a copy of *The Wall Street Journal* because, well, because that was what she always did. Craig liked to read it in the mornings so she read it to him when she visited, every single page and every single article. Leaving Max in the car with the windows cracked, even though it was chilly, she wandered into the hospital to sit by Craig's bed. "Hi, sweetheart," she said as she sat down and took his hand. "Sorry I didn't make it yesterday, did you miss me?"

He didn't answer.

She didn't expect him to.

"I brought the paper and Max, he's out in the car, he misses you." Julie opened the newspaper and began to read it to him. "Let's see what's going on in the world today." Just about at the end of the first section, she heard Rick coming down the hall. Julie stopped reading so she could listen to the sound of his voice. She didn't turn towards the windows but she didn't turn away either as he came into view.

Mason felt awkward and uncomfortable as he passed the window of the Coma Ward and saw her there. The woman he'd been sleeping with was holding her husband's hand; he couldn't help but take in the gleam from the stone on her finger. When he asked her to marry him, Craig Miller went all out with the rock. It was the first time he saw her wedding rings, as her hand lay over Craig's. He almost felt guilty. Julie glanced at him as he passed by but she didn't smile and she didn't wave. He kept walking and she went back to reading the paper aloud. As his voice faded down the hall and away from her ears, the news of the world didn't seem so important any longer.

Julie let the paper fall to the floor as she picked up Craig's arm, lay down by his side, and put it around her. "I miss you. Things are such a mess; I don't know what to do anymore." She said

174

tearfully as she laid her head on his chest. The next words were so hard she didn't know if she could do it and couldn't imagine having to do it were he awake. "I know we never talked about this so I don't know what you'd want me to do. I wish you could tell me. Would me want me to be alone? Maybe you would, you were always so possessive, I don't know. I wish I did." She paused again and then forced herself to go on. "But, you see, I'm so sorry about this, my love, but...I've met someone." Julie whispered and wiped a tear away from her eye. "He...makes me feel...alive again. His name is Rick and he's a doctor of all things. I know you'd be laughing your ass over that, my love. If you can hear me you probably are."

Outside the Coma Ward's open door, Richard Mason stood listening to her. He wasn't on his way to do anything important and, being the sneaky bastard he was, he simply crept back here. He hadn't meant to actually spy on her or eavesdrop on such a personal conversation and he knew he should walk away from the door. Of course he didn't.

"For whatever its worth, I think you'd like him, he's a lot like you." She snickered a little and wiped another tear away. "I don't know what to do. I'm so tired of being alone and lonely. So tired of being without you but you're not coming back. I'm not giving up on you I won't leave you alone. Never. I won't. What do I do, Craig? My life has become an absurdity. I need something...someone...to hold on to. I just keep drifting but I don't know to where." She could cheat. She could sit here and tell him that if it was ok with him that she date Richard Mason then Craig should lay there and do nothing. That would be the sign. She let out a near cackle as the thought kept going through her head in Craig's voice. Asking him to squeeze her hand, well, she'd done that half a million times and gotten no response. Why should now be any different? "He makes it better. I think I could love him but I don't think he'll let me."

It was at that, that Rick turned and slipped away from the door knowing he'd stayed far too long.

A short time later, Julie kissed her husband good-bye without any resolutions. The elevator seemed to take forever as she stood there shifting from one foot to the other and trying to look around inconspicuously to see if anyone was looking at her. Suddenly, visiting with Craig made her self-conscious, sitting there holding his hand and talking to him all the while wondering if Doc was going to poke his head into the room or worse yet, if he'd talked about her and their little fling making the staff suspicious. Her heart began to race as she started to curse the closed elevator doors. Just when she decided she'd take the stairs down the two flights they opened and there was Evelyn Sinclair, Chief of Staff and Chief Administrator of The Mountainside.

"Mrs. Miller," Sinclair tried to make her tone light and pleasant even though she already felt the tension. She'd had many run-ins with the woman since Craig Miller took up residence at The Mountainside.

"Doctor Sinclair," Julie returned in the same tone as she hesitantly boarded the elevator. "How are you?"

Sinclair pushed the button for the Lobby, "I'm fine. How's Mr. Miller?" That was a stupid question. Mr. Miller's condition would change when he died and not a moment before. She noticed the small set of stitches in the woman's forehead, "What happened?"

"I'm alright and Craig's the same," Julie turned to look at the doors. Of all the rotten luck in the world! She'd rather the doors opened and Doc was standing there. Evelyn Sinclair was the reason Julie waited so long to make a move on the Doc. When no one noticed you it was easy to observe everyone else and it was clear to Julie that Doc had the hots for Sinclair. He was always checking her out, making crass sexual innuendos and double entendres to her. Most of the time he only served to irritate Doctor Sinclair but there were a few other times when she zinged him back then walked away leaving him grinning as he licked his chops watching her ass sway from side to side. Julie didn't know the history between Doctors Mason and Sinclair but it was clear in Doc's eyes what he wanted out of her in the future. Sinclair was even the reason Julie darkened her normally pale strawberry hair, she was hoping Doc would find the darker color more attractive since Sinclair had a beautiful head of wavy black hair to go with those big brown eyes. "You?" The Muzak in the elevator seemed too loud, Julie pulled at her ear, shook her head slightly and started swaying the tiniest bit on her feet.

"Busy," Sinclair chimed, "never a dull moment around here."

Before she could stop them or even think them the words just slipped out of her mouth, "Doctor Mason keeping you on your toes?"

For a second, Sinclair balked, to the best of her recollection Mrs. Miller never once mentioned Mason, "He does his fair share, why? Did you have a problem with him?"

Julie tried to recover as the Lobby button lit up, "No," she smiled and touched the stitches, "I just saw him recently, that's all."

Sinclair's eyes turned upward and thought those stitches looked like Mason's work, he always tied sutures in the Vertical Mattress style. She also thought he might have taken one too many of his pills before stitching up Mrs. Miller as there was a double-stitched patch of skin. "Are you sure?" She got lots of complaints about Mason and was ready for whatever the normally very vocal Mrs. Miller had to say about him.

Julie took a deep breath as the doors opened, "Nope, that's it," she forced a smile as she took a step across the threshold and fished in her purse for her red-lensed glasses. "Have a nice day, Doctor Sinclair."

Exiting the elevator after her Sinclair stammered, "You too, Mrs. Miller." She watched the woman weave a slightly uneven path to the front doors and out to the parking lot.

In the car, Max was waiting and had to pee; Julie felt ill as she put him on the leash and walked him around the grounds of the center for a few minutes grateful for the stupid sunglasses as they were hiding her red swollen eyes. However, they were doing nothing for the breath catching in her lungs. Julie tried to chalk it up to the exceptionally cold late autumn day but that didn't explain her rapid heartbeat.

Climbing into the car, she lit another cigarette and found it lightly sweet. "There must be something wrong with my taste buds." She licked her lips before drawing in another drag. "Well, Maxie, looks like we're on our own with this one." She gave the dog a pat on the head. "Daddy wasn't any help." Julie slung her arm around Max's neck and gave the dog a big hug, he, in turn, licked the side of her face and then nuzzled his muzzle against her hair. "It's you and me, kid, you and me against the world. What do you suppose our odds are? Slim to none?"

The dog let out a bark.

"Put your seatbelt on, time to go." Max grabbed the strap with his teeth and brought it towards her, Julie clicked it into place. "Safety first." She drove out of the lot.

If Craig wasn't going to be any help then she would have to make a decision on her own. She knew one thing; having Rick's warm live arms around her was better than being in Craig's half-dead ones. Pulling out of the lot, Julie went straight towards town, she drove past The Doc's house with the most dreadful feeling that she was only staring at shadows. Nevertheless, shadows were a start, where there was a shadow there was light. On down the street she parked in front of the El Royale Hotel. "Be a good boy, I'll be right back." She told the dog. It

178

was five o'clock and the night manager, the one she knew so well, was just coming on duty. "Good evening, Leroy."

"Evening Miss Montague." Leroy said with a smile. "Always a pleasure to see you. What can I do for you this evening?"

With a nervous stomach she walked up to the desk altogether uncertain of what she was doing. Julie looked around the lobby of the old hotel that was probably built somewhere around 1940. Her home away from home. Then she looked back at Leroy as she fished in her purse and produced the key card. "I'd like to turn in my reservation, Leroy."

"Something wrong, Miss Montague?" The night manger asked in a concerned and surprised voice. She'd been his very best customer for over a year now and if the staff had done something to make her turn in her key then he wanted to know about it. "Something we did?"

"No, nothing like that." She looked down at the little white card she carried around for so long. "I think, maybe, I just don't need it anymore."

Well, in that case, maybe it was good news. Maybe the pretty lady with the strange eyes finally found what she was looking for. He took the keycard from her hand and punched her name into the computer. "We certainly are sorry to lose your business, Miss Montague."

"I like this old place," Julie said to him. "Sorry to leave it but, well, that's just the way it is." The card gone from her she felt unsure but relieved just the same. "Been a pleasure, Leroy."

"Wait, don't go yet."

Julie turned around.

"It's only the 15th; I owe you two hundred bucks." He said with a smile and opened the till.

Julie hadn't thought about that and she could use the cash.

"Do you want to go up and get anything?" The whole staff knew what Miss Montague kept in the nightstand drawer of Room 404. Like her, it was legendary.

Julie looked up toward the ceiling with its faded painting of the Twelve Olympians and Mount Olympus thinking of the room three floors above and the contents thereof. "That's all right, Leroy, you keep it." She said with a wink and took the money he was handing over. "See ya 'round."

"Take care, Miss Montague." Leroy said knowing he'd probably never see her again.

Max barked as she walked out of the hotel and looked down the street. "One more minute, Maxie." Julie walked the four doors down to the bar.

"Evening, Miss." Tony said with a smile. "Martini?"

"No, just a shot of gin, please." Julie said and sat at the bar rather than in the corner booth.

"A little early tonight," Tony remarked putting the shot in front of her. He still didn't know her name but he knew she drank a gin martini and this was the first time she'd asked for just the gin.

"I'm not staying, just stopped in for this on my way home."

"You all right tonight, Miss? I mean, if you don't mind my asking." Tony inquired. She looked a little different tonight. She looked pale, even for her light skin, yet there was a glow in her cheeks and sad uncertainty in her oddly hypnotizing eyes.

Julie knocked back the shot. "I think maybe I'm going to be all right. See ya 'round, Tony."

"Yeah, see ya Miss." Like Leroy ten minutes before, Tony knew he was never going to see her again. "You take care." He called after her and then picked up the money she left on the bar along with the shot glass.

Julie was halfway back to the car; she could hear Max barking as he saw her coming toward her when she heard a voice that made her blood run cold.

"Evening, Mrs. Miller."

Julie didn't have to turn around. "Good evening Trooper Ritter." She kept walking.

"You just come out of the bar?"

What a stupid question. "I imagine you saw me." The car was only two car lengths away now.

"I did, you're not going to drive are you?"

She watched him do this to Rick and she wasn't going to be his next victim or his repeat victim. Julie stopped walking and turned around to face him. "That's my car, I'm going to get in it and drive away now. If you ask my for license and registration I'll give them to you, they'll check out but you already know that." She said in a clear calm voice. "If you want to give me a breathalyzer that's fine as well but we can just go back into the bar and Tony can attest to the fact that he served me one shot of gin. That hardly qualifies me as drunk."

In the car, Max barked louder and scratched as the windows as he tried to get out. The dog even tried to squeeze itself through the inch crack she left in the window.

"Just lookin' out for your well-bein' Mrs. Miller, that and along with the well-bein' of the general public." Ritter smiled something near friendly and gestured toward the street. "You don't look drunk so I don't think any of that will be necessary."

"Thanks." She said snidely and began walking to the car.

"That dog licensed?"

"Yes and registered with the State of Vermont, Trooper. He's a lethal weapon." She said in almost a taunting tone. "If that will be all I'll be on my way now."

"How's Doctor Mason?" Ritter called after her not wanting to get too close to the car and the snapping jaws within. "You two seemed very cozy."

"Which night would that be?" Julie shot back. "Last night or Tuesday night?"

"Both." Ritter answered in the same cold voice and took a step toward her. "He's a drug addict, Julie. He's arrogant, self-righteous, and self-centered. He'll never love you. He's already in love with himself."

"It's Mrs. Miller to you, Trooper Ritter and I didn't ask for your advice."

"You should listen to it....Mrs. Miller," he took another step and leaned toward, "seems a little formal, don't you think? I have been inside you."

"Weren't you lucky?" Julie spat not wanting to be reminded of the night and if she needed such a reminder, she could look at the stitches in her head and the bruise around her neck. "Leave me alone. Leave Rick alone. We haven't done anything."

"How's Craig?" Ritter asked. "Still a vegetable?" He laughed a little and then smiled. "You, Julie? How are you feeling these days? Huh? How's your head?" He took another step. "Mason stitch it up for you?"

Julie felt threatened. She'd felt threatened when he said 'good evening Mrs. Miller' but now he was too close. Ritter probably thought he was safe from the pit bull that was currently going

182

out of his mind penned up in the car, as she couldn't get to the door handle just yet. The Lexus had several features. Holding her keys, she clicked a button on the chain and the remote door slid open. Max flew out of the car, bounding toward Ritter whose eyes went wide as his face went white. Jaws snapping, just itching to rip off a good chunk of flesh, the dog leapt at him. Ritter put his arms up to cover his face.

Julie grabbed the collar, pulling the dog short of his goal. Max was not happy. "Namaste." She said through tight lips and held on to the leash. The dog pulled on the leash, barked, and snapped at the cop but he stayed at his mistress' side. She waited until the detective lowered his arms. "I say another word and he'll rip your throat out right here, right now. If I were you, I'd turn around and leave."

Ritter didn't need a big public scene and people were staring at them and the dog. With no badge to flash and hide behind, he was just another thug on the street. "I'll be seeing *you*, Julie."

"Not if I see you first."

Ritter stuffed his hands into his pockets and made his way off down the street.

"Good boy, Maxie. Good boy." Julie patted the dog's head as he stopped pulling on the leash and her heart began to slow down. That is a very dangerous man, she thought as she stood there watching to see if he'd turn back. He did, about halfway to the bar; Ritter turned around and then turned back just as quickly. "Let's go home."

Chapter Thirteen

Opening the front door of the house Julie felt an icy chill along with the sense that she wasn't alone. "Hello?" She called out. She looked down at the dog but he was all right. The door had been locked. The alarm was set. Yet, she couldn't shake the feeling that someone had been in here. "Hello?" Now Max's ears pricked up and he alerted. "Do you hear someone?" Julie didn't hear anyone but she smelled them. Hanging in the air, just as though it were any ordinary morning and Craig had come bounding down the stairs fresh from the shower the scent of Grey Flannel Cologne wafted over to and enveloped her. "Craig?" Julie looked over to the stairs with the faint hope that she would see him standing there hale and hearty with his arms open and a smile on his face.

The house only echoed its silence.

Of course he hadn't been here! That was stupid! She just left him at the hospital an hour or so ago and he was still in a coma. He didn't just get up, grab a cab, and come home between then and now. It was only her mind playing tricks on her. Yet, she shivered as she locked the door. Was that a draft she felt? An errant wind from in the house? *Probably! It's a damn old house, Julie-Baby!*

"Cold in here, huh?" She asked Max who only sat there staring at her and if a dog could look concerned then Max did. Julie turned on the heat for the first time this year, she usually cuddled up by the fire, but she had the sudden urge to hide in her room for the night. Maybe that was it, maybe there was a window cracked open in the bedroom and it was blowing the scent of the cologne down the stairs. She couldn't remember if she'd opened the bottle today to take a sniff from it. Turning up the thermostat, she saw the little red light on the phone blinking telling her she had a message.

The mechanical woman's voice spoke to her. "You have...two...unheard messages. First unheard message received today at 3:15 pm..."

"Hi, Jules, it's Tim. Sorry I missed you. I'm going to come down and see Dad for a while this weekend, I was hoping my room was still open? Give me a call. Hope you're ok. Bye."

"Second unheard message received today at 4:36 pm."

"Hi, Julie, it's Rick. Look, I'm sorry, I have to back out of our date tonight...I ah, I got a big case and I can't get away. I'll call you later."

"End of unheard messages."

Feeling oddly deflated and relieved at the same time by Rick's message—with the nagging suspicion that he was lying in the back of her mind making those goose bumps rise further—she put the phone down. "Looks like it's just you and me tonight, Maxie." It would probably be good for them to spend a night or two away from each other and get some perspective. Clearly, they were moving too far too fast and a break was in order.

Wandering unsteadily into the kitchen, she groped for the wall to keep herself on her feet and thought that shot must have gone to her head. Trying to keep her eyes focused, she fed the dog and looked in the fridge but wasn't hungry. The last thing she ate was dinner last night but just the thought of food was enough to start her stomach tumbling. Max, however, greedily gobbled down every kibble she put in the bowl then looked up at her for more. "I thought they said you were a Pit Bull but I think you must be at least half pig." She commented with a laugh looking at the empty bowl and refilled it halfway. She grabbed a bottle of SoBe LifeWater from the fridge and a package of grapes. Leaving the dog to finish his dinner, she wandered through the empty house to the living room where she thought she might gather some of her candles to take upstairs for the night. "MAX!" Julie screamed as the plastic bottle of water and bag of grapes tumbled from her hands. "Oh Maxie you didn't!"

The dog stopped in mid woof and came running to her side.

On the hearth floor laid the photograph of Julie and Craig on their wedding day. The glass smashed to bits, the photograph mangled as though the dog had chewed on it. "Bad dog!" Julie admonished heavily. Max lowered his ears and his tail as he looked up at her. Julie stared back at him. When Max was caught doing something wrong he whimpered and then went and hid. Now, the dog wandered over to the broken bits of her wedding photograph, sniffed at it and began to let out low gruff barks. "I know you did it." She said to him. It's just that I didn't notice it earlier, that's all. Rick was here and...and he checked the windows in the living room, and he would have said something if the photograph was on the floor. Maybe he didn't notice either. Julie looked back to the mantle and thought how odd it was that only the photograph was broken when there were two jar candles in front of it and they were fine. If Max had jumped up here, wouldn't he have knocked everything down or at least out of place? The candles were exactly where she'd left them. "Get away from there, you've done enough. Go back to your dinner." She shouted at the dog and began to pick up the broken glass. The photograph was not salvageable and she wept a little at that. She'd have to get in touch with the photographer and see if he still had the negatives so she could have another one made up. With the mess cleaned up, Julie gathered her candles, water, and grapes before wearily making her way up the stairs for the night.

In the bedroom, she thought the scent of Grey Flannel was stronger. It was still early but she wasn't going anywhere and she wasn't expecting any company. Julie kicked off her shoes, took off her jeans, and relieved herself of the sweater before sitting down at the vanity to brush her hair. The bottle of cologne sat there, where it had since the day Craig last left this house, but now the cap was off. She looked over to the window

186

by the bed to see it cracked open. She didn't remember leaving it open, she reached it out shut it and the keep the cold night air at bay. It was starting to sprinkle out there. Julie picked up the little dark grey bottle and smelled it contents before she put the cap on and put it back on the tabletop.

Taking off the wedding and engagement rings, she reached for the box but it was gone. "I left it right here," she mumbled to herself, "right next to Rick's...where's the ring?"

Yes, before she left to go to the hospital, Julie was certain she put the white box on the vanity right next to Rick's High School Ring. Then again, she did feel sick and dizzy and maybe... "Maybe it fell on the floor." Pushing the stool back, she got up and then got down on her hands and knees in her bra and panties to crawl around the bedroom floor. She searched every inch from under the vanity to between it and the bed to under the bed and came up empty. "What the hell?" Getting back up again wasn't as easy as getting down and her already sore joints protested at the indignity. "I need a massage." She grumbled as she used the tabletop to help pull herself up while trying to fight off the returning feeling of vertigo.

If they weren't on the floor, then... she opened the center drawer of the vanity and there was the white box. She must have put it back after all. Julie opened it and put the wedding and engagement ring inside. Rick's ring wasn't in the drawer. It wasn't in the bathroom. It wasn't in the nightstand. "Well it didn't just get up and walk the fuck away." Oh, Christ, if he asked for it back what was she going to tell him? Throwing up her hands in exasperation, she shook her head, nearly stumbled backward as a result, and had to grasp the wall again, that's when she saw the wastebasket. There was Rick's ring staring up at her. "Oh, no, no way, I did not throw it out." She said to herself as she retrieved it.

Maybe she did, maybe accidentally, after she'd been sick, maybe...

The phone began to rang, the sharp tone made her jump as it pulled it out of her thoughts. "Hello?"

"Hey, Jules, how are ya?"

"Hi, Tim." Julie said a little relieved. "Coming this weekend? I'm sure your father would like that." *If he knew, if he understood.*

"Yeah, I thought maybe I could stay with you?"

"You know your room is always here and ready for you." *For as long as I own the bloody house, anyway.* "When are you coming?"

"Probably won't get there until late Friday night, thought I'd stay the night, visit with Dad a while on Saturday and head back on Sunday." He ventured. "Is that ok? Too much? You got plans? I'm not kickin' your boyfriend out, am I?"

"It's fine," Julie said to him.

"No plans?" Tim asked. "No boyfriend?"

"None."

"Aww, Jules," he said in that way that only a 17 year-old boy can say it. "Bingo? Bowling? Something? Anything?" He didn't see her very much and his mother hated her but Tim liked Julie, she was always good to him. He felt bad that she was stuck with his useless lump of a father, shut away in that house and wasting her life. "Ya gotta get out of that house, Jules."

"Sorry, Tim, you'll just have to suffer with me for the weekend."

"I'll bring some movies."

"I'll bring the popcorn. See you Friday night." The line went dead in her hand and Julie put the phone down. He was a good kid, it wasn't his fault his mother was a royal bitch. She'd get his room ready before Friday, change the sheets, and open the

188

windows for a bit. Taking off the bra, she slid a nightgown over her head before pulling back the covers and climbing into bed with her remote control. Max wandered into the room and jumped up on the bed to lie down beside her. Wanting a cigarette she reached for her purse but it was downstairs and the cigarettes were in the car. "Shit. You're losin' it, Julie-Baby, you know that?" She mumbled and opened the nightstand drawer to pull out a fresh pack. If they were in the purse downstairs then she'd go get them but she didn't feel like wandering around outside in her nightgown. Opening the fresh pack, she poured the last of the gin into the water to give it a little kick and then turned on the TV just as it started to rain.

**

Richard Mason canceled his date with Juliette Miller for several reasons but the main one was so that he could meet with a private detective at 7 o'clock. Mason wanted to find out what was going on before he went any further with her. Second reason was the conversation he'd eavesdropped on upon earlier today. The part when she told Craig that Rick probably wouldn't let her love him just stuck in his craw. Who was she to say something like that? To her husband of all people—yeah, he was in a coma, so what? She couldn't possibly know that about him.

But she did.

She was right on the money.

He liked her. Yep, he liked her a lot. He loved being with her and being *in* her. He found her infuriatingly interesting and he could see them spending a good amount of time together. She made him want to do things like connect and reach out, to kiss, cuddle, hold, and make love. Julie made him want to go so far as to do things for her such as putting the toilet seat down. Nevertheless, that didn't mean he'd follow through and eventually, he'd find a way to fuck it up. The kicker was he'd do it on purpose either to actually drive her away or just to see how much she could take. Mason doubted it was in him to allow someone to love him because way deep down inside, Richard Mason considered himself unlovable. Julie obviously didn't feel the same but what the hell did she know? She was crazy. There was, however, a small part of him thought he might like to try and to do it before it was too late, before that part of Life passed him by altogether.

"Let me get this straight, you want me to *tail a cop*?" Lucas Buck, the PI Rick was hiring, asked as they sat in the far corner booth of a local diner. He'd done a lot of strange work for Mason in the past but this was beyond the pale. "Are you serious or is this one of your little games? I've heard all sorts of shit about this guy—and you—but him, well, he's bad news, ya know."

"I am serious." He said. "Can you do it?"

"*Can* I do it?" Lucas scoffed. "Yeah. *Will* I do it? I don't know. What's going on? What are you really looking for?"

Rick tried to think of how to put this. "Ritter's been following a woman I know."

"Girlfriend?"

"Loosely." Rick agreed.

"Just knockin' boots, huh?" Lucas asked and popped a pickle chip into his mouth. "She hot?"

"Her name is Juliette Miller." Feeling a little guilty, he pushed a small folder toward the PI. Inside were Julie's address, phone number, social security number—courtesy of the hospital's records,-- and photograph he'd gotten off today's surveillance tapes at the hospital. Inside were also the names and addresses of the bar and El Royale Hotel.

Lucas opened the folder. "Sweet," he exclaimed as he looked at her picture. "Good goin'. You wanna know if he's puttin' it to her too?"

"He already did," Rick said bitterly. "Pay attention, your target isn't Julie, it's Ritter. I gave you that so you have a starting point. Find out why he's following her, IF he's following her."

"Maybe he just thinks she's hot, Doc, I already do." Lucas said grinning down at the photograph.

"Yeah, would you stand outside my window and watch us? All night? How about my car?"

Lucas thought about that and the idea was not without its appeal but it wasn't exactly his style either, in fact it was downright creepy. "Peepin' Tom, huh? Lotta guys get off on that, they're usually harmless."

"He is *not* harmless." Rick asserted. "I think he's stalking her." That was why he gave Lucas the name and address of the El Royale Hotel. He wanted to know if anyone had seen Ritter around there other than the one night he spent with Julie. The neighbors around her house were probably too self-involved to notice but the desk clerk there, he was sharp, and he'd remember.

"All right, you got it." Lucas agreed finally. He liked working for Mason it was usually fun and had a fair amount of kicks but looking at Mason's face now this was different. This Ritter, Mason found him a real threat either to the pretty woman or to himself. "I'll have something for you by this time tomorrow, not sure what or how much but something."

Mason sat there watching Lucas leave the diner wondering which way it went down. Who was Ritter really following? Him or Julie? For how long? The thing that kept coming back to him was Julie's insistence that Ritter had been in the bar 'lots of times'. Rick, didn't go to the bar 'lots of times', true he went

191

more frequently over the last few months but, if Rick didn't see Ritter then maybe it was because Ritter wasn't there except when *Julie* was there. The son of a bitch made Rick's life and lives of his friends and colleagues absolutely miserable over nothing. He had the power of the badge on his side but Rick was damned if he was going to let Ritter use it against Julie. Maybe he wouldn't let her love him but that didn't mean he'd stand by and watch her get hurt.

It was still fairly early in the evening and Rick thought about getting together with Julie but then thought better of it. Still, he said he'd call her later so he would. He'd tell her he was still at the hospital and maybe he'd see her tomorrow. That was what his intentions were when he pulled the cell phone out of his pocket and dialed her cell phone. One, two, three rings and he was told that Julie was away from her phone, please leave a message. Away from the phone? Wasn't the whole point of a cell phone? The fact that it was small and portable and you could keep it on you at all times? He left a short message then tried her house line only to find it busy. At first he didn't know what the strange sound in his ear was, it was rare that one heard a busy signal these days with Call-Waiting and surely she had that. It was standard on most lines.

Getting up from the table to make his way back to his car, he told himself he'd try again when he got home. At home, cold and shaking from the short walk from the sidewalk to his front door with the rain coming down the way it was, he popped a frozen dinner into the microwave and waited until after he ate it to try Julie again. Maybe she got the message about him canceling the date and she didn't want to talk to him, if that was the case then he didn't want to look needy. Wiping the last of the tomato sauce from his whiskered chin with the back of his hand and tossing the plastic container into the trash, a strong crash of thunder echoed the little container's landing. He looked toward the window to see the little rainstorm was churning things up good out there.

With a bad feeling in the pit of his stomach, he used the kitchen phone to try Julie again. She must be home by now, well that was, unless she decided to stop by the bar or the El Royale after seeing Craig and breaking the bad news to him. The house line was still busy. The cell phone only told him to leave a message. "Julie its Rick call me when you get this." Wondering where she was and if she was even at home who she could be talking to for so long, he watched the rain fall against the window. With a cluttered mind and concerned heart, he sat back down on the couch to turn on the TV. Monster Trucks were on tonight and he didn't want to miss that.

Just after the first commercial, the phone rang, thinking it was Julie he didn't look at the Caller-ID. "Hello."

"Hey, Doc."

Familiar greeting but not Julie's voice. It was Lucas.

"I know I said I'd call you tomorrow with something but I thought you'd want to know this right away."

He turned down the volume on the TV so he could easily hear over the gritty roaring engines. "What is it?"

"Your buddy, Trooper Ritter. He isn't Trooper Ritter anymore and he hasn't been for a while." Lucas said as he stared at the computer monitor. "He's a Private Eye, lost his job with the State Troopers for disorderly conduct."

"He's *not* a cop?"

"Nope, he's not a cop." Lucas agreed. "I'll let you know when I have more..."

"Do you know where he is, right now?"

"I haven't gotten a tail on him yet, I was just doing some legwork on the Internet." Lucas tried to explain. "Doc? Mason?" There was no answer.

Rick hurriedly dialed Julie's numbers again and got the same response, which was no response. Leaving the TV on behind him, he grabbed up his keys and headed for her house. Upon arriving he looked around for a familiar car but didn't see it, he also didn't see any lights on in the house. He rang the bell, banged on the door, he looked in the front window but didn't see anything. "Julie!" Rick shouted before ringing the bell once more. No one answered but the car was here and the dog was barking upstairs.

The skies opened on his way here and the rain was coming down in sheets as lightning crackled overhead. A bright bolt light up the night and Julie's yard. The gate was open and he went around to the rear door, it was locked, the kitchen light was on and he could see the photograph lying on the top of the trash. "Julie!" He shouted out with more urgency and slammed his fist against the door. Max came bolting into the kitchen from out of nowhere and threw his firm little body so hard against it that it made Rick stumble backward and down the steps. The dog hit the door again as he barked and howled. "Julie!" Coming back up to the door he watched in amazement as the dog took a third run at it, Max leapt into the air, not trying to break the door or smash the window but grab the lock with his strong jaws. This time he got it. Pit Bulls never let go once they get their teeth around something. Hanging by the knob of the lock of the back door the dog started to thrash about, swinging its hind end up into the air until the lock turned and the door opened. Rick didn't know if he should go in or not with the dog standing there barking and staring at him but then Max took off back into the quiet house and he followed. "Julie? Come on answer me!"

The dog waited at the bottom of the stairs then looked up them anxiously.

She's up there. He's done something to her and she's up there.

Afraid of what he was going to find when he reached his destination, Rick forced his legs to go up the steps one at a time keeping an eye on the dog who headed for the master bedroom. Heart in his feet and stomach in his throat he peered around the corner. The bed was empty, the covers thrown back. On the nightstand were a pack of cigarettes, an empty bottle of gin and empty bottle of LifeWater along with his High School ring.

Julie was sprawled out on the floor face down in a puddle of her own vomit.

"Oh shit, you crazy bitch." Rick muttered thinking she'd drank herself into a stupor. He got down on the floor and turned her over. Her face was red, covered in her own blood; it soaked her chin to chest and stained the pretty white satin nightgown. "Julie! Julie wake up!" Rick leaned down to see if she was breathing and was met with an oddly sweet scent under the gin and cigarette smoke. Maybe it was the water. Julie was very still, she was barely breathing and her eyes didn't respond to the light when he opened the lids. Pulling the cell phone from his pocket, he dialed 911. "This is Doctor Richard Mason; I need an ambulance at 12 Chapman Lane...."

Chapter Fourteen

From across the street, Ritter watched while Mason hurried out of Julie's home next to the stretcher on which Julie was laying. She was loaded into the ambulance; Mason left his car behind and climbed into the back with her. Siren blaring and lights flashing, the ambulance took off headed for The Mountainside Wellness & Research Center.

That was unexpected. Ritter thought it would be at least two more days before Julie realized she needed medical attention and three or four after that before she actually went for it. He hadn't counted on her smoking all of the tainted cigarettes in such a short period of time. Another unexpected thing was the sudden appearance of the stepson who never visited his comatose father but would be arriving---or would have been arriving depending on things went—this weekend. He listened to her phone conversation with the young Timothy Miller, the phone messages left for her and found the one from Richard Mason of particular interest. The last thing he wanted, though he expected it, was for Mason to back off the relationship. With hot and ready sex like Julie gave out, what guy in his right mind would give it up? Then again, Richard Mason wasn't in his right mind and probably never had been. The last interesting thing was that Julie had been trying to call Mason's home line just before she went down. He heard her collapse and thought about going in, but decided against it as he listened to her throwing up and then struggling for breath with lungs full of poison smoke.

Waiting a few moments, he pulled away from the curb in the heavy rain.

II

Rushing through the Emergency Room doors of The Mountainside, Mason was met by Doctor Sinclair. "What's going on?" She asked hurriedly looking down at the pale woman on the stretcher. "Friend of yours?" She looked again. "Mrs. Miller? What happened to her? I just saw her this afternoon." Doctor Sinclair ran into Julie Miller this afternoon and she was in far better shape than she was tonight.

"Dunno, get out of the way." He said gruffly and pushed past his boss as the stretcher followed. The EMTs began to turn right. "No, follow me." Mason ordered glancing back over his shoulder. "I want her upstairs not sitting around in this death trap."

"Mason!" Sinclair said sharply.

"What?!" He returned in kind, as he turned quickly to look at her. "She's sick; she doesn't need to wait around here for someone to say it....*I just said it.*" He huffed. "That's still good enough around here, right?" Mason hobbled off after the stretcher to the elevator.

"She has to be admitted!"

"Later!"

Everything went well on the hurried ride to the hospital; Julie's vitals were weak but holding. Respiration and oxygen levels were low. Blood pressure was on the low side of normal, temperature right on the money, pulse also on the low side of normal. Her color was off she was pale. She didn't vomit on the ride, at least in part due to the fact that mostly she didn't wake up.

Waking up.

In a hospital.

Julie was going to freak out.

Exiting the elevator and walking past Mason's office, his team watched him rush by them. They were here staying late on another case that Mason couldn't be bothered to tend. "Is that?" Steward asked.

"More importantly," Wylds interjected, "is he?"

They watched Mason pass by the office with the EMTs and the woman on the gurney. A second later, he was back outside the glass and giving the 'get off your ass and come with me sign' with his hand.

"Most days he can't learn their names. Since when does he escort them in?" Wylds asked.

"Beats me," Steward replied, "but it looks like we're on so let's go."

Rushing out of the office, Wylds grabbed up a clipboard with fresh paper. "What's going on?" She asked as she started to put pencil to paper.

"Female, late thirties, symptoms began with body aches, headache," Mason started and then began to think. She said she was coming down with flu. "No fever, cough, or congestion." The EMTs turned the gurney into the nearest room. "Other symptoms include," What? "Unsteady gait," he said thoughtfully as he remembered Julie weaving her way around his apartment this morning and saying she was a little, "lightheadedness. Culminating in bloody vomit and loss of consciousness."

"How long was the onset?" Steward asked as he watched Wylds and Goodspeed help the EMTs get the woman onto the hospital bed.

"A day? Two?" Mason wondered aloud. "I want an ultrasound of her carotid artery." He looked from her to his team, "you'll need to keep her sedated or she'll jump out of that bed the second she wakes up and go screaming out of here."

That seemed a little detailed and coupled with the way Mason rushed in with their new patient, "Friend of yours?" Wylds asked.

"Sort of," Mason said grumpily. "Ten milligrams lorazepam." He ordered.

Wylds looked up at him. "Are you trying to keep her sedated or unconscious?"

"Whatever works best, let's start with this." To the blank staring eyes of his colleagues he added, "She's latraphobic and she doesn't know she's here and she won't know until or unless she wakes up. If you'd like to avoid that rather unpleasant scene, give her the shot."

Like the rest, Wylds had never encountered an latraphobic mostly because latraphobics did everything possible to avoid the doctor. "If she's out of it she can't tell us what's wrong with her, what her symptoms are." Wylds protested. "You don't have any idea what's wrong with her, it could be a drug overdose for all we know. How are we going to treat her if we don't know...."

"I know," Mason said in a raised voice, "Ok, I know what her symptoms are. Just keep her in a happy haze. It's not an OD." Wylds gave him a nasty look. "You can trust me on that one."

Wylds felt sorry for the woman as she pushed the plunger into the IV.

"Why the ultrasound?" Steward inquired.

"Take a look at her neck." Mason pointed to the unconscious Julie and watched as Steward turned her head to move her hair. "It's a couple of days old but the artery could be pinched. She lost consciousness but doesn't know for how long and, judging

199

from the way she's been stumbling around, may be experiencing some feeling of vertigo." If the artery were pinched, that would account for many of Julie's symptoms but not the bloody vomit. He couldn't shake the feeling that Ritter had done something to Julie. "I want a full blood work-up. While you're doing that, Wylds," he put his hand in his pocket and tossed a set of keys at Steward, "you two go check out Julie's house."

"Keys?" Steward asked nearly stupefied as he held them up to the light. "We don't have to break in this time?"

"No, go ahead, you're black, but you can still use the front door." Mason told him then reached inside the table near Julie's bed for pad and paper. "There's an alarm," he said and scribbled down the code, "don't forget to reset it." He held out the paper to Wylds.

"You have keys to her house and the alarm code?" Wylds asked. "Who is she?"

"Julie Miller," Mason said to her annoyed, "the code." He shook the paper at Wylds. At least they wouldn't have to worry about Max, Animal Control took him away promising to take good care of the dog until Julie came home. Wylds took it from his hand. Still certain that Ritter had done something to Julie, Mason stopped wanting to tell them to check for all known toxins. Ritter might be a brute and he might be a bully, but a murderer? Even Mason had a hard time swallowing that one. Better safe than sorry. "In the master bathroom you'll find out why this isn't an OD." He asserted. "Bring a garbage bag."

"A garba-" Wylds stopped and capitulated. "All right, whatever you want, you're the boss."

"That's right, I'm the boss. Could use more of that around here." He advised and then thought. "Near the bed there's an empty bottle of gin, a bottle of water and a pack of a cigarettes."

"You want those too? Just what are we looking for here?" Steward asked still not believing he was holding the keys to Mrs. Miller's house. "Molds? Air bourn toxins? What?"

"Anything you can find. You," he turned to Wylds, "I want a full tox-screen and blood alcohol content too. You're gonna find pot, I don't care about that. I'll be in my office." He was hoping she'd come back stoned and drunk out of her mind but had the sneaking suspicion he wasn't going to get that lucky.

At his white board, Mason popped two Oxycodone and began to write very carefully. Just what were her symptoms? He told Wylds he knew but that was just to shut her up. Standing there in front of the blank white board, Mason realized, he'd been far too interested in the fantastic sex he was having with Julie over the last few days to note any symptoms.   She'd been complaining the last day or so....what did she say?

He wrote:

BODY ACHES
HEADACHE
FATIGUE/RUNDOWN

Yes, that was right, Julie had been sure that she was coming down with the flu.

What else? She'd been unsteady on her feet early this morning; he gave himself an ego stroke by telling himself that it was his doing that she was walking funny this morning.

UNSTEADY GAIT
DIZZY
LIGHTHEADED

What about dinner last night? She didn't eat much. So what about...

LOSS OF APPETITE

What about this morning? He'd accidentally hit a big nerve to be sure but did that explain her explosive anger? How about a little later in the morning when she broke into tears over Craig? What about this afternoon when he saw her visiting Craig and, for whatever reason in her head, she let out a cackle? Was she hallucinating or were her emotions out of whack?

MOOD SWINGS?

Then there were the obvious symptoms;

BLOODY VOMIT
LOSS OF CONSCIOUSNESS
RESPIRATORY

On the ambulance ride her breathing had been very shallow and labored, currently Julie was on oxygen though she was holding her own.

"All right, Mason," Sinclair said as she came into his office, "I assume Mrs. Miller is at least settled into a room, mind telling me what's going on?"

"She's sick, isn't that obvious?" Mason snapped.

Sinclair pursed her lips and drew in a breath. "Any idea what's wrong with her? Were you with her when she collapsed?"

"I found her on the floor," Mason said through tight teeth. He didn't want to explain his relationship with Julie Miller to Evelyn Sinclair.

"Where?"

Mason hung his head. "Her bedroom."

"Oh, I see." Sinclair mused. "How long has this been going on? If you're...involved...with her then you shouldn't be treating her."

"What do you care?" Mason snapped. "Just watching the hospital's ass or are you jealous? If you are then kiss me and let me know and if not, there's the door, use it, and let me do my work."

"I'm going to use the door, but she still has to be triaged."

"You have all her information; it's the same as that vegetable upstairs." Sinclair made her way to the door. "Hey!" Sinclair turned around. "You saw her this afternoon? That's what you said, right?"

"Yes, she seemed fine to me." Sinclair agreed. "We rode down in the elevator together and I even walked with her to the front door."

"She wasn't unsteady on her feet? Didn't say she had a headache? Looked pale? Slurred speech?"

"She wasn't drunk if that's what you're asking me." Sinclair admonished. Had she been swaying in the elevator? Perhaps she had been, yes, she was, and Sinclair thought she was just swaying to the Muz-ak in the elevator. "Maybe swaying...just a little but other than that, no she was," then she thought for another second, "she was fine," she said again, "I don't know, it's probably nothing but to you nothing is always something."

"What is it?" Mason snapped.

"She seemed...high. Not on drugs but I don't know. She just seemed...happy." That was a big change; usually Julie Miller was as grumpy as Richard Mason. "Things were funny to her, maybe a little too funny." Sinclair ventured. "But laughing isn't a crime and since when I see her, her eyes are usually red and swollen from crying I thought it was a good thing. You probably see catastrophe looming on the horizon."

Her eyes should have been red and swollen from crying because even though she laughed, nearly cackled, when Mason saw her, Julie was crying. "Get outta here." He grumbled and went back to the white board. He erased the question mark next to MOOD SWINGS.

Sinclair took a few steps toward him. "Before I go and I know I don't have to remind you of this," she rolled her eyes and put her hand on her hips. "But it is illegal to sedate a patient for the sole purpose of keeping them in a hospital against their will. It's called assault and, even, unlawful imprisonment."

"She can have me arrested after I find out what's wrong with her."

"That's what I thought so I overrode you, Mrs. Miller won't be receiving any further sedatives until after she's woken up, told us what's wrong with her...."

"Julie's not a doctor. She doesn't *know* what's wrong with her."

Not caring for Mason's use of Mrs. Miller's first name with such familiarity, Sinclair overrode him. "AND then she can tell us whether or not she *wants* to stay here."

"She doesn't know what she wants," Mason said knowing his words had two meanings and seeing the same in Sinclair's eyes. He thought it best to continue with the medical argument rather than getting personal. "She's latraphobic." Mason explained. "When she wakes up she's going to go tearing out of here."

"That's her choice. Not yours." With that, Sinclair turned and left the office.

That gave him a little more than two hours to solve the puzzle. Not a lot of time.

**

"So who do you think she is? You think she's, ya know...*her*?" Wylds asked.

"Her?" Steward replied in the same snippy tone. "If you mean do I think Mrs. Miller is the woman Mason has been sleeping with then the answer is yes I do." Steward turned the key and opened the front door of Julie's home. "Nice digs." He said upon entering and turning to the alarm panel.

"What are we supposed to be looking for?"

"No clue. Let's find the master bedroom and start there." Steward suggested. In the bedroom, Steward bagged up the empty bottle of gin, bottle of water and cigarettes before the shiny silver ring caught his eye.

"Well, Mason was right," Wylds said coming out of the bathroom with a Hefty bag. "Not a drug overdose, would you look at this? There must a hundred prescriptions in here and I don't think any of them have even been opened."

"Would you look at this?" Steward countered and held up the ring. "Guess who it belongs to."

"I don't know...who?"

Steward held the ring and read the inscription; "Richard Mason, it's his high school ring. Hate to break it to you, Wylds, but it looks like Mason and the beautiful Mrs. Miller are serious." He listened while Wylds let out a long wistful sigh. "Yep, looks like you're just going to have to be happy with Goodspeed. Mason is otherwise engaged."

Feeling a tinge of guilt, Wylds looked longingly at the silver ring in Steward's hand. She had her chance with Mason and he

205

wasn't interested or at least he pretended he wasn't. She had Goodspeed now and they were very much in love, somehow that didn't stop this from stinging any less. "Other than this...stuff." She gestured to the room. "What are we supposed to be looking for?"

Steward shrugged his shoulders. "Not sure, Mason did order a tox-screen so let's do the usual..."

"Collect spores, molds, and fungus?"

"You got it Egon."

**

Wylds ran into a miffed Sinclair in the hall and then stood outside Mason's door looking in at her boss, she saw him staring at the White Board and knocked before she entered.

"The ultrasound?" Mason asked holding his hand out for the file Wylds was carrying.

"Showed some minor damage to the carotid artery, some pinching, but it's nothing that would cause her symptoms other than a headache and maybe some lightheadedness."

If Mason could take those two symptoms off the list then what was he left with?

"Bloodwork's back too."

"And?"

"Blood alcohol level is low; maybe she had a shot or two over a period of time. Tox-Screen's clean, you were right about the pot; THC levels are nearly off the charts. Couple that with the cigarettes she smokes and it could be lung cancer. Other than that it's just some aspirin and probably good old Tums."

"It's not lung cancer," Mason countered, "she's having trouble breathing right now but, trust me, last night she didn't have any problems with that." It wasn't alcohol poisoning either.

"Her red blood cell count is done, she's anemic, is she on any medication for it?"

"Wouldn't matter if she were." Mason mused. Nope, whatever pills she might have been given were sitting snug in her medicine cabinet, unopened and unused. "She wouldn't take it."

"Her white cell count is down too. You sure you wanna take cancer off the table?"

Yes, yes, yes, he wanted to take cancer off the goddamn table! Just because he wanted it didn't make it so. "Get a chest X-Ray. Hurry while she's still sleeping."

"I'm on it." Leaving the file behind, Wylds left the office.

**

Ritter slunk around the halls of The Mountainside Wellness & Research Center in faded blue jeans, faded yellow jacket, a very authentic looking paste-on mustache, and baseball cap. No one noticed him as he hung around in the hall outside Julie's room or down the hall from Mason's office. He watched the doctors dope up an already unconscious woman, heard Mason bark orders, and saw Steward and Wylds leave. Ritter thought about following them, but then decided against it. They'd do their standard search of her home, maybe they'd find something useful and maybe they wouldn't—he was sort of hoping that they would, for Julie's sake, but if it didn't happen then it didn't happen. Either way nothing interesting would happen there. Not much of interest would happen around Julie until she woke up.

If she woke up.

Ritter wandered down the hall a small ways, he'd know when she woke up because he'd find Mason hurriedly stumbling down to her room. He wouldn't miss the show when she opened her eyes and, from what he overheard from Mason and the others, it could be quite the show indeed. Instead of following Steward and Wylds, or Goodspeed who was just down in the lab running boring tests until the results came up and then he'd be on his way to Mason's office. Ritter camped out in the waiting area just out view of the big window-walls behind which sat The Great Doctor at his White Board; he was alone in the room and mumbling to himself. He looked damn irritated, frustrated even.

Cup of fresh coffee in hand, he picked it up along with the newspaper in the coffee shop downstairs, Ritter settled back on the bench against the wall to wait and watch.

**

"I got the results of the chest x-ray back and...what the hell is all of that?" Goodspeed asked as he took in the sight of the bottles of pills on the conference table.

"Contents of Julie's medicine cabinet," Mason said.

"Yeah, and half of these are B-12 prescriptions." Steward said as he looked down at the table.

"Well, that helps to explain the cell counts, she has vitamin deficiency anemia." Goodspeed said as he sat down, "the x-ray's clean. For a smoker, she's got great lungs."

"Don't I know it?" Mason remarked.

Steward and Wylds had been able to separate the bottles and boxes into groups the two largest being the prescription bottles full of B-12 nasal spray and a prescription folate supplement.

"This one's from 1998." Steward said as he shook his head unable to believe what he was looking at.

"So that's it then, right?" Wylds said looking from the pills to the White Board. "It's Aplastic anemia. Her red and white blood cell count is low so are her platelets and obviously she's already prone to it."

Scanning the lab work results for the umpteenth time Mason looked up. "Aplastic anemia doesn't have this sudden of an onset. It doesn't account for the bloody vomit."

"Argue with the technician if you want...oh wait that would be me." Goodspeed said. "I did the tests right, you can double check if you want. You've got something better, let's hear it."

Aplastic anemia fit perfectly but it didn't sit right with him. Maybe he just didn't want it to be Aplastic anemia because there was treatment but no cure other than a bone marrow transplant. Julie smoked. She hated doctors, wouldn't take her prescriptions. She drank like a fish. Chances of her going to the top of donor list were remote. Chances of her wanting to be on it were even less. However, if Julie wasn't Julie and she was just some Jane Doe off the street he'd say... "Get a bone marrow biopsy to confirm."

Wylds' turn to speak. "We'll have to wait until she wakes up for that."

"Do it...NOW." Mason ordered. "If we wait for her to wake up we'll never get it, she won't consent."

"If nothing else, it's invasive and it's painful." Wylds argued. "Why not start with a CT-Scan of the underarm; we'll get a look at her lymph nodes. If it confirms the blood work then we'll go for the biopsy."

"Who's in charge here? You or me?"

"You are but..."

"Then do what I tell you do, damnit!" He looked down at his watch. "No! Wait, another twenty minutes, wait."

"What?" Steward asked resuming the seat he was just getting up from. "I thought you said..."

"I know what I said. But you're going to have to put her out for this and..."

"Put her out?" Steward asked suspiciously. "The last I checked we generally use local anesthesia for this."

"Not this time, you're going to use general." Mason said in a defiant voice. "Since she's already out that would be redundant, now wouldn't it?"

"Mason, Sinclair said..."

"I know what Sinclair said!" He railed and reached into his pocket for that friendly little amber bottle, the one that never let him down. Popping a pill into his mouth he said, "We all know what she said but I'm in charge, not Sinclair." In the back of his head he could hear Julie screeching at him; *I'm not your fucking patient!* "If she sees a needle she'll go out the damn window if she has to. You're going to wait another twenty minutes; she'll start to wake up..."

"We put her out again for the biopsy and instead of twenty minutes you get another hour, is that it?" Wylds asked. "You know you really can't keep her here."

Mason looked around; he looked at the ceiling, the floor, and the walls, back at the team. "Anyone else hear that? The *same old echo* seems to keep repeating itself."

"What's with you and this woman?" Steward asked. "Who's she to you?"

"What business is it of yours?" He snapped.

"If you're invol-"

"Damn, there's that echo again."

"So you are...involved....with her?" Wylds asked wistfully.

"What? The Aussie Stud not punching your buttons lately?" He looked from Wylds to Goodspeed and back again. "Not curling your toes and makin' you throw Frisbees around the room?"

Wylds blushed and became flustered. "He's doing just fine." She stuttered and looked at her husband with loving eyes. "I just meant..."

"You don't want me to lose my happy-go-lucky attitude, is that it?" He snapped again. "Figure if Julie dies then I'll go back to being the same old bastard I always was?"

"She's not even dead and you're doing it already." Steward admonished. "We found your ring in her bedroom, maybe you should take yourself off this case."

The suggestion was met by a long moment of dead and uncomfortable silence. "Go get ready for the biopsy." Those around him expressed their displeasure with a round of grunts and groans as they stood up. "No one wears a white coat when they go into the room." He advised. "Coats off."

"It's hospital policy," Steward reminded Mason.

"Not in her room, she sees those coats and it'll only help to set her off. If she doesn't see them, then she just sees the three of you and not three big scary doctors."

With three white coats laid over the Nurse's Desk, Steward, Wylds and Goodspeed walked into Julie's room just as she was starting to come around. "He's going to get sued." Wylds said as she pushed the sedative into the IV. "But it won't be the first time."

Julie's eyes that were just starting to loll open rolled closed. "Well, he's got another hour." Goodspeed said.

"So do we, let's get moving." Steward added.

An unconscious Juliette Miller was prepped for the procedure before Wylds inserted a rather large needle deep into her thigh and through the bone to remove a sample of the marrow there within. After that, they left her to sleep and went back to Mason's office to await the results of the biopsy and the swabs of Julie's home. The house came back clean, there were no known toxins present. Mason looked at that and put it in the back of his churning mind. Just because they were undetected didn't mean they weren't there. It all depended on the results of the biopsy.

**

From his place in the hall, if he craned his neck just right, Ritter had a good view of Mason sitting behind his desk, wheels turning behind those blue eyes, as he started to sweat. A woman came rushing up the hall with a slip of paper in her hand and he leaned forward.

**

"Here the results you wanted, Doctor Mason." The lab tech handed him the sheet then turned and left the office.

"Well?" Steward asked.

Mason looked down at the paper. "It's positive." He said unhappily. "Aplastic anemia." It felt wrong. It looked right. It looked perfect.

Too perfect.

"Start treat—" Mason's beeper went off followed by the others. "She's awake." He mumbled. "Oh, this gonna be fun."

Scrambling down to her room, they found Julie screaming at the top of her lungs. "LET ME THE FUCK OUT OF HERE! YOU CAN'T KEEP ME HERE!" She was engaged in a near fistfight with an orderly and a nurse, both of whom were trying to keep her in the bed. "LET ME GO! YOU SON OF A BITCH!" The orderly made the mistake of getting his hand too close to Julie's mouth. She bit down hard.

"OW!" The orderly wailed and yanked his hand out of her mouth only to have it come back covered in blood saliva. "You bit-"

"Uh-uh-uh." Mason said from the doorway. "Must always be nice to the patient."

"Really?" The nurse rolled her eyes. "You handle this one; she's right up your alley, Doctor Mason." The two of them stormed out of the room.

Yes, as a matter of fact, this one is right up my alley and I've been up hers. I like it that way.

"Back off, I got this." Mason said out of the corner of his mouth to his team standing behind him. The last thing Julie needed was for three people in White Coats to come busting through her door. "Coats off before she sees you."

"Do-c? Do-c, what's going on? Why am I here? WHAT HAVE YOU DONE TO ME?" Her hip was killing her! She felt like she'd been hit by a slow moving car. It was hard to catch her breath but that wasn't slowing her down too much.

"If you don't calm down, I'll have to give you another shot." He warned.

213

"Like hell you will!" Julie, free from the grasp of the orderly and nurse, threw the blankets back and jumped out of the bed only to fall on the floor.

"That better?" He asked as he wandered around the bed. He wanted to help her up but he didn't want to be bitten by her. "Floor more comfortable for ya?"

"Don't just stand there you idiot! Help me up!"

"Nope, not if you're going to run out of here." Julie kicked him in the shin of his bad leg. He gritted his teeth instead of backhanding her.

"You can't keep me here! I know my RIGHTS!"

"Yeah? Do you know you're sick as hell?" He shouted back. "Do you know I found you passed out on your bedroom floor soaked in a puddle of your own bloody vomit?"

"What?" Julie's last memory had been of being in bed. She felt sick, she was going to throw up, she got out the bed, and then...she was here.

"Yeah, how 'bout that?" He mused. "Now, I could be wrong, but I thought you told me that you had to be bleeding out of your eyes before you saw a doctor. Does throwing up blood count or...not?"

"No, it doesn't. It's not the first fucking time." She snapped. "Help me up or GET OUT OF MY WAY!" The yelling hurt her head and made her chest hurt. Her hand began to go to the space between her breasts but it was rudely yanked away as the other was brought upward.

The Doc hauled Julie to her feet by her wrists. "You're going to be back in that bed and you're not going to give me any shit, you got that?" He hissed.

"Mason!" Steward said in a low voice from the doorway not understanding the little game that was about to be played out in front of them.

"Fuck you," Julie said through slotted lips that pulled back into a cold grin before she hauled off and spit in Doc's face.

Mason was angered and surprised but not so much so that he didn't have the presence of mind to block her next kick with his cane. "Later," he said in that same hiss. "Right now you're going to get in that bed." He increased the pressure on her wrists and she let out a little cry. "Am I understood?"

Julie's weird and wild eyes scanned the room looking for help. She saw three people standing in the doorway but didn't know who they were at first because she was so used to seeing them in those damn white coats. "What's wrong with me?"

"That's what I'm trying to find out but I can't do that if you don't...*get back in that bed.*"

Julie brought her eyes back to him. "I'm not staying here, Do-c."

"All right," he said, "you made me do it. I tried to be nice, Julie-Baby." The hand that had been holding his cane dropped it to the floor and grabbed her sore neck. Julie let out a whimper and the strength went out of her knees.

"Mason!" Was called out in unison by the three other doctors standing in the doorway watching their less-than-sane boss choke his patient. "Let her go!"

Mason turned his eyes to them. "Back off!" The tone of his voice was enough to cause the three of them to take a step back. "They're not going to help you, Julie-Baby. But I am." One hand clamped on her already wounded throat and the other holding her wrists safely in place, Mason backed her up to the bed until she fell on it. "I got these for you." He said with a grin and reached for the restraints on the rails of the bed.

215

"NO!" Julie screamed or tried to anyway. The air getting to her lungs, which seemed to be not enough to begin with, was now slightly choked off even more by his hand. She bucked, kicked, thrashed about, spit, and tried to bite Doc in a scene right out of *The Exorcist*, the only thing seemingly missing was the pea soup vomit. In the doorway, the doctors looked on in stunned amazement as Mason harnessed the writhing and protesting Julie to the bed. He didn't once let go of her throat. He got the first hand free, pinned the other down with his knee, grabbed the freed fighting, clawing, hand, and tightened the strap with just one of his hands. He repeated the same with the second then loomed over her. "You know, when this is over and you're better," he whispered in her ear, "I'm going to strap you down like this in my bed."

"In your dreams, Do-c." Julie returned in a threatening tone.

"Yours too." He countered. "Behave or I'll have to spank you." He got off the bed, his heart racing, and his pulse pounding. "Now that I have your attention, you have Aplastic anemia." He began and sat in the chair next to her. "Do you know what that means?"

"I don't give a damn. LET ME GO!" She pulled at the leather restraints on her lower arms until the muscles there popped and every vain was visible.

"Keep it up; you'll break your arms." He warned. "They're not going to give way no matter what you do."

"You CAN'T KEEP ME HERE!" She railed and began to thrash about violently on the bed once more. "It's ILLEGAL!"

"I know," He agreed, "that's why I went to the trouble of having you committed for 72 hours." That was an outright lie but she didn't know that. "Hate me, Julie-Baby?"

"With a passion...Do-c."

"Fine, if I have my way, you'll live long enough to hate me for the next forty years or so." He got up and walked out of the room.

"I HATE YOU DO-C!" Julie screamed.

"Shut her up." He said to Steward on his way through the door. "She's disturbing the entire floor."

"When Sinclair finds out about this you're going to lose your job." Steward said. "You assaulted her!" He said in an incredulous tone, "Right in front of all of us, are you crazy? Scratch that we all know you're fuckin' crazy, I guess the question is; how crazy are you...over her?" Steward paused and waited for an answer but didn't get one. "If nothing else, she's right," he pointed toward the woman struggling to free herself from the restraints, "you don't have a Court Order, and you *cannot* keep her here even if it is for her own good."

"So I'll get one," Mason told him, "in the meantime, shut her up, and start treatment."

Chapter Fifteen

Since they arrived here nearly three hours ago, Mason felt as though he were being watched. He didn't see anyone familiar or out of the ordinary but he felt the weight of their stare and it put him on edge. That didn't help his little display in Julie's room which got him called here, into Sinclair's office and she was steaming. Those perky little breasts were heaving and her jaw was set tight as she glared at him from behind her desk.

"What did I tell you, Mason?" Sinclair asked rhetorically. " You've really just gone way over the top this time. Now I've got people coming to me and telling me that you actually physically assaulted Julie Miller? In front of witnesses?"

"I had to get her back in the bed," he told his boss. "I didn't hurt her."

"You don't know that."

"Yes, I do."

"You grabbed her by the throat knowing she has a pinched..."

"I know what she's got," he said angrily, "I did not injure her further." It was just part of The Game Julie-Baby played but he wasn't sure how to explain that to Sinclair. "If I didn't do that then she would have run out—"

"That doesn't give you the right to trample all over her rights." Sinclair asserted as she stood up from behind the desk.

"I don't give a damn about her rights."

"I KNOW!"

"What good are rights if you're not alive to enjoy them?" He countered.

For that Sinclair had no answer. "I should have you arrested, right here, right now, just to cover the center's ass." She said in an exasperated tone. "I let you get away with a lot around here but this is going too far."

"I just want to make her well," Mason said in a much softer tone. "Julie understands that."

"How, Mason? How in Gods' name does Julie Miller understand that your grabbing her by the throat and strapping her down to a bed is in her best interest? How does anyone understand that?"

He thought about it for half a second. "She likes it." That was true enough. The whole time he was arguing with her, staring into those wide frightened frenzied eyes, all he could hear was Julie telling him that Craig used to throw her over his shoulder if he had to in order to get her to a doctor. She was used to it, she was accustomed to having someone, a man, take charge. "It's a *game*."

Sinclair blinked and sat down again as she picked up on the tone of Mason's voice. "Maybe in bed," she lead.

"Not just in bed but believe me she loves it there." He said with a sly grin. "You can't let her run out of here just because she's scared. She'll die if you do that then you'll need a really big sling for the center's ass."

"She'll sign an AMA slip I'm sure," Sinclair said snottily. The idea of Julie Miller and Mason in bed together was enough but the image of bondage and role-playing was really just too much.

"Only if *you let her*!"

"Mason...."

He was at the end of his rope. The way she was looking at him, well, the idea that was sleeping with Julie Miller didn't sit well with Evelyn Sinclair that was clear in those blue angry eyes. "I'll get a damn Court Order just don't let her leave. "

"I'm not going to let you wake up a Judge at," she looked at her watch to see it was nearly 11:30 pm, "it's way too late, you'll only make them angry."

"Why are you stonewalling me?" He stood there staring daggers at a woman who usually invoked different feelings in him. " Don't you want her to get better? I've done way worse than this over the years."

"You can say that again." Sinclair sighed.

"I've done way worse than this over the years." He said in a mocking tone.

"Cute but no cigar. What I want or don't want is irrelevant, it's what Mrs. Miller wants that counts. Call me crazy," she lifted her hands in the air as she shook her head and rolled her eyes, "I don't think she wants her doctor assaulting her." *Or her Lover for that matter.*

Everyone kept tossing that word around, assault. In his mind what he'd done was far less than that and for a greater purpose. The way they said it you would think he beat her to a pulp. "I did not hurt her, it only looked that way. I told you, it's a game."

"The twisted bitch is right up your alley," Sinclair mumbled under breath.

'"What did you say?" He took a step toward her. "I didn't catch that." But the truth was he heard it just fine. "You got a problem with me and Julie then spit it out." He challenged. "But don't let it cloud your medical judgment. You know I'm right about this. Just give me 24 hours to start treatment and see if it works."

Maybe Mason was right, maybe she was letting a few old lingering feelings get in the way of Julie Miller's treatment. Sinclair looked down at the file. "It's pretty cut and dry that Mrs. Miller—"

"Julie," He asserted as he grew angrier, "her name is *Julie*."

"Ok," Sinclair said in a calmer voice trying to keep her star doctor calm and on point, "Julie's got Aplastic anemia," she said thoughtfully. "Are you trying to tell me it's not?"

Was he? Aplastic anemia was a lovely fit—well, IF the pinched carotid was the explanation for the fatigue and lightheadedness--but it didn't explain the bloody vomit, the sudden onset, or the mood swings, or the respiratory problems. "I don't know." He admitted. The more he thought about it the less Aplastic anemia fit.

"You don't know? Are you serious or are you just yanking my chain?"

"Serious," He mumbled. "Even if the tests are right the anemia could only be a symptom of a larger problem. Look at the file, the first round of tests came back, the change is minimal. She isn't responding."

Sinclair looked at the file again and the numbers were not encouraging, Mason was right, but what could she do?

"She has to stay here until I find out what's causing the anemia."

Sinclair hung her head. "You can't get a Court Order for this, no judge is going to give it to you." She leaned across the desk. "Look, I'll give until she wakes up but that's it. This is a hospital not a prison. If you're lucky, she'll sleep through the night even after the drugs wear off and you'll have her until tomorrow morning. If you can't convince her to stay on her own then it's over and you have to let her walk out of here." She advised.

"Go home and get some rest, hope that she forgives you when this is over."

**

For a change of pace, it was his staff who went home while Mason spent the night at the hospital. They were all sure they'd made the right diagnosis and that Julie would respond to treatment within the next few hours. From there on end, the stop-gap measures would be used until a bone marrow donor could be found. Mason sat in his office going over all of the results from Julie's recent tests looking for whatever it was that he was sure he was missing.

Wylds was such a good little doctor, she wrote down the contents of Julie's refrigerator for him; milk, eggs, cheese, broccoli, romaine lettuce, orange juice, 14 bottles of LifeWater. The list went on and on and extended to the meat in Julie's freezer, most of which was liver. He looked at it and the black hefty bag sitting in the corner of his office. Julie wasn't stupid just crazy. She knew she was sick, she understood what it meant, but instead of taking the drugs prescribed she tried to compensate and correct the problem with her diet. If she'd been able to avoid the prescriptions for ten or more years she must have been maintaining fairly well. So what happened?

Ritter.

Mason just couldn't shake it, could not rid himself of the dark sneaking suspicion that the ex-cop really had gone out of his mind and tried to kill an innocent woman. He would kill her if he couldn't find out what was wrong with her.

The phone in pocket began to ring and he answered it looking at the Caller ID to see it was Lucas. "Yeah, what's up, Lucas?"

The PI had become alarmed when Mason hung up so abruptly and then didn't answer either phone. "What's going on? You hang up on me and...."

"Kinda busy here," Richard said with frustration, "it's late, you got something for me?"

"Oh yeah," Lucas said on the other end. "When I couldn't get a hold of you I decided maybe I should do some work."

"I am paying you."

"That too," Lucas agreed. "Where are you?"

"The hospital, why?"

"Good, you're not far. Get down to the El Royale, there's something you've just go to see to believe."

"What is it?"

"Just get down here." Lucas hung up the phone.

Putting the phone back in his pocket, Mason popped a Oxycodone and looked toward the conference table with the Hefty bag next to it, then to the papers scattered on his desk. He was still unable to get rid of the sense that someone was watching him. It gnawed at the back of his mind and distracted him from his work. Maybe getting out of here for a few minutes would be good, get some fresh air and a new perspective. He stopped by the Nurses' Station and was told Julie was resting comfortably, she hadn't woken or given them any trouble since her mega-outburst. Mason walked away from the station to stand directly on the other side of the glass and peer inside. She looked a lot more peaceful than she did an hour ago, even if her arms were restrained to the bed. Almost as though it were a reflection in the glass, he could see her, Julie's pretty face twisted and gnarled in anger as she told him where to get off and lashed out at him as though he were an attacker rather than a doctor. Could fear really do that to someone? Maybe. But could fear without a rational basis do it? Maybe Julie had a horrible experience with a doctor at some point and that was what started it all. What did it matter? When the meds wore off she'd go right back up the wall, turn into a spitfire from hell. Right now, she was still, she was quiet, and she was beautiful. He couldn't stop thinking about how much he wanted her, that same little spitfire, out of that bed and back in his own...where she belonged. That wasn't going to happen if he couldn't fit the pieces of the puzzle together in time. "She wakes up call me on my cell." He said to the nurse before leaving.

**

Ritter watched Mason leave and wondered where he was going. He saw him get the phone call and then wander down to Julie's room, thought about following him but thought he'd use this opportunity for something else. It was near mid-night, shift change. The nurse's station outside Julie's room was empty. He sauntered past and into Julie's room where he drew the blinds. She looked like shit. She was pale and covered in sweat. She'd vomited again but no one seemed to notice as there was a great blood red and bile green mass drying on her sheets. Seemed he brought the right tool for the job, she must be very thirsty. She put on quite a show with Mason earlier, kicking, screaming, biting and hissing like a little demon. Even Ritter was shocked by the level of contempt she showed to the man currently sharing her bed. An outsider would have thought that Julie had never even laid eyes on Mason before she woke up in the feared hospital bed. The lame bastard handled it well although Ritter doubted Mason's underlings and colleagues saw the same. It was a while ago that they gave her the last shot of whatever sedative they were giving her to keep her quiet. He thought it a shame that she so was scared of Mason, it was funny as hell too from his particular point of view, but if she weren't afraid then she'd be awake. If she were awake, Mason would surely notice that Julie was starting to hallucinate by now. He gave that a little nudge earlier tonight and intended to keep it up for the next night or two—then his plans got blown by the impending visit of the stepson and he thought he'd have to put them on hold for the weekend.

224

Ritter didn't have to break in to Julie's house today, he found the Hide-A-Key easy enough and her alarm code...piece of cake. He got it right on the second try, his first try being Craig's birthday. The alarm off, the dog out with Julie for the day, he looked through her things for an hour or more before making his way to The Mountainside which was where Ritter had been sure she was going. He saw the bottle of Grey Flannel on the vanity and splashed some around the room, down the stairs and in the living room. There the wedding photograph caught his eye, if it were to be broken Julie would be very upset. So he smashed it. Looking down at the broken glass and scratched photograph he wondered just how far gone she was, if it looked to her like someone had broken in here then he was screwed. That's when he got the idea of making it look like the dog did it. He picked up the photograph, crinkled it up in his hand and then chewed on a corner of it for a few seconds before straightening it out and putting it back in the busted frame.

Back up the stairs to replace the bottle he left the cap off and saw the ring sitting beside the ring box. Seeing red and the image of Mason deeply inside a place Ritter believed that he should be, he almost pitched it out the window but settled on the garbage can instead. Then he put the ring box back in the center drawer, didn't take much to figure out that's where it belonged as the space it left was perfect. Again, maybe, in a chemically induced haze, Julie would take these things as signs from Craig. If he was dead it would be an absolutely perfect and Ritter was working on that. Craig was nothing but a useless lump of human flesh anyway so who'd give a damn if he finally gave up the ghost. He had a good plan in mind but implementing it would be most difficult. Yet, if he were smart and cunning enough, perhaps in the end Ritter could make it appear that Mason was responsible for the deaths of Mr. and Mrs. Craig Miller. Better that than risk the chance the fair Juliette would actually fall in love with that bastard Mason.

To that end, Ritter tried to warn her this afternoon. He'd been very earnest and sincere in his warning and the sharing of his belief that Richard Mason was incapable of loving anyone other than himself.

There wasn't much time, shift change would be over soon. Ritter reached across the sleeping woman and undid the restraints around her wrists. Underneath the heavy buckle a deep impression had been left on both arms even though the thick sheepskin should have prevented just such a thing. She was wiry one. He never saw anything like it when she had the nerve to spit in Mason's face, even he did a double take. He smiled as he ran his hand up her limp arms. The flesh was soft and supple. He followed it all the way up her forearm, under the Johnny, over that struggling chest to those breasts he'd had the pleasure of biting on a few nights ago. "Hey, can you hear me?" Ritter whispered into her ear. "Julie-Baby, can you hear me?"

Was someone calling her name? Did someone want her? What was that sound?

"Julie-Baby?" Those whispering words were closer to her skin as Ritter took in the sickly scent of her. Yes, gone was the intoxicating cinnamon that filled his head to bursting the last time his hand rested here. That didn't stop the skin below her ear from tasting as delicious as he remembered, a little sweet, a little salty, a little more would be good. His cock began to tingle between his legs.

Julie's head was heavy on her shoulders as she rolled it toward what she thought was the sound of a voice. Her eyes opened but all she saw were fuzzy shadows.

"Thirsty, baby?" Ritter took a step back from her so he could gauge those eyes that were opening to take him in. Hazy and distant they were, he was near certain she couldn't really see him. His hand remained under the Johnny cupping that perky little breast. That tingling cock was waking up with a hunger making him wish he had more time than just the few precious minutes of shift change. He'd like to put it to her while she

226

couldn't resist, right here in this bed. Right here, where Mason would come back through that door and sit by her side never knowing Ritter fucked the snot out of her. The thought almost drove him wild as he fought to stand there and keep speaking quietly. All the while getting as good of a feel as he could.

There was something pressing against her lips. Something, some familiar smell, and something else...something tickling her nose.

"Go on, Julie, drink it. You must be thirsty after all that screaming." Not to mention the puking but since she didn't seem aware of that he thought it best to leave it unmentioned. Ritter didn't want her coming around fully, screaming and alerting the whole floor to his presence.

More out of reflex than anything else, Julie's mouth closed around the straw and she began to suck the cold liquid into her mouth. Coke. Cold, icy cold, Coke. It tasted so good and quenched the fire at the back of her throat as it went down removing the horrid salty taste from her mouth.

"That's right, drink it up. Feels good, huh?" Holding the cup to her mouth, he slid the free hand away from the soft supple breast and down the flat of her stomach. "That feel good too?"

Julie hardly noticed that hand that was so quietly molesting her. It was the liquid that held her attention. It was impossible to suck through the straw and breathe at the same time, Julie didn't know what to do. She didn't want to stop drinking the blessedly cold soda but air was always good. Eventually air won out. She stopped drinking in order to take in a great whooping breath through her mouth. There was something in her nose, something that was blowing a funny smelling thing into her. The air getting to her lungs seemed as heavy as her head and Julie soon began to cough harshly. Instinct brought her eyes upward toward the voice, so kind and so light, for help. She couldn't see a face. Her eyes didn't want to focus as hard as she tried she just couldn't make them. All she saw were blurry colors; yellow and blue, in the impressionistic shape of a man or two. "C..craig?" Julie croaked between coughs.

Ritter smiled a cold grin. At first the sounds of her coughing alarmed him and made him think that someone was bound to come rushing in here. Then again, this was a hospital, people hacked, coughed and sneezed all the time and no one came. "A little more, huh? Have a little more, Julie-Baby. It'll make you feel better." He put the straw to her lips and Julie sucked in more of the tainted Coke. Wandering the halls, lurking, and watching, a little while ago Ritter came to the conclusion that it was probably best if Julie died. It really was a mercy killing. In his eyes, Ritter was saving Julie from two Great Evils; that of wasting her life on the hopes that a nearly dead husband would return to her hale and hearty, the other, of course, was Richard Mason. What kind of a life could a man like him offer a woman like Julie or any woman? Just a bunch of sarcastic misery. Mason didn't deserve Julie, she was crazy as a loon but she hid it well. Wasn't everyone crazy in their own way? Sure they were, look at Mason. The man spent his life halfway off his rocker and got kudos for it. That didn't make it right. He could never love Julie the way she needed a man to love her and Mason didn't deserve the chance to even try. "Stay away from him, Julie-Baby." Ritter whispered in her ear. "Mason, he's evil. Don't let him near you."

There was only air coming through the straw now and making a loud sucking sound. Craig took the cup away. "Love...him."

"He doesn't love you, he's trying to hurt you." For added emphasis his hand found her nipple and gave it a good twist. Julie let out a painfully small cry as though she couldn't get any air into her lungs at all.

Outside the room he could hear faint voices. Shift change was nearly over. It was time to go. "I love you, Julie-Baby, *you do*

228

what *I tell you* to and everything will be fine." Ritter slipped out of the room before shift change was over.

**

The drive to the El Royale was short especially at this dead hour when there was no traffic on the road except for him. Mason parked right in front of the place and walked in. Lucas was standing at the front desk chatting with the night manager. "Well, look who it is. Sorry, my friend, she's not here." The night manager said to Mason. "Not coming back either. She turned in her key earlier today."

"Excuse me?" Why would she do that? Why would Julie give up her room? It was her Safety zone, her little nest, the place where she could go and the troubles of the outside world didn't matter. Not what other people might have picked for such a place but to Julie it was comforting in its own demented way. Did she find another Safe Zone? For half a second the idea that he might be that new Safe Zone went zipping through his mind;

I think I could love him but I don't think he'll let me.

"Sad day around here." The night manager said with a shrug and watched the older man that Rose seemed so taken with turn and look at the PI. "You two know each other?"

"He hired me," Lucas said. There wasn't any sense in lying to Leroy about who he was or what he was doing, Leroy spotted him soon after meeting him. The night manager didn't know much about the woman who called herself Rose Montague other than the sounds that came from her room and how frequently they did so. She paid her bill, kept her room clean and that was all Leroy really cared about.

"So I suppose you want to know about the other guy?" Leroy asked and then stuck out his hand. "By the way, my name's Leroy."

229

"Mason," the two men shook hands. "What other guy?"

Leroy told a fascinating story about Patrick Ritter, he didn't know the brute by name but he surely knew his face by photograph. Ritter started renting room 404 several months ago. "That's the room next to where Rose had been staying."

"Rose?" How long had she used that line; A rose by any other name. How often? Julie never gave him a false name, Richard just started calling her that on his own. "Montague?"

"That's what she says, I didn't ask for ID." In his business, when it came to customers like Rose asking for ID would put him out of business. Wasn't any of his concern who his clients were outside of this place so long as the bill got paid and the room wasn't trashed. "Sorry to see her go, she kinda brightened up the place a little." He looked around at the old building. "Anyway, that guy," he pointed to the photograph of Ritter on the desk, "started coming around a while ago, always took the room next to hers, tried to make sure I'd keep it available whenever he wanted to use it but I told him that was four hundred a month and he'd slip me a fifty here and there to put people in other rooms if possible." Leroy laughed. "Like we've got the 'NO VACANCY' sign up." He laughed again. "Weird thing, except for one time earlier this week, they never seem to run into each other. He always," Leroy leaned forward and whispered, "I mean he *always* got here about fifteen minutes *after* she arrived...every time. Don't you think that's weird?"

"Nope," Mason said without thinking and felt the acid in his stomach start to bubble and churn. "What else?"

"Come with me." Lucas said and lead Mason to the elevator. The ride up was full of memories for Richard Mason and ones that he'd rather enjoy alone rather than here with Lucas. "Check it out." He'd asked Leroy to let him up here and only forty bucks did the trick, Lucas would put that on Mason's bill. "See anything?"

He looked around at the room which was only a room and not a suite like Julie's. It had a bed and a bathroom, a table and two chairs off in the corner but other than it was unremarkable as far as Richard could see. "No. You got me down here for this? You could have told me on the phone."

"Nah, wait." Lucas slid his pack off his back and put a laptop on the bed. Turning it on, he shone a flashlight along the baseboards. "How about now? See anything?"

"Rat gnawings?" Mason asked in a huff as a few small holes caught his eye.

"Those holes, there's five of them. Three along the baseboard and two up higher, see them?" Lucas shone the light along the wall which Richard assumed ran along Julie's bedroom and sitting room. There were two pinholes about four feet from the ground and if Richard guessed right one was located just below the mirror on the bureau in the bedroom and the other behind the TV in the sitting room. "He's a sneaky bastard, your Ritter." Lucas shut off the light and began hooking up the laptop as he'd done earlier. "You were right, he's been spying on your girl."

"On his belly?" What could Ritter possibly see from down on the floor through such small holes. The other two made more sense but, still, they were so small it would be damn difficult to see through them.

"Nope, on the bed. Watch." Taking what looked to Mason like nothing more than an long electrical cord, Lucas stuck one end of it through one of the holes and hooked the other to the laptop. He turned the computer around so Mason could see it. "Perfect view, wouldn't you say?" Mason stood there looking at the large and crystal clear image of Julie's room. "Just use the mouse to change the camera angle," he moved his hand over the pad and the picture moved up, down, and side to side. "Can even zoom in if you want." Lucas elbowed Mason. "Probably did a lot of that, from what I understand the action in that room was pretty hot and heavy, classic hardcore material."

"This thing records?" If the damn thing did then Ritter had him on tape with Julie. What might Ritter do with that? The full impact of the situation started to fall on him. Ritter sat here, night after night, probably jacking off, watching Julie do her thing. How many months? Four? Five? Maybe even half a year? If Julie got into his head so quickly and deeply with him only running into her once, what had she done to Ritter's head while he sat here watching her fuck the Flavor of the Night? Especially since Ritter tried to be that satisfying flavor on so many occasions.

"Oh, yeah, sure it does. Hey, if anyone was in there right now you could hear them, this baby's got a microphone."

"You're sure Ritter has one of these?"

"Pretty standard for most PIs, Mason." Lucas assured him. "What else would the holes be for?"

Had he really come back here to watch her do whatever guy she picked up while she turned Ritter down? How sick did someone have to be to sit here and watch that? How angry did they get doing so? How obsessed? Maybe, when he showed up on the scene, Ritter finally decided that if he couldn't have her no one could and Mason sure as hell wasn't going to.

"Kinda twisted, huh?"

"KINDA?" Mason returned. "It's sick is what it is."

Yeah, it's sick. So is Julie and Ritter did it! So come on, Old Man, what did he do to her? What looks and smells like Aplastic anemia but isn't? As he racked his brain for the answer, his cell phone went off. "Yeah?" He listened. "What? She stable?" A pause. "I'll be right there."

"What is it?" Lucas asked quickly.

"Julie went into convulsions," Mason said uneasily, "They gave her valium to stop them and she stopped breathing, they had to intubate her." The bloody vomit was back too but Lucas didn't need to know about that or anything else for that matter. They found her convulsing on the bed, her vitals sky high, and her restraints undone. The nurse reported Julie hadn't given them any trouble other than to mumble incoherently, something that sounded like 'Craig' though it could have been 'Rick' considering their relationship.

"She all right?"

"What do you care? You don't even know her."

"No," Lucas said thoughtfully, "but I'd like to." He added hopefully.

"Back off buddy, she's mine." Mason warned. "All mine. You find out where Ritter is."

"Aww, that's easy, he's at The Mountainside."

Mason ran out of the room so fast his bad leg didn't have time to notice the pain.

Walking swiftly as possible through the halls his eyes kept darting about to every corner and every face he saw. Ritter was here somewhere. He was watching and he was waiting for Julie to die. For him to fail to save her just so Ritter could have the last laugh.

Some fucking joke.

Playing around with an innocent woman's life, that just wasn't funny.

Chapter Sixteen

On his way up to Julie's room, Mason alerted security to be on the lookout for Ritter who was undoubtedly in some type of disguise. He didn't have to describe Ritter to Andy Defresne, head of security, the man was well acquainted with Ritter and promised to alert the guards and keep a closer eye on the security cameras stationed around Julie Miller's room and Mason's office.

In Julie's room, he found his new patient nearly unresponsive. She wasn't yelling. She wasn't fighting or telling him to go fuck himself. Julie didn't have the strength for anything like that. Lying there on the bed with the IV in her, intubation tube down her throat and monitors hooked up to her, the most she could manage was turning her head toward the sound of his voice. Those translucent eyes, the ones that were nearly colorless, were now nearly black as their pupils were fully dilated and they didn't seem to show any sign of recognition. Mason wondered just how many of him she was seeing if she was seeing him at all.

"Can you hear me?" He asked as he leaned over the bed.

The voice seemed to come from so far away as to hardly be noticeable. Only a wish on the wind. It was so hard to breathe, there was something long and hard stuck in her throat, and it was most uncomfortable. She tried to talk but that thing in her throat stifled her voice. So thirsty! Where did that Coke go? Had it been here at all? Where was here? Why was everything changing around her? She had no clue. Julie tried to clear her throat if only to get rid of the thick paste building up there and in her mouth, a low guttural sound came out from her throat. That was a little better but not by much. With the effort it took to perform that simple task, the room did not spin so much as it began slowly turning like the Earth on its axis. The things about her that had been changing and morphing before her eyes, take for instance the chair in the corner. One moment it was a chair, blue, quilted pattern, rather comfortable looking, ordinary in every possible way. The next minute it was a monkey, a blue quilted monkey with an oversized mouth that had once been a footrest, it flopped open on its hinges like a marionette operated by an insane puppet master. Its crazy legs became paws as it danced around the room, the armrests turning into monkey arms and flapping around over the top of its quilted blue head. The Monkey-Chair began to cackle in that monkey-way; "Hee heeh HEEE!" It danced its way over her and Julie tried to scream but that damn thing shoved down her throat prevented it.

"They're going to take you down for some tests now," Mason explained though he didn't know why, surely she couldn't understand him. "They'll bring you back soon." He watched while Julie and all of her accoutrements were wheeled out of the room back to MRI and then to Ultra-Sound, he wanted to get a good look at her stomach and her brain. The bloody vomit had to be attributable to something and now she was hallucinating so that meant, whatever it was, it was now affecting her brain. This was a fine time for his underlings to take the night off but that was about to come to an end. Just after midnight he called each one of them and told them to get their prissy little asses back to the hospital, Julie didn't have much time left. Her last blood work came back and not only was the treatment not working she was getting worse; all cell counts were down including platelets.

It had to be a toxin but which one? Mason had no clue and so he ordered another tox-screen but this one was broad spectrum, they weren't to search for illegal drugs but poisons. There were thousands out there and not all of them would show up in the blood. It was one in a 10,000 chance he would get it right. To better his odds and on the off chance Ritter had been able to gain access to Julie's house, he ordered the gin bottle, water bottle and cigarette butts tested.

Whatever it was, it had to be something easy to get. Something easy to administer. Something as undetectable as possible; no color, no odor, no taste.

Or maybe

Maybe

Something....

...Slightly sweet...?

Richard's nostrils flared as he remembered leaning over her tonight in her bedroom and smelling that underlying odor of sweetness beneath the bloody bile. If that were true then that could narrow the search considerably.

"Are you Doctor Mason?"

Mason was shaken out of his contemplative daze as he sat at his desk tossing a ball between his hands and looked up. "Where'd you come from?" He did not see the door open but then again he was lost in thought.

"Are you Doctor Mason?' The man asked again.

"That's what it says on the door, isn't it?" Mason snapped suddenly uncomfortable with the presence of the stranger in the room. There was something oddly familiar about him as he stood on the other side of the desk; something about his face or maybe it was his hair that for some reason seemed uncharacteristically long. "Who are you?"

The man just stood there looking at him for a long moment before he spoke again almost as though he were trying not just to read Mason but to understand him. "Woman, down the hall," he said slowly, "says her name is Rosie, she's calling for you."

Mason looked down at his watch and thought it possible Julie was back from the tests by now but unlikely she was saying anything since she had a tube down her throat. "Who the hell are—" Mason stopped and looked around the empty office. A cold chill ran up his spine and forced him out of the chair and to the door where he looked out into the empty hall. He looked back to the office to see if the man was still standing in there somewhere, perhaps he'd ducked into the middle office but, no, it was empty as the hall.

Feeling as though he needed a sweater to bring him warmth, Mason made his way back down to Julie's room. She appeared to be resting comfortably with the tube still down her throat. Standing at her bedside, she didn't turn her head to look at him or even seem to notice he was there. Julie's tripping eyes were fixed on the far corner of the room and Richard wondered what she was seeing over there.

"Julie?"

She hardly noticed when the wind whispered her name. The Monkey-Chair had ceased its crazy dance but now there was a light in the far corner. A ball of light that was growing in size and intensity. She watched it until it engulfed the whole far wall and then reached out to her. In the middle of the bright light was a hole of blackness wide enough to walk through. Something was coming; it was coming into this room from another world. She tried to hold her hand up against the light but it was so heavy and it took so much effort just to raise it off the bed she soon dropped it to the mattress.

"Julie, what do you see? What is it?" Stupid. Even if she could hear him and wanted to respond, she couldn't with that tube down her throat.

Out of the middle of the black hole with its shining aura of golden light a figure appeared in silhouette. On the monitors, her heart rate and blood pressure began to rise. Whatever it was it was coming to get her, it was going to drag her away to some horrible dark place where she would pay for all her Lustful Sins for the past year and a half.

"Julie?" Richard watched as the machine, which should be breathing easily and steadily for her, started to ring its alarms. Julie was breathing on her own and she was trying to do so faster than the machine was set to allow. "Stay with me, Julie-Baby, if you can hear me, just relax, don't fight." He unstrapped the mask around her mouth and pulled the tube from her throat. Julie sucked in a great gasp of air and began to cough. At the sound, Richard felt a great wave of relief. She was breathing on her own and that was a very good sign.

The dark silhouette stepped closer and Julie saw that God picked a most appropriate person to escort her to Hell. "-reg." She mumbled.

"What? Julie? Look at me, Julie."

"Hiya, Julie-Baby." Craig said to her as he stepped out of the harsh light. "I miss you." He stood by the bed and held her hand. "I'm so sorry I had to leave you."

On the other side of the bed, Mason watched Julie's right hand rise up into the air and hang there as though someone were hold it up for her. Or, maybe, as though the muscles therein had contracted and frozen in that position. "Julie!"

It was Craig and he was healthy and standing on his own two feet. He needed a haircut, Julie had been meaning to get to that this last week or so, but she didn't have the time. "G-go wit u." Julie mumbled though her parched throat begged her not to do any such thing.

"No, you stay here." Craig soothed. "With him." He looked to the distraught man on the other side of Julie's bed. "Look at him, Julie-Baby, look at his face. Go on, look. Listen to his voice."

Whose face? Whose voice? Julie didn't know and it was so hard to turn her head but she managed it because Craig asked her to. On the other side of the bed, holding her other hand was something that looked like a man. He had silver hair and a painted face. It was the deepest blue Julie had ever seen and it covered his entire face. Over one eye and extending down half of the cheek was a black patch, almost triangular, dotting the edge were blue jewels that shined and glimmered as they caught the light. The lips moved and the wind spoke again. "Julie?"

"Look at him, Julie-Baby." Craig said very tenderly. "Look at those eyes and the furrowed brow. He loves you, he's not ready to admit it, but it he loves you."

The arm in the air rose a little higher as Craig brushed his lips across the back of Julie's hand. Her throat hurt, it was ON FIRE! So hard to talk. "You...u said...don't trust him."

"Don't trust who? Ritter? Did Ritter do this? Did you see him? Julie?" Mason asked in urgency. She didn't answer him and when her head turned back the other way and the palm of the hand hanging in the flattened out as though she were holding it against something, he couldn't shake the feeling that someone was standing on the other side of the bed. He could feel them, almost see them. That was crazy but this whole situation was insane. It was just a hallucination, that's all; there wasn't some invisible person standing there, not in reality, only in Julie's head. "Julie?" *Don't you die on me, Julie-Baby, please don't you die on me. I'll go crazy if you do. I'll do anything, just stay here with me.*

"I didn't say that," Craig smiled sadly, as he held her hand to the place where his heart once beat only for her, but now it beat no longer. "I love you, I don't want you to be alone. I want to stop doing the things you do, they're bad, Julie-Baby, very bad. You're so much better than that. I'm sorry I left you alone so swiftly. I know those men don't make you happy but some day he might."

One more turn of the head to look at the Blue Man on the other side of the bed. Before her eyes, the blue paint morphed away into tiger stripes. Orange, white and black, covered his face in a perfect tiger pattern which included whiskers, leaving only those haunting blue eyes behind to hint at a human being. Gazing down at her hand, the one in Richard's, it too began to turn. It was as though the stripes which she was sure covered his entire body were moving toward her, replicating on her, and then taking over. With quiet amazement, she watched the stripes work their way up her bare arm.

"Bye, baby, I love you." Craig whispered on the other side. "Always."

On the bed, Julie started to cry. Her dilated eyes welled up with heavy tears, which spilled down her cheeks as she stared up him. She didn't have to turn her head back to know he was gone or that she would never see him again. Hallucination or not, Craig Miller had come to say good-bye and in the part of her mind that was still holding on to reality, Julie knew that if she ever got better one of the first things they would tell her was that her husband had passed away. Doc's soft hands brushed the tears away from her cheeks as he brushed a kiss atop her forehead. "Rick," Julie mumbled with rasping breath.

Another wave of relief. "Right here."

Did her breath have a sweet smell? After all that vomit?

Rick leaned in closer. "Say my name again."

It was difficult but Julie croaked it out one more time. "Rick."

Not Doc. Not Do-c. Rick. He smiled unabashedly. "That's right, it's me, it's Rick. Who were you talking to?"

Julie drew in a harsh breath, let it out, and tried for a second. "Craig," came the long low rasp. "He's gone."

Gone? The word had finality to it. "He's fine, Julie, he's right where you left him." *Where the hell else would he be? It's not like he got up and went out for ice cream.*

"Drink. Where...Coke?"

Where's the Coke?

He took a whiff of the air and yes, it did smell sweet. Too sweet for mere Coke. "Did someone bring you a Coke?"

Julie licked her dry lips with her dry pasty tongue and nodded her head. "More...pl-ease."

Who brought her a Coke? Ritter. Richard looked around the room and then to the garbage basket on the other side of the bed where there was a yellow paper cup with a straw sticking out of it. The bastard got in and gave her another dose of whatever it is that's killing her. But he left it behind. "I'll be back." He grabbed the cup out of the trash and headed to the lab.

Unwilling to trust the work to a Lab Tech, Mason promptly booted the night tech out of the lab. He found the other items he wanted tested still waiting including Julie's latest blood and urine samples. What about the word URGENT stamped in red letters on the work order, didn't the lab Tech understand? "Son of a bitch." Reaching into his coat pocket he took out that heavenly little amber bottle. Feeling the weight of it in his hand as he looked down at its friendly shine and wanting to take just the edge off the pain he felt—which, strangely enough, didn't seem to be emanating from his leg at the moment. Mason put it back in pocket unopened. He would live with the old annoying pain for now he needed to keep his head clear.

Down the hall from where Doctor Richard Mason sat sequestered in the hospital lab, John Ritter watched him work. When was the last time the Great Doctor Mason ran a *lab test* himself? He must really be hooked on the Fair Juliette. The clock was ticking, time was running out, and even if he did find the answer Ritter doubted he would be in time. Wasn't it a damn shame about Craig Miller? Poor bastard had only been 40 and spent the last two years of his life in a coma before suffering a massive heart attack only twenty minutes ago.

Pity.

If the Fair Juliette did recover, how would she handle that news? Surely, The Widow Miller would go into mourning thereby freezing out the Great Doctor Mason. Therefore, as far as Ritter could see, he was still ahead of the game. All possible outcomes considered he still came out on top.

In the lab, Mason continued working away with a look of pure consternation. A few moments later that look of worry and determination faded away as Mason took some slip of paper from some machine and read it. Ritter leaned forward to watch. Was Mason...crying? Was that it? The Old Man's face fell and then he hung his head, the paper slipped to the floor and then his shoulders started heaving.

"Sorry, Doc." Ritter muttered.

Raised voices were coming down the hall on harried feet; he looked up to see Wylds, Steward, and Wylds making haste down the corridor toward the lab. Each complaining about having been woken up and dragged into the hospital in the middle of the night and each stopped dead in their tracks at the sight of Mason alone in the lab. "Oh my god," Wylds stuttered looking at her cantankerous boss who now appeared broken and shattered as he sat there red-eyed and fishing in his pocket for his bottle. Mason's mouth hung open long before his hand was ready to place the pill inside.

"Guess he found it," Steward said quietly.

"Guess it's not good." Wylds agreed.

This time he not only saw someone on the other side of the door out of the corner of his eye but he had the time to try to pull himself together before they entered the lab. "It's Benzene." Mason said as he cleared his throat hoping to take the surrealist feeling of the situation away with the rough sound.

That wasn't good but there could be several reasons Julie had Benzene in her system and chief among them was the fact that she smoked. "Well, of course she's got some Benzene in her system, she smokes." Wylds said hoping that Mason was just overtired and not thinking straight.

"You're not understanding me...."

Steward interrupted, "Come on, Mason, how much time do you think Julie Miller spends in an industrial setting? How else would she come into contact with high amounts of Benzene? I thought you said she's an unemployed English teacher not a factory worker."

"Poison." Mason sighed and brought his hand to his aching head. "Everything you two just said is exactly why Ritter figured we'd never look for it." He couldn't help but feel he had been outsmarted but the oaf of an ex-cop.

"RITTER?" The three team members exclaimed in unison.

Steward continued. "What's he got to do with any of this?" He watched those gathered frown at the bitter memories that went flooding through their minds. "Why didn't you tell us about this before now?" He looked at the other two whose mouths were hanging open. "If nothing else, we wouldn't have left here thinking things were under control. We would have stayed. Didn't you want us here?"

Excellent question and the answer was 'no'. Mason let them go home tonight without a big hassle because he wanted to handle the situation himself. In other words, he was acting more like a Lover than a Doctor. He wanted to be with her, to protect her, to look and watch over her just as much as he wanted to cure her. For a Doctor that was no-no, the desire to cure must always come first and when it didn't then things became hazy. "Long story," Mason said more to himself than to his team. "I'll fill you in some other time. Ritter figured we'd never look for it *because* she smokes and doesn't spend *any* time in an industrial setting." Just before the team came through the door, the results came back to him. Benzene was an insidious poison and unless the victim knew what they had inhaled or ingested chances were, it might never be discovered. Benzene metabolized quickly and because of it was virtually undetectable in the blood, though one might find it in the urine if they caught it quickly enough and knew what to do look for. Nothing in the gin, the alcohol destroyed any detectable trace of the poison but not the poison itself. The cigarette butts, out of three in the ashtray, one had nearly quadruple the amount of Benzene that it should have. The last pack of cigarettes in the empty carton yielded one spiked cigarette. Mason found the pinhole in the bottom of the pack and wondered how many tainted cigarettes Julie had smoked. The disposable cup found in her room came back with traces of Benzene. Somehow, Ritter got into the house and he spiked her cigarettes which was why the onset was nearly unnoticeable at first but then hit like a ton of bricks. Ritter had probably been hoping to drag it out by poisoning the cigarettes but Benzene was one of those chemicals which was far worse when inhale than when ingested. The fiend probably figured that since Benzene was present in every cigarette brand and no one immediately keeled over and died from it that it was all right to up the dose on her. Poor Julie, the chemical wouldn't even stain the cigarette paper, there wouldn't be so much as a watermark to let her know that something may be wrong.

The fact that she suffered from anemia to begin with was of no help, it only aided the toxin in working quicker and spreading faster. The Benzene turned relatively simple Vitamin Deficiency Anemia into Aplastic Anemia.

The immediate problem was this; Benzene had no known antidote. Several types of treatment were shown to ease symptoms and make the patient more comfortable but on the whole the body either dealt with the toxin or it didn't. In small quantities, this was not a problem and the body usually absorbed and rid itself of the poison. Lasting effects included liver and kidney failure and several types of rather nasty and aggressive cancers. Even if she lived and the Benzene did not kill her outright, Ritter still may have handed Julie a death sentence. Her immune system was shot; she would still need the bone marrow transplant to deal with the Aplastic Anemia. Thankfully, he'd already took care of that and he'd found a readily available donor for Julie. Still, in the end, no matter what Richard did, what he tried or how brilliant he was, that bastard Ritter probably still took twenty years off Julie's life.

"There's no cure, no treatment." Wylds said what the others were thinking. "There's nothing we can do for her."

"Nope, not much." He agreed disheartened. "Start flushing her system, we'll see if that helps. Give her Valium to keep the convulsions down and deal with the hallucinations. Just keep pumping fluids into her. Other than that, all we can do is wait." No matter whom the patient was the waiting was the toughest part of his job but now it seemed especially cruel.

"We're on it." Wylds said easily. "If you need anything..."

"Julie needs a bone marrow transplant, she'll be stable enough soon, I hope. Come get me when she's prepped."

"Ok," Wylds said slowly and with much thought, "but who's the donor?"

"You're looking at him." Mason was exhausted and he stumbled back to his office while the team went off to treat Julie. He would go down to her room in a few minutes, after he caught his breath and faced the situation. He was falling in love with her and now he was going to lose her. While Mason wouldn't say that he could see a bright sunny picket fence future with her, he could see himself spending an incredible amount of time with her and being not miserable about it.

Ritter.

Climbing onto the elevator was when Mason got it.

Ritter.

The insane brute wanted to take something important away from Mason, something Mason loved and would never be able to replace or get back.

Julie.

Just like Ritter thought Mason was responsible for him being kicked off the police department.

Ritter graduated from brooding bully to obsessed stalker to attempted murder in the space of a few months. The real problem was that Mason couldn't prove any of it. Medicine was simple, take a bunch of educated guesses, run a bunch of tests, see what pops, then cure, treat or watch them die. The Law was different; it required a different type of proof. What did he have? Nothing. He could tell law enforcement officials that Ritter rented the room next to Julie's at the El Royale but he could not prove Ritter drilled the holes in the wall or that he had been stalking her. As far as The Law was concerned, that was just a coincidence. He could not tell the police that Ritter pulled him over and impersonated a Police Officer without Julie to back him up and in her condition that wasn't going to happen any time soon. He could not put Ritter inside Julie's house unless he was dumb enough to leave his fingerprints behind.

Maybe Ritter had been that stupid or, in his case, maybe he had been that overconfident.

It was starting to look as though, if Julie died, Ritter would get away with murder.

The elevator doors opened on the third floor and Mason was in no mood for company as two doctors whose names he couldn't remember got on the elevator. Just past them, at the doors of the coma ward, someone was being taken out on a stretcher with a sheet over their face.

"I've tried to get in touch with his wife several times," the first doctor said to the other, "I just can't reach her and, while she's a royal bitch," he grumbled, "Mrs. Miller is always responsive."

Mason stumbled back against the elevator wall.

"Doctor Mason, are you all right?"

"Julie Miller?" He croaked.

"Yes, her husband just passed away. Do you know her?"

"She's on the second floor." He looked down at the smaller doctor who was looking up at him with a mixture of concern and suspicion. "You can't get a hold of her because she's admitted for Benzene poisoning."

"Oh my." The second doctor exclaimed. "She's so young. What happened?"

"What'd he die of?" He asked as he regained his composure. "How long ago?"

"Massive heart attack." The first doctor said. Now Mason remembered him, his name was Annaballini. "About a half an hour ago. Night shift is so slow; they're just moving him down to the morgue now."

247

What if Ritter killed Craig Miller? "Any history of problems with his heart?"

"Amazingly enough it's about the one thing that wasn't wrong with him." Annaballini nearly scoffed. "It was a shock to all of us. I suppose it will be a relief to Mrs. Miller, well, after a while anyway. He really could have lived like that another ten years or more."

"Blessing, is that what you're telling me?" The elevator doors opened.

"For her, I would hope. Keep me posted on her condition?" Annaballini asked.

Mason stepped off and then turned back as the doors began to close. He shoved his cane into the doors to keep them open. "Test Miller."

"For what?' Annaballini asked.

"Someone tried to kill his wife, Julie Miller was poisoned. If he didn't have any heart problems..."

Mason was crazy as a loon but the man was so often right that you just had to forgive him for being insane. It couldn't hurt to run a few extra tests on a dead man. "I'll consider it."

Ritter used Benzene on Julie and he would use something equally easy to get and virtually untraceable on Craig. "Digitalis." Mason said and then let the elevator door slide shut.

The man in his office. The one who said Rosie was calling for him. It was Craig Miller that was why he looked so oddly familiar.

As soon as the thought fully formed in Mason's mind and began to settle in, he dismissed it. "Too many Oxies." He mumbled letting himself into his office. "That's all. Dead men don't pay people visits." Even if Craig Miller did reach out from beyond (or just short of) the grave, how would he ever know to call his Julie-Baby 'Rosie'?

Chapter Seventeen

"You're sure you want to do this?" Wylds asked as he stood over Mason with one of the World's Largest Needles.

"If you ask me that one more time I'm gonna have to deck you." Mason returned. The one good thing he'd been able to ascertain from all of those tests was the fact that he was a perfect match for Julie. He didn't think twice about stepping up to the plate, after all, he did want her around even it would be twenty years less than anticipated.

Three hours had passed, Julie grew a little worse. Her breathing became shallow and normally he, like 90% of other doctors, would prescribe ephedrine to open the air passages and help her breath easier. In cases of Benzene poisoning this almost always proved fatal and the chemical tended to induce a sudden and massive heart attack. In her state Julie wouldn't survive that. Lying there on the bed, bathed in sweat, Julie gasped for air with an oxygen saturation rate of only 89%. Mason put her, not on oxygen but *in* an oxygen tent. It was old-fashioned but it would work and it would be the most comfortable option for her. In the tent she was hallucinating, she was talking to someone that no one but she could see. Mason wondered if Craig came to pay her another visit. IF the man had visited his office then surely he'd stood by his wife's bedside, come to say good-bye. What other Words of Wisdom might the man have had for her? "Would you get on with it?"

"It's not like you to be so self-sacrificing." Steward said from behind his surgical mask.

"Are you gonna do this or not?" Mason bitched as he laid on the table ready to be put out for the procedure. "If not, I'll find another team. I don't have to explain to you what you already know or justify it."

The transplant team was waiting, Julie was waiting. Her vitals were holding but who knew for how long. The transplant was her only shot at effectively dealing with Benzene in her system. It wasn't a cure, it wasn't even a recognized treatment but it would do wonders for the Aplastic Anemia, which in turn, would do wonders for the effects the poison was having on her.

"All right, here we go." Wylds said as she took in a breath and watched the anesthesiologist place the mask over Mason's face. "You know the drill, breath normally and count backward from one hundred."

On the table Mason nodded knowing that soon the gas would have him under.

"You're doing a really good thing." Wylds said in a soft voice as she stared down at him, "That really isn't like you." His eyes were closing, she leaned in close to him. All she could think of was the ring they found by Julie Miller's bed. For years she had a crush on her mentor. Even after she married Goodspeed her heart never let go of the faintest hope for just one clandestine night with Mason but it never happened. Never even came close and she'd made her intentions well-known to him on more than one occasion. "You must love her, huh?" Her eyes shot upward to look at Steward and her husband, Goodspeed, to see that they were just as intrigued as they were repelled by her unethical question. They leaned over the table to see if Mason would nod or shake his head before the gas took hold.

Mason mumbled something and it did sound like 'umm-hum' but no one could be sure.

"All right," Wylds said a little sadly as she stood up again, "let's get to the business of saving the future Mrs. Mason."

Goodspeed laughed. "Yeah, right. The woman might be crazy but no woman's *that* crazy."

An hour later, Mason woke up in a hospital bed with both hips screaming. Reaching down below the blanket he felt a triangular pattern on each hip. Six harvests altogether. "How are you feeling?" Steward asked as he got up from the chair where he'd been waiting for Mason to wake up.

"How's Julie?"

"Getting better," he said with encouragement.

"Ritter?"

"Nothing to report, if he's around, no one's seen him. I put a security guard outside Julie's room and," he glanced toward the window walls, "Yours. Just in case."

"Your concern for my safety is touching." He mocked and reached for the pitcher of ice water. It was cold going down his dry throat. Anesthesia so often had that bitter little side effect and it was a hard thirst to quench, just as hard as the Morning After Fire which burned at the back of the throat after a long night of drinking. The cold water sliding down his throat, he understood how Julie drank the Coke Ritter offered her, she probably even asked for more.

Steward had something else to tell his boss. A decision had been without him and Steward doubted Mason was going to like it but there were ethics and legalities to consider. "We had to call the police," he began and watched Mason's eyes grow wide. "We didn't tell them anything about Ritter but, you have to admit that it's clear someone tried to kill Julie Miller." He said rationally. "As physicians we have to report suspected attempted murder." Of course the police wanted to interview Julie but she wasn't up for questioning. "They want to talk to you. We told them about your...relationship, with her. They think you might be able to offer some insights."

"What am I supposed to tell them?"

"Just what you know. They fired him for a reason, right?" Steward asked. "Who's to say they won't believe you?" Steward started to walk away then turned back. "Doctor Annaballini asked me to tell you that...you were right." He'd almost forgotten about that. Shortly after Mason was wheeled into Recovery, Annaballini came rushing down the hallway looking for him mistakenly believing Doctor Mason was the doctor and not the patient. He gave Steward the message to pass on when Mason woke up. "What does it mean?"

"It means, get those cops in here."

**

The Mountainside Wellness & Research Center started to crawl with cops about a half hour ago then, not long after that, it started to swarm with them. There were two uniformed police officers stationed outside Julie Miller's room replacing the Rent-A-Cop who'd stood there for an hour or so before them. Another two outside of Mason's room and one outside his office. Major Case came in and took over, they took Craig Miller's corpse back to their high-tech lab. How could anyone know he'd been poisoned? It was a coincidence that Craig Miller died while his wife was so ill in the same hospital but after being in a coma for so long, surely it couldn't be any big shock to anyone.

His ex-Brothers In Blue, were questioning every nurse, doctor, orderly and food server they could find. Ritter knew if he stayed in the hospital much longer they'd find him. He'd heard his name bandied about several times in the course of listening in on their conversations. The place was too hot and he decided to leave. He'd go home and play it cool. They were bound to come looking for him and it was best if they found him just where they thought they would, this would help him avoid suspicion. *Why, yes, officer, I've been here in my little house all night. Julie who? Sorry, I don't know what you're talking about.*

If they dug around enough they'd come up with something that linked Ritter to Julie and, as he walked out of the Emergency Room into the cold November night with his head down and baseball cap slung low on his head, he started to come up with ideas. If they found he'd been poking around into her financial background well that was no big deal. *Oh, yes, officer, that's right. I totally forgot. Yes, Susan Miller did hire me to look into Julie's affairs some months ago. Here's my file if you want it.*

If they linked him to the bar well, so he tried to pick up the beautiful woman once or twice and was once successful. Tony might clue them into that though he doubted Julie-Baby would under any circumstances even if it meant setting free the man who tried to kill her. *Tony's bar, you say? Yes, I've been there often, it's just down the street, officer. Yes, I did see Julie Miller there once or twice, is that a crime?*

If they linked him to the El Royale he could be royally fucked. He'd have to get back there and patch up those holes. He could always look at the cop and say; *I never noticed any holes in that room. I have no idea what you're talking about. I stayed there a few times when I got too drunk at Tony's to drive or stumble back home. Is that a crime, officer? No, I never saw Julie Miller there.*

Who was to say otherwise except Leroy the night manager who once saw them come in together? So what? Two patrons walked through the door at the same time, it wasn't like Julie was hanging all over him or something.

But there was the gin bottle and the cigarette pack and the broken picture frame and the bottle of Grey Flannel. All of them had his fingerprints on them. It was just a matter of time before they found them. Would Julie Miller go so far to keep her dark secret that she would say she'd invited Ritter into her home? The crazy bitch just might. If that were the case, then Mason would go up the fucking wall!

Nice fantasy but the husband was dead. Julie had no reason to keep her secrets now.

Looking around feeling as though he were being watched but seeing no one in the parking lot, Ritter opened the door of the gray Ford and climbed behind the wheel. Turning the key and putting the headlights on he backed out of the space toward the exit of the parking lot.

He got as far as the streetlight before the police cars swarmed in on him.

They'd been waiting for him to get scared enough to leave the hospital. Ritter hadn't even suspected that the janitor hanging around the emergency room was an undercover cop.

Ritter was pulled from his car, thrown to the ground and then in handcuffs as he was told he was being arrested for the murder of Craig Miller, the attempted murder of Julie Miller and stalking Julie Miller, he had the right to remain silent, anything he said could and would be used against him in a Court of Law.

"Got him."

Someone said and Ritter looked up to see a uniform talking into a cell phone but looking up toward the hospital. In cuffs and squirming, Ritter followed the uniform's gaze only to see Mason standing in third floor window looking down, watching, and smirking at him being taken away. Mason had the nerve to wave to him. He stood there until Ritter was loaded into the back of a cruiser and the cruiser was out of sight.

"You feel better?" Spaulding asked as he came up behind Mason to watch the last of the scene play out.

"Loads." He said with a sigh of relief. "I honestly didn't think they'd believe me."

"Excuse me," came a male voice from the doorway, "are you Doctor Mason?"

The voice was almost familiar and Mason half-expected that when he turned around he'd see Craig Miller standing there. The young man he saw was close but not Craig. "Yeah."

"I'm Timothy Miller, I got a phone call, they said my Dad, Craig Miller, died," Tim said the word easily, like Julie part of him had just been waiting to say it, and, god help him, it felt good. The next did not feel so good. "And my stepmother, Jules, is here in the hospital, she's sick. They said you're her doctor. What's wrong with her?" Tim took in the sight of the hospital johnny on the doctor. "What's wrong with you?"

"Long story, how much time have ya got, young man?" He sighed good-naturedly. It looked as though there was someone in the world who cared about what happened to Julie Miller other than him. That was good. "Come on, let's go see your stepmother." His hips hurt and the pain transferred down both legs, Mason slung an arm around the kids shoulders in what appeared to be a very fatherly gesture if one didn't know he was looking for the added support the boy could provide with ease. Kid looked like a linebacker.

Chapter Eighteen

Two Weeks Later

"Would you stop fussing over me, Doc?" Julie complained as she sat on the couch. "I can get up and get a drink."

"I can get it, you stay there." Julie came home only three days ago and the day after that was Craig Miller's funeral. It wasn't a somber occasion, the mourners gathered were there to celebrate Craig's life and not grieve his passing which had happened some time before that day. That day was physically and emotionally exhausting, for Julie. Richard not only went to the funeral and stood by her side, (unheard of for him even if it was a close friend who passed, he had to be dragged to his own father's funeral) he stayed with her, here in her house and in the bed she once shared with Craig. Julie curled up on him and slept peacefully in his arms for the first time in nearly two weeks. While he stayed awake for a while, holding her, stroking her, and listening to her breath, it wasn't long before Richard fell into a deep satisfying sleep that lasted through the night.

Ritter was in jail. The press was outside Julie's house, Rick's house, and The Mountainside. Up here in the Vermont mountains, Julie's escapades became the Scandal of the Decade (if not the Century). Upon her leaving The Mountainside an entire horde of reporters was waiting at the front and back doors, they followed her home and shouted questions. They even had the audacity to shout at her before and after Craig's funeral yet retained the good sense to shut up during it.

The local police confiscated Ritter's computer and came across nearly 40 recording of Julie Miller with different men in room 404 of the El Royale Hotel. They found footage of Julie going to the hospital, the grocery store, the dry cleaner, the park with her dog and even footage taken inside the bar of her sitting and drinking alone or with the impending Flavor of the Night. Ritter's fingerprints were found all over Julie's house, including the front doorknob, the alarm panel, the bottle of Grey Flannel and the outside of her lingerie drawer.

All of those combined would convict him of stalking and breaking and entering. Minor crimes in the State of Vermont. If his videos didn't have sound it would stop there but the Vermont State Troopers and the FBI became involved and called his crime Wire Tapping. A much more serious offense.

He might have gotten ten years in prison if the police hadn't also found Ritter's fingerprints on the bottle of gin Julie had been drinking from. Ritter immediately claimed Julie invited him to her house and they had sex in her bed, that was why his fingerprints were all over the house and on the bottle. Julie denied it but it was her word against his and since one of those sex tapes had Ritter on it doing his thing with the Fair Juliette, things didn't look good for her in the local press. She was a loose woman who's word meant nothing. All of that would either be explained away or come down to a simple case of He Said/She Said.

Ritter couldn't account for his fingerprints being found on a syringe that had contained digitalis and which was found in the sharps container of Craig Miller's room. He never thought they'd look for it so he didn't bother with the millions of surgical gloves that surrounded him.

Ritter also couldn't account for his fingerprints unexpectedly being lifted from the disposable cold drink container Richard found in the wastebasket of Julie's hospital room. Hell, he didn't think one could lift prints from a thing like that. Seemed there'd been a few advances made in forensic science since his unfortunate departure from the force.

All in all, Ritter was looking at hard time on charges of Attempted Murder and Murder in the First Degree.

Soon the reporters would go away for a while but when it came time for Ritter's trial they would come back. When that happened they would bring the national papers and TV crews with them. Hell, *Dateline* was already putting together a story on 'The Video Vixen' as the media was calling Julie. Rick would ride it out with Julie until it was over and the two of them could find a little peace again.

"Are you ready for your interview tomorrow? Don't you think you're pushing it?" He asked as he came back into the living room with one of those bottles of LifeWater she seemed to like so much.

She had a big interview tomorrow, Willington Community College was still looking to fill their position in the English Department and Julie had been lucky enough to wrangle another interview in the face of the scandal. "I'll be fine, it's just an interview." She was still weak and tired very easily, Doc said that would happen for the next month or so and after that she'd begin to feel more like her old self. "No one says I'll get the job." She didn't know who'd hire a woman whose sexcapades had been broadcast all over the State of Vermont. It was a miracle she got the interview let alone getting the job.

"No one says you won't," he countered, "I don't think going back to work so soon is such a good idea..."

Julie sighed. "Is this Doctor Mason or Rick talking?"

"Both," he admitted, "I'm your Lover I'm allowed to be concerned about you and fuss over you if I want."

"So you are," she smiled and moved across the couch to cuddle next to him. He put his arm around her shoulders and drew the blanket over her. "I'm glad you're here. Thank you."

He was equally glad to be where he was, here with her. Life was fragile and he shouldn't wait. He shouldn't be afraid. He almost lost her, like Life, Time was a precious thing. He reached in his pocket and produced the high school ring still on the chain. "What do you say, Rosie? Wanna be my girl? For real this time. Just you and me, nobody else."

Julie reached for the ring. "I thought you'd never ask."

He looped it around her neck and kissed her long and deep. His lips tingled and his heart beat double time. As many women as he'd slept with, both serious and just for the night, no woman ever made him feel like this. No woman set his body, mind and soul on fire like Julie. No set of lips ever said; *I want you*, the way hers did.

No matter how brief it might turn out to be, there was a future here. One that wasn't lonely or filled with self-inflicted misery. She once said that we were all damaged and lost. We were all human. With her that was all right, there was no shame in being damaged or lost or human. She accepted him with open arms, warts, flaws, self-righteous arrogance and all. He wanted nothing more than to reach out to her, one human being to another and confess all that he felt. "Don't leave me, Rosie."

Looking up at him and into those beautiful shining but slightly confused blue eyes, she smiled for him. Rick said over and over that Craig visiting her in the hospital was just a hallucination, maybe it was. But, whatever it was, it was right. It was good. She could see it in Rick's steely blue eyes. He did love her. He just wasn't ready to admit to it yet. "Never." She promised and kissed him again.

The End

Other Books by Lisa Beth Darling

Fiction:

The Heart of War

Child of War-A God is Born

Christmas Eve on Olympus

Child of War-Rising Son

Women of War

Kingdoms of War

Sister Christian; Genesis

Sister Christian; Sins of the Father

On a Hot Summer Night

Dream Weaver

The Limikkin

OBSESSION

Non-Fiction:

The Shame of Eminent Domain

A Window to Magickal Herbalism

Sex, Love, Magick

Visit http://www.moonsmusings.com

www.ingramcontent.com/pod-product-compliance
Lightning Source LLC
Chambersburg PA
CBHW072213170626
46813CB00003B/913